"Don't touc[h]

"Don't give me orders," he said, his voice soft and menacing. He pressed her head down against his chest. "I can't take much more of this, Sally. When you want me to touch you, I don't trust myself. When you don't want me to, I lie awake nights thinking about it."

She struggled against his grasp, but he tightened his arms around her and kept dancing.

"Jake, let me go."

"I can't. Not yet."

"You can, and you will," she demanded.

He stopped dancing. "Oh, the hell with it." He scooped her up in his arms and headed for the barn door.

"Where are you taking me?" she protested, her voice muffled against his chest.

"Where do you think? Out behind the barn. I'm either going to kiss you until you say uncle or beat the living hell out of you. I haven't decided which…!"

Dear Reader,

When we ran our first March Madness promotion in 1992, we had no idea that we would get such a wonderful response. Our springtime showcase of brand-new authors has been so successful that we've continued to seek out talented new writers and introduce them into the field of historical romance. During our yearly search, my editors and I have the unique opportunity of reading hundreds of manuscripts from unpublished authors, and we'd like to take this time to thank all of you who have given us the chance to review your work.

In Lynna Banning's heartwarming first book, *Western Rose,* a rancher agrees to court his neighbor's strong-willed daughter in exchange for a prime piece of land. But complications arise when he actually starts to fall in love with her.

And be sure to keep an eye out for our other three March titles. *Fool's Paradise* by Tori Phillips, the charming tale of a noblewoman and the jester who becomes her protector. *Warrior's Deception* by Diana Hall, a medieval story about a marriage based on lies. And *The Pearl Stallion,* a tale of adventure from Rae Muir.

Four new talents, four great stories from Harlequin Historicals. Don't miss a single one!

Sincerely,

Tracy Farrell
Senior Editor

Please address questions and book requests to:
Harlequin Reader Service
U.S.: 3010 Walden Ave., P.O. Box 1325, Buffalo, NY 14269
Canadian: P.O. Box 609, Fort Erie, Ont. L2A 5X3

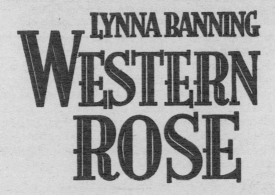

LYNNA BANNING
WESTERN ROSE

Harlequin Books

TORONTO • NEW YORK • LONDON
AMSTERDAM • PARIS • SYDNEY • HAMBURG
STOCKHOLM • ATHENS • TOKYO • MILAN
MADRID • WARSAW • BUDAPEST • AUCKLAND

ISBN 0-373-28910-3

WESTERN ROSE

Books by Lynna Banning

Harlequin Historicals

Western Rose #310

LYNNA BANNING

has combined a lifelong love of history and literature into a satisfying "early retirement" career as a writer. Born in Oregon, she has lived in Northern California most of her life, graduating from Scripps College and embarking on a career as an editor and technical writer and later as a high school English teacher.

An amateur pianist and harpsichordist, Lynna performs on psaltery and recorders with two Renaissance ensembles and teaches music in her spare time. Currently she is learning to play the harp.

She enjoys hearing from her readers. You may write her directly at P.O. Box 324, Felton, CA, 95018.

For Clarence Woolston and Suzanne Barrett

With special thanks to
Janice Bennett, Nancy Greenman,
Jean Banning Strickland and Floyd Strickland,
Mary Banning Yarnes and Lawrence Yarnes

Chapter One

Klamath County, Oregon
1886

Jackson Bannister reached a long arm across the scarred oak table and poured himself another two fingers of the Silver Cup's best bourbon. "I can't make it through another summer without water for my stock, Tom. With the drought, all my wells are going dry. I need that piece of yours down by the alder grove. That land has a year-round spring—hell, the grass is up to my stirrups!"

He paused and drew in a long breath. "How much?"

Thomas Maguire looked steadily into the desperate eyes of the man seated across from him. "Like I said, Jake—that land's not for sale. But—" he reached for the half-empty bottle that stood between them "—maybe we could make a deal."

Jake watched Tom pour out a generous slug of the amber liquid and swallow it in one quick gulp. "Deal? What kind of deal? Hell, Tom, you don't need that parcel. You've got water enough to swim your herds in just for Sunday fun, while I've got cows so skinny by the time I drive 'em to the railhead to sell, I barely make expenses. Why not just sell it to me?''

"I told you before, son, that land's not for sale. Sure I feel for you and for your cattle—poor thirst-crazed beasts that they are. And that piece is honey-rich, it is.'' Tom paused, tapping one finger against his drink. "And, seein' as it lies just where our two spreads join up, why, I don't blame you one bit for wantin' it.'' Tom's eyes twinkled.

Jake clanked his glass onto the tabletop. "I don't just *want* it, Tom. I've got to have it. Just name your price.''

Tom exhaled a long breath and shifted his bulky frame in the battered oak chair. A slow grin spread over his face. "Well, now, Jake, I been savin' that piece for a reason. You see, when I die, my spread'll be divided between Louisa and Sally. Louisa, now—with every cowpoke within ridin' distance comin' callin' every Sunday—I expect Louisa'll be married and have a brood of her own when I leave this earth.''

Jake sighed with impatience. What the hell did Tom's daughters have to do with the parched land of his Bar Y range and hundreds of head of scrawny cows bawling with thirst? "I'm listening, Tom.''

"Well, Jake, it's like I said. That hundred acres is not for sale.'' His voice contained a hint of laughter. "But it could be yours, just the same.''

"What? You want to ride that one by me again, Tom?''

"You heard me right, Jake. You can have that land. But—''

Jake blinked. "But?'' he prompted. He'd known Tom Maguire long enough to know there'd be a catch; the only question was, how big? Negotiating with Tom was like playing poker with a short deck. The canny Irishman always had a surprise or two up his sleeve.

"But," Tom reiterated, his voice dropping into a confidential tone, "I'd like to get my daughter settled first."

"Settled," Jake echoed uneasily. He tilted the oak chair back from the table, lifting the two battered front legs off the floor, and rested one shiny leather boot against the table. "Settled," he repeated.

"Aw, you know, Jake—married!" Tom eyed him over the edge of his glass.

Jake blinked. "So?"

"So," Tom enunciated slowly, "you marry my daughter, you get that hundred acres."

Jake frowned. "Now, why would you need to horn-swoggle a man into marrying Miss Louisa? Hell, she's pretty enough to get damn near any man she—"

Tom Maguire coughed. "Not Louisa," he said, the skin under his red-gold sideburns flushing. "Sally."

"Sally!"

Tom took another generous swallow of bourbon. "You remember Sally, don't you, Jake?"

Remember her! Hell, yes, Jake remembered her. Last time he had seen Sally Maguire she was maybe fourteen or fifteen, a gawky tomboy with a mass of curly red hair and, he recalled with a frown, a temper to match. Once at a dance, Jake had stumbled onto the Maguire girl with young Tommy Pcarson's hands all over her. He'd paddled them both good—Tommy for being a randy little kid too big for his britches and Sally for innocently leading the boy on. If he hadn't stepped out behind the barn for a smoke, the girl might have got herself in real trouble. But had the little spitfire been grateful? Hell, no. The instant he'd released her, she'd socked him a good one right on the chin. That girl had a temper like a wildcat. And on top of everything else, she was flat chested as a skillet.

Jake tossed off the last of his bourbon and stood. "No offense, Tom, but no piece of land is worth that."

The older man flinched. "Now, Jake," he coaxed, "what's wrong with Sally? It's true, she ain't as pretty as Louisa, and since their ma died Sally's sort of—well, got used to havin' things her own way an' all. But, hell, Jake, she's a rare woman."

"Then how come all the young bloods around here aren't begging for her hand?"

Tom winced. "No guts."

Unexpectedly, Jake laughed. He leaned down toward Tom and clapped him on the shoulder. "Well, you're honest, I'll say that for you." He chuckled. "But I'll tell you something, Tom. For most men, taking on a wife is trouble in itself, but taking on Miss Sally—"

"You're just the man for Sally," the Irishman interrupted. "You marry her, and I'll give you that land."

Tom looked expectantly at the owner of the spread next to his. The tall, well-muscled man across from him was lithe and toughened. On foot or on horseback, Jake moved with an unstudied animal grace that Tom had always secretly admired. Jake Bannister could outride and outthink any man in the valley. Sally would like that; he'd bet money on it.

Tom prided himself on his ability to judge both horses and men. And women. He smiled as he remembered Marie. His wife had been a lot like Sally—headstrong and sometimes too smart for her own good. But she'd known a good man when she saw one. He and Marie had been happy all their years together. Sally, though, was another matter. Oh, she was no fool. And

Jake—well, they didn't come any better than soft-spoken, imperturbable Jake Bannister. Every rancher in the valley respected him. Sally would see that right off.

And that would solve everything. Jake would have water for his stock, and Sally would have a good man. Tom could rest easy knowing she'd be well taken care of for the rest of her life.

Satisfied, the older man nodded. "You and Sally are a lot alike, Jake. You're both tough, strong-minded. And deep down inside you both care about things—the land, makin' a life out here. Maybe even each other, someday."

Jake repressed a snort. "Tom, she's not grown up enough. She's half wildcat and—"

"Well, now," Tom pursued doggedly, "how long has it been since you've seen her, Jake? You've been gone back East since she was fourteen, and just before you got back, she left for St. Louis, been at that teachers college for the last two years. She's comin' in on the train tomorrow. Gonna teach school right here in Honey Creek."

Jake stared into the older man's eyes. True, he hadn't seen Sally Maguire for some years. At his father's invitation he'd left the ranch he'd run for him and gone back to Philadelphia to attend college. Then the elder Bannister had sent him on a European tour. Jake had gone just to please him, surprising himself by enjoying the opera in Italy as much as mountain climbing in the Austrian Alps.

But he missed ranching. When he'd returned from Europe he'd persuaded his father to let him take over the Bar Y. He'd been back in Oregon for just a couple of years. And that meant Sally Maguire was, let's see,

about twenty-three now. Aw hell, she was an old maid!
No wonder Tom was desperate to get her married off.
He didn't want her on *his* hands for the rest of his life,
either!

But Lord, how he needed that land. One hundred
acres of succulent, hip-deep grass, good year-round
water and—best of all—it butted up against his own
sprawling spread.

But marry Miss Sally? Most of the men in the valley—possibly the entire county—crossed to the other
side of the street when they spied Sally Maguire coming down the plank sidewalk.

Tom's voice took on a dulcet tone. "Jake, you know
your wells are all pumpin' dust, and the only spring you
got left is peterin' out. Your creek'll be goin' dry before
the end of the summer. Your cattle are gettin' mighty
thirsty."

Abruptly, Jake lowered his muscular frame into the
chair and stared across the table at Tom. He reached
again for the bourbon. Suddenly, at thirty-two, he felt
old and tired. "True," he acknowledged. "Last year I
lost close to fifty head to drought. The rest were so
scrawny I couldn't find any buyers." He groaned. Another year like that would bankrupt him. The Bar Y
land stretched all the way from the Maguire place to the
Big Horse Mountains and beyond, four thousand acres
in all. It was the biggest spread in the valley, but he
needed water. Damn, but he needed that land of Tom's!
But, great balls of fire . . . Sally?

Jake downed a healthy slug of the whiskey. "Tom, I
don't love Sally. I don't even know her! And she probably doesn't come close to remembering me. It won't
work. She'd never agree."

Tom's lined face split into a wide grin. "She's not to know, my boy. You just court her and let nature take its course. And when you two are married, I'll give you a hundred-acre wedding present." His grin broadened. "But," he cautioned, "don't let on to Sally. She's got her heart set on teaching school. She's a little crazy that way about things she makes up her mind to do. I figure about one term will get it out of her system, and after that . . . well, you know." He rolled his empty glass between his thumb and forefinger. "Let nature take its course."

Let nature take its course! Jake snorted inwardly. With a screeching, flat-chested hellcat like Sally Maguire? Not a chance. Nobody could change as much as she'd need to in just nine years; it'd take half a century at the very least!

Then a thought lighted his brain. If he knew Sally, she wouldn't *want* to get married. Women like that, they get started teaching school and they like it. The next thing you know they're eighty years old and still unmarried.

He leaned toward the older man and licked his lips. "Tom, I'll make you a deal. I'll court her, and eventually I'll do the honorable thing and ask her to marry me—you have my word on it. But if she refuses, I want the land in exchange for my trouble."

"Done!" Tom chortled. He grasped Jake's hand and shook it hard. His face shone with anticipation. He knew Sally better than Jake did. Hell, he knew *Jake* better than Jake did! If he played his cards right, Sally would end up with a good ranch *and* a good husband. He almost laughed out loud, then caught the thoughtful expression on Jake's face.

Instantly Tom sobered. "Sally's been in St. Louis all summer, visiting my sister. She's coming in on the noon train tomorrow. She's gonna need a mare to ride to the schoolhouse this fall. You got any for sale?''

"Sure, Tom." Absently Jake withdrew his hand from the Irishman's callused grip. "There's one thing I'm curious about, though," Jake said slowly. "What's 'Sally' short for, anyway?''

Tom hesitated a split second. "Sultana. Sultana Marie. Her mother got kind of crazy around the time she was carryin' her, and when she was born, Marie named her after some Arabian princess she read about in a book." His voice softened at the memory. "Marie was like that—kinda spur-of-the-moment."

Sultana. Jake rolled the name around in his mind like a shot of Silver Cup bourbon. Sultana Maguire. No—Sultana Bannister. Mrs. Sally Bannister. He'd ask her to be Mrs. Sally Bannister and she'd laugh in his face, and then he'd have his land from Tom, anyway. Jake smiled, already planning how he'd graze his prize bull on that rich grass next spring.

Abruptly his mind ground to a halt. But court old maid Sally Maguire? Next to losing his herd this summer, he could think of nothing worse.

Sultana Maguire carefully rearranged the folds of her dark green velvet traveling dress for the fifth time in as many minutes and resolutely set her lips in a straight line. She hated this dress. It was high necked and hot, and she was laced into a corset tight enough to strangle a pig. The minute she got home she would throw it in the stove in the corner of the kitchen and burn it up! Aunt Josephine had bought it for her at Brading's Department Store in St. Louis and had insisted Sally wear it on the trip home to Oregon.

But Aunt Josephine knew nothing about trains or perspiration or dust. Or life, for that matter. Aunt Josephine had lived all her days as a well-to-do, citified maiden lady and would certainly disapprove of almost everything out here in the West. But, Sally thought with a secret smile, what she did not tell her, Aunt Josephine would never know. She would burn that corset the instant she could get it unhooked!

She hated getting all gussied up. Her aunt meant well, and she had been extremely generous, sending her back to Oregon with a trunkful of clothes suitable for young lady teachers in the East. But she wasn't in the East now. She was in Oregon. Or she would be in just a few hours. And once she was home, she could shed all these frills and fripperies, pull on her beloved denim jeans and an old flannel shirt of her father's and feel human again. At least until the school term started.

A grimy-faced boy of about eight peeped at her over the top of the leather seat. "Are you goin' to Honey Creek, too?"

Sally smiled into the round blue eyes. "Yes, I am."

"We're goin' to live with my grandpa. He has a horse!"

"That's nice," Sally responded as the face disappeared. That child might be one of her pupils, she thought with a stab of apprehension. She admitted she was a bit unorthodox when it came to classroom learning. She hoped his mother would not object to her teaching methods. A new teacher, particularly one educated at an eastern college, would be viewed with both awe and suspicion, especially by ranchers with little schooling themselves.

The train jolted, then resumed its rhythmic swaying, and Sally let her eyelids drift shut. She would be the first trained schoolteacher Honey Creek had ever had. What would teaching be like? Would any of the children know their letters? Would they come to school regularly? Most of the ranchers lived too far out for their children to attend school in town; ever since she could remember, the ranch children had been tutored at home.

A tremor of fear curled into her belly. She tensed her stomach muscles to conquer it and resolutely gazed out the train window. The landscape had changed from rolling green hills to an endless flat, brown plain. They were getting close to Honey Creek.

She had a hard time admitting to herself when she was frightened, but she did it now. She wasn't just frightened, she was scared to death! She wanted so much to be a success. She *must* be a good teacher. She must! At twenty-three with no interest in marriage, she was well on her way to being a maiden lady like Aunt Josie.

She shut her eyes tight. She *had* to make a life for herself in some way or she'd spend the rest of her days keeping house for her widowed father. And that, quite simply, would not be enough for her. She wanted to be involved in something challenging, something meaningful. And nothing was as challenging, or as satisfying, as helping a mind to grow.

Sally opened her eyes and watched the parched grassland roll past the train window. As the hours passed, she thought about her plans, her hopes for the coming year. One winter, when she was just sixteen, the "town" teacher had contracted pneumonia. Sally had taken over the younger children's classes, and she had treasured every moment in the drafty church hall that housed the lower grades. Her students had made significant progress in just a few short weeks, and then and there she had decided this was to be her life's work. She had been certain of it. In fact, since her mother's death, it had been the only thing she *was* certain of. She could never let her life slip by just keeping house for her father.

The dirt-streaked face reappeared. "Do you got any children?"

"No," Sally responded, keeping as straight a face as she could manage. "I don't. Do *you?*"

The eyes blinked. "Nah, I don't got any, I *am* one!"

Sally laughed as the head disappeared. A moment later it popped back up. "Lady, does you got a mister?"

The round eyes widened as his mother, a plump woman in a plain gray traveling dress, yanked sharply on her son's arm. The grimy face vanished.

Sally stifled a snort. Did she have a mister, indeed. No, she didn't have a mister. She was the acknowledged spinster of Hope Valley. Her father always said she had a mind like a new razor and a spine of spring steel, neither of which was particularly admired by menfolk. But that didn't matter a whit. She was dead set on teaching school. In fact, she was determined to be the best darn schoolteacher in Klamath County!

She reviewed her attributes with matter-of-fact acceptance. Yes, she had a temper, and she was far too outspoken for a lady. But that was before she had gone east to school. She was mature now. More polished, thanks to Aunt Josie. Now her biggest worry was not her temper, but her corset. She squirmed uncomfortably as the whalebone stays bit into her flesh.

The coach car jolted again, and the train began to slow. Sally stared out the window at the landscape rolling past. The sagebrush-dotted plain was broken by occasional green patches where willows and alders grew along a riverbank. She loved this country. There was something rough and unspoiled about it. Something free.

A surge of joy flooded her chest. She was coming home! At this moment she felt an outpouring of love for everyone in the valley.

Well, maybe not everyone. She had known most of the townspeople all her life. Reverend Mathews, Chang the barber next to Baker's General Store, the ranchers from all the spreads in the valley—she'd missed every single one of them!

Except for Jackson Bannister. She drew in a breath and frowned. Jackson Bannister she would hate for the rest of her days. He was arrogant, and he was a bully. She would never stop hating him. Never. And she would never forgive him for what he'd done.

She had been fourteen. The Pearsons had held a square dance in their new barn, and Sally and her sister, Louisa, who was four years younger, had begged to go. Sally loved to dance. She knew all the steps to the quadrilles and schottisches George Peterman scraped out on his fiddle, and all the square dance calls, too. Her energy was inexhaustible. And for the first time in her life, she had worn a dress just like a grown-up, a blue-checked gingham with a flounced skirt.

Everything had been lovely until she'd bribed Tommy Pearson to kiss her out behind the barn during one of the fiddler's breaks. Jake Bannister had caught them. He'd walloped Tommy, then closed his hand over her wrist and yanked her away from the goggle-eyed boy. Then Jake had whacked her, too. Just once, on her bottom, but hard.

Humiliated and mad enough to kill, Sally had spent the rest of the evening sitting in the buckboard nursing her temper and her sore buttocks.

Even now the incident seemed as fresh as yesterday. What right had Jake to paddle her? True, he was an old friend of Pa's, but that didn't give him the right to act as her protector. She didn't need protecting! And what was *he* doing out behind the barn, anyway?

Sally's cheeks burned at the memory. She would never forget her mortification at Jake's hands. She hadn't seen him since then—he'd gone back East shortly after the incident. But she knew she would never forget it. And she would never forgive him. Never. She didn't like Jake Bannister, and she didn't care who knew it.

The train slowed again, and Sally heard the high, mournful whistle signaling their approach to the station. Honey Creek, at last! She forgot Jake and gazed eagerly out the window as the town slid into view.

There was the Silver Cup saloon, next to the hotel. And there was Baker's General Store, where she had bought hundreds of sticky penny candies as a girl. There was old Mr. Baker now, a splotched apron tied about his thick middle, sweeping the board sidewalk in front of his store in his continuing battle with the town's dust.

The dirt-smudged face popped up in front of her again, the blue eyes regarding her solemnly. "How come you doesn't have a mister, lady?"

"Jason!" The woman hissed at her son. The child disappeared.

How come? Sally echoed, her lips twitching into a smile. Because she didn't want one, that's how come! Because, my young friend, most "misters" over the age of twelve were tongue-tied dullards who smelled like a stable and pranced after a girl expecting her to...to what? To get all gussied up for them, she huffed. Ridiculous. Not one of them was worth getting trussed up in a whalebone prison for. She didn't care *what* Aunt Josephine said.

Sally snapped open her reticule, withdrew a small hand mirror and peered into the glass. After more than a week on the soot-filled train, her ordinarily clear skin looked a bit gray. She discreetly moistened her handkerchief with spit and rubbed it over her cheeks. Her mouth was a bit too generous, she thought, but her teeth were white and even. She inspected her nose critically for a telltale freckle. Nary a one, she noted with satisfaction, recalling the hours in Aunt Josephine's boudoir with a paste of lemon juice and oatmeal plastered over the offending blemishes.

But her hair... Sally sighed. The thick, dark red tresses crowned her head in an ample bun so heavy it made her neck ache. Clear, turquoise-green eyes looked calmly back at her from under the brim of the silliest hat in all of St. Louis—a fluffy, dark green concoction Aunt Josephine had fallen in love with at Brading's. One iridescent green peacock feather swooped rakishly over her curved dark eyebrow and bobbed annoyingly against her nose. Sally blew it away from her face with a gust of breath blown upward through pursed lips. How Aunt Josephine would flutter if she could see her now, Sally thought with wicked delight. When she got home, she would burn the hat, too.

"Honey Creek!" The burly conductor tramped through the lurching car, announcing their arrival. When the train bumped to a stop, Sally took a deep breath, picked up her traveling valise and moved to the door of the car.

* * *

Jake watched the three passengers descend the iron steps to the station platform. He had talked Tom into letting him meet the train and drive Sally out to their ranch in his buggy. After all, it might take a while to court a crotchety old maid like Miss Sally; he figured he might as well get an early start. He'd need water for his cows come summer.

She was not on the train. His eyes scanned the travelers again to be sure. None of the passengers even remotely resembled the Maguire girl. It had been close to ten years since he'd seen her, but he remembered what she looked like—all arms and legs and straight as a branding iron. And about that friendly, too.

Jake stepped down from the buggy and inspected the travelers more closely. A plump matron shepherded two whining children into the station house. A frail, gray-haired lady in black stepped quickly past him and flung her arms around a dusty cowhand. The third figure, dressed in dark green, stood with her back to him, tapping her foot impatiently on the platform. A fashionable, extravagant-looking feathered hat rode high on the proud, dark head.

Elegant, Jake observed in appreciation. But definitely not from around here. The dress nipped in the girl's figure sharply at the waist, outlining a lusciously curved body that took Jake's breath away. Whooee! Must be a new calico queen down at Charlie's Silver Cup. Didn't know her yet, but would sure like to. Old Charlie could sure pick—

The girl made a half turn toward Jake, and he studied her profile. A straight chin, full lips and a stylish, heavily veiled creation on top of her head, the feather bobbing enticingly toward the perfect nose. His eyes moved lower, to the curve of her breasts, the inviting buttocks, impudently accentuated by a gathered bustle. Jake felt his loins tighten.

Damn. What a time to be courting Sally Maguire. It'd have to be hands off this beauty, he guessed. Just his luck.

Then the girl made another quarter turn and faced him. The green-blue eyes looked directly into his, and Jake's heart stopped. Behind her, the train rolled past the station and chuffed its way on down the track and out of town. The rhythmic sound faded, and in the ensuing silence Jake stared at Sally.

"Damn," Jake swore. It couldn't be...

"Mr. Bannister?" The cool, controlled voice sliced into his brain.

Jake opened his mouth, but nothing came out.

Sally took a step forward. Jake scrutinized every inch of her, letting his gaze move slowly from her feathered hat to her full lips, her slim neck, her... It couldn't be, but it was. Sally Maguire, in full feather.

Oh, boy. Jake's brain sang. *There is a God, and he is definitely on my side!*

"Close your mouth, Mr. Bannister. It's me, Sally Maguire."

For the first time in his life, Jake was tongue-tied.

"Mr. Bannister?" Sally repeated.

Under the brim of his gray Stetson, Jake's gaze traveled over her in disbelief. "Jake. Call me Jake."

"Jake," she repeated after him. He watched her mouth form the word.

"My," she observed in an icy voice, "how you've changed!"

How *he'd* changed! Startled, Jake burst into rolling laughter. "*I've* changed?" he said when he could talk.

Lord, just look at her. She made his mouth go dry. "I thought you would be..."

Sally shot him a cold look. "You thought I would be what?" she demanded. She blew the peacock feather off her nose. Of all the people in Honey Creek, why was *he* here at the station, spoiling her homecoming? The elegant gray Stetson tilted back on his dark head with a certain careless panache. Just the sight of him made her mad as a hornet.

"Older," Jake enunciated carefully. And flatter, he added to himself. And not so...

"I'm twenty-three years old," she snapped. "That's old enough to recognize a snake when I see one."

The deep blue eyes blinked. "Miss Sally?"

"Don't you 'Miss Sally' me," she said, her voice frost filled. "What are you doing here, anyway? Where is my father?"

Jake chuckled. So, the duckling had become a swan. He wondered if Tom Maguire knew what a beauty his daughter had become. Then he shook his head. Yes, she was grown up now, a real looker. On the outside, anyway. Inside, he'd bet she was still a hot-tempered little hellcat who needed a lesson in manners. For all intents and purposes, Sally Maguire hadn't changed a bit.

"Mr. Bannister, I asked you a question!" Sally's voice rang with impatience.

"Jake," he responded automatically, struggling to tear his eyes from her lips.

"Where is my father?" Her imperious tone snapped Jake to inner attention. If he was going to marry this girl, graze his prize bull in the promised hundred acres, he'd best not let her get the upper hand. It was time to take charge. Jake grinned. It was time, he reminded himself, to start courting.

"I'm here to meet you, Miss Sally," he said evenly. "Where's your baggage? I'll load it onto the buggy."

"You?" Incredulous, Sally stared at him. Why would her father send Jake Bannister of all people to meet her? The tanned, fine-featured visage of the man staring at her stirred disquieting memories.

"Why not? I've got two legs and two arms, like most men. Where's your trunk?" he repeated.

"Arms and legs don't make you a man," Sally scoffed. "A man is—"

"Going to drive you home, Miss Sally." His quiet voice knifed through her sentence. "Now shut up and tell me where your—"

"I'd rather walk home than ride in a buggy with you!"

Jake gave her a level look. "Suit yourself. You want me to load your trunk, or do you want to carry it with you?"

Sally stamped her foot on the platform. Fury boiled up in her throat, and she opened her mouth to speak, then snapped her jaw shut.

"Get in the buggy, Sally," Jake ordered.

Surprising herself a little, she obeyed, pointing out her black trunk as she swept in front of him and climbed up into the runabout.

Jake ambled over to the baggage at the edge of the platform, upended her trunk with little effort, then dipped his body and levered it skillfully onto one shoulder. He moved toward the buggy.

Sally sat motionless on the tufted leather seat. Why on earth would Pa send Jake Bannister to meet her? Was her father ill? Or maybe injured? Or had he gone a little crazy since she'd been gone and forgotten how much she detested Jake?

The mare shifted slightly as Jake dumped the trunk down onto the rack and secured it with a length of rope. Sally picked up the reins to steady the horse. Suddenly a wicked thought wormed its way into her brain.

In the next instant she snatched up the buggy whip from the seat and snapped it over the mare's head. The horse jolted into action and trotted smartly out of the station yard and onto the road.

Jake stared after her, openmouthed. Why, that little hellion! Then his eyes narrowed, and he swore softly. A slow smile broke his thinned lips into a curve.

"Miss Sally," he said as the buggy disappeared behind a cloud of gray dust, "for a schoolteacher, you have a heap of learning yet to do. I think I'm going to enjoy teaching you some of the facts of life."

Grinning, Jake tipped his Stetson over his eyes and headed for the Silver Cup saloon. There was nothing he liked better than breaking a high-spirited filly. Miss Sultana Maguire was in for the surprise of her life.

Chapter Two

Tom Maguire pushed his battered Stetson up with one finger and opened his eyes as his older daughter clattered into the yard driving Jake's shiny black buggy. He blinked, lifted his long legs from the porch railing and clunked his chair into an upright position. Sally was home! And just look at her! His heart swelled with pride as he took in the trim figure in the green velvet dress. Why, she'd become a real beauty, he acknowledged in disbelief.

Then he frowned. Sally was alone.

Tom caught the bridle and steadied the mare as his daughter descended from the buggy. "Welcome home, honey-girl." He clasped her into a bear hug, and a lump as big as a hen's egg lodged in his throat. He hadn't felt this quivery inside since Marie died. Why, you old fool, he thought. Don't you get all teared up and spoil her homecoming.

"Oh, Pa, I missed you so much!" Sally clung to Tom's rough wool shirt.

"Honey-girl," Tom rasped, patting her back with his huge, gnarled hand. "Things haven't been the same since you left."

Sally looked up at him and laughed. "No burned suppers? No broken ribs?" she teased.

Tom grinned. "No fun at all," he admitted.

Unwilling to let go of her father for a moment, Sally closed her eyes and breathed in deeply, savoring the pungent smell of tobacco and leather she always associated with him. Then she opened her eyes and gazed about her. Oh, everything looked so green, and smelled so good—the vanilla scent of the roses trailing along the fence, the sharp smell of green grass, even the dust kicked up by the buggy mare, it all smelled of home. During her two-year absence she had missed everything more than she cared to admit.

"Where's Louisa?" Sally inquired.

"Upstairs, gettin' dressed up to welcome you home. She's pretty as ever. Got every cowhand in the valley dancin' to her tune." Tom held Sally at arm's length, looking at her with admiration. "But now that you're back, she might have some competition."

"Oh, Pa. You know the men around here never took to me much. I'm too outspoken and hot-tempered, I guess. But I don't much mind, really. There's never been a one of them I'd care to settle down for."

"Sally!" Louisa emerged from the house in a cloud of ruffled petticoats and yellow dimity. The screen door slammed behind her as she flew into Sally's embrace and kissed her soundly on both cheeks. "Sally! Oh, Sally, I'm so glad you're home!"

Sally laughed and gave Louisa a hug. How she adored her younger sister. Her cloud of fine gold hair, her delicate, ladylike ways, and above all her quietness, had assured her belle-of-the-ball status since she had turned twelve. Sally had never minded playing second fiddle. In fact, she rather enjoyed it. She was proud of Louisa's feminine accomplishments. And because Louisa attracted hordes of beaux who came calling every Sunday afternoon, all Sally had to do to assess the prospects was to rock back and forth in the porch swing and keep her eyes open.

And her mouth shut, she acknowledged ruefully, which she found extremely hard to do. Men surely didn't like a woman who talked a lot. At seventeen, Louisa had been demurely quiet, a sharp contrast to Sally's tomboy ways and waspish tongue. Nineteen now, Louisa was even more beautiful, Sally thought with fondness. She gave her younger sister another squeeze. "The boys still come courting thick as flies?"

"Thicker," her father interjected. "It's honey that attracts them, daughter. Not vinegar."

"Oh, Pa. I'm a schoolteacher now. I'm never going to marry." Oh, the cowhands and ranchers were a good sort, but they lacked—what was it, exactly? Polish. Education. And wit. Not one of them failed to lapse into tongue-tied silence after five minutes in her company, and silence Sally found boring as one of Reverend Mathews's Sunday sermons.

"Well," her father ventured, "maybe after you've been back for a while, you'll change your mind." Abruptly he glanced at Jake's buggy.

"Where's Jake, honey?"

Sally's dark brows rose, and she widened her eyes in studied innocence. "Jake?"

"Jake Bannister. That's his horse and buggy."

"Oh, I imagine he'll be along in a while." Sally worked to make her voice light. "He had an errand in town."

Tom peered at his daughter. "I'll bet," he said, a smile tugging at his mouth. "Okay, honey-girl. Shorty can drive the buggy over to the Bar Y after supper."

Sally caught Louisa's hand and headed for the porch steps. "Thanks, Pa," she called over her shoulder. "Could Shorty carry up my trunk now?"

She turned to her sister. "Lou, come and help me unpack. I've so much to tell you, I don't know where to begin."

Tom shook his head at the retreating figures of his daughters. He'd bet money Jake's "errand" in town would give him one whale of an appetite. He'd better ask Martha to set an extra plate for supper.

"Lordy," he muttered under his breath. This might be a tough campaign for old Jake. He chuckled. Maybe some of the boys'd care to lay some wagers on the outcome?

Sally bounded up the hall stairs two at a time. "Lou, hurry up! Wait till you see what I brought you from St. Louis!" She burst through her bedroom door and stopped short.

Everything was just as she remembered it. Her heart swelled as she gazed around at the familiar furniture—her narrow, quilt-covered bed with its slightly saggy center, the tall walnut chiffonier she'd inherited from Aunt Emma, her father's oldest sister, the armoire in the corner that she knew held her jeans and flannel shirts and leather riding boots. She blinked back tears of joy. Dear Lord, it was good to be home. She turned to Louisa.

Her sister's blue eyes studied Sally's green velvet traveling dress and the matching peacock-feather hat.

"You certainly look different, Sally. Aunt Josie must have had a field day!"

"Aunt Josie had conniption fits every time we went out of the house. First I had to wear a corset. Then it was pantalets. And finally—" Sally rolled her eyes upward "—hats. Heavens, how I hate getting dressed up for everything!"

Louisa laughed and gave her a hug. "I bet the men noticed you," she ventured. "Knowing Aunt Jo, she must have introduced you to everyone in St. Louis. Did you have a beau? Or maybe two or three?"

Sally sniffed. "None that mattered. None that stayed long after I opened my mouth," she amended.

Louisa's blond eyebrows quirked upward, and Sally studied the floor rather than meet her sister's penetrating gaze. Lou always saw more in what Sally *didn't* say than what she did. She gestured at the doorway when Shorty clumped up the stairs with her trunk. "C'mon, Lou, help me unpack."

The two sisters chatted as they lifted garments out of the trunk and laid them in Sally's chest of drawers. Louisa wanted to know about everything—St. Louis, the train, the shiny buggy in the front yard. "Did Jake meet you at the station, Sally? Where is he?"

Sally swallowed. She hated to confess to Louisa that she'd deserted Jake, but once Lou got her teeth into something, she never gave up until she had the whole story. "I...I left him in town."

"You didn't!" Louisa's hands stilled on the nightgown she was folding.

"I most certainly did," Sally snapped. But underneath her air of bravado, a flicker of unease crept in. And Louisa didn't help matters much.

"Oh, honey," her sister moaned, "you're so smart and so dumb sometimes. If you think you've gotten away with anything when it comes to Jake Bannister, you've got another think coming."

"I don't care," Sally blurted. "It was worth it. I'd give anything to have seen his face, but I didn't dare look back."

Louisa shook her head and refolded the gown. "You haven't changed too much, Sally," she remarked to her sister's back. "Just on the outside. On the inside..." Her voice drifted off.

Sally turned toward Louisa and grasped both her hands. "I don't want to change, Lou—you know that. I want to be me—just me—no fancy feathers, just rags and bones, as Pa used to say. You know me better than anyone, Lou. You know that's what I've always wanted."

Louisa raised shining eyes to meet Sally's. "Yes," she said, her voice quiet. "I know."

By suppertime Jake had still not made an appearance.

"Who's the extra plate for?" Louisa inquired as she helped herself to a dainty portion of fluffy mashed potatoes.

"Jake Bannister." Tom reached for the blue-patterned china serving dish. "I figure he'll show up here sooner or later."

Sally's fork clattered to her plate. "But Pa! You said Shorty would drive the buggy over after supper!"

Tom sighed. "I know I said that, honey. But I can't do that. You know Jake—he'll have to have some words to go along with it."

Louisa sent a sidelong glance toward Sally. "I told you you'd be sorry."

"I won't either," Sally replied.

Unperturbed, Louisa continued her calm perusal of her older sister. "Well, when Jake does get here, I don't want to miss it," she observed mildly. She nibbled at the mound of potatoes on her fork. "When he rides in here madder than a hornet, your not being sorry won't matter a whit."

Sally glared at her sister. Louisa was the only member of the household—perhaps the only person in the entire valley—Sally could not intimidate. "Oh, for heaven's sake, Lou, what can he do? I'll say the mare got spooked and bolted, and that will be that."

"No Bar Y-broke mare ever bolted," Tom contradicted. "It'll only be a matter of time before Jake comes for his buggy—it's still sittin' in the front yard." He chuckled softly. "I don't want to miss the fireworks when he gets here, either." He scooped a double helping of snap beans onto his plate. "I'm sure glad you're back home, honey-girl. There hasn't been any fun worth spit around here for an age!"

"Nobody," added Louisa, her tone matter-of-fact as she cut her roast beef into tiny bites, "nobody has ever crossed Jake Bannister and gotten away with it."

Sally shifted uncomfortably on the upholstered dining room chair.

"Besides, honey," Tom remonstrated, "it wasn't smart to one-up the best horse breeder in the county. You're going to need a good horse to ride to the schoolhouse. Jake said he'd have some ready for you to look over tomorrow. You just need to go on over and pick yourself out one you like. That is, if he'll let you on his property after what you did to him this afternoon."

"Oh, for heaven's sake," Sally fumed. "Why all the fuss? I'll just apologize. Then what can he do?"

Tom and Louisa locked glances. After a long moment, both pairs of eyes swiveled toward Sally.

Sally sniffed. "Oh, pooh to you both." She clanked her knife and fork onto her plate and stalked into the kitchen.

"Just leave 'em in the sink," Martha called from the dining room. "Won't need any help tonight, seein' as how you'll be—" The housekeeper's voice stilled as Tom gave a loud cough.

Sally felt her cheeks flame. Despite her bravado, she was growing more nervous with each passing minute. No one ever *had* crossed Jake and gotten away with it. And from the stories she'd heard from Shorty, the hired man, and the other hands gathered around the cookhouse dinner table, Jake's retribution more often than not exactly suited the crime perpetrated against him or his ranch. Once, at gunpoint, he'd forced a cheating cardplayer to tear up the ace he'd hidden in his sleeve, chew it up and swallow it.

Sally suppressed a shudder, then squared her shoulders and marched into the parlor. He couldn't very well force her to eat a horse and buggy, could he?

An hour passed. Louisa settled onto the couch next to Sally and took up her crocheting.

"Coffee?" Martha inquired. The bulky housekeeper set the cups and the sugar bowl and cream pitcher down on the carved walnut sideboard.

Sally fidgeted, watching the lace edging take shape as her sister's deft fingers wove the silvery hook under and over the thread. Martha poured coffee and handed out the cups, then settled into the rocker by the fireplace.

Tom puffed on his pipe and kept his eye on the front door.

Sally squirmed in the silence. It was plain they were all waiting for Jake.

"It's getting late, Pa. Isn't anyone going to bed?"

"Not sleepy," Tom responded.

Louisa's voice sounded airy. "This piece is almost done. I think I'll just stay up a bit and finish it tonight to add to my hope chest."

Martha nodded and rocked forward to pour more coffee. The clock on the mantelpiece ticked ominously in the quiet. Ten o'clock. Ten-fifteen. Ten-thirty.

At last Sally could stand it no longer. "I don't care *what* Jake Bannister does tonight—or any other night, for that matter." She rose, stretched purposefully and shook out the folds of her bombazine skirt. "I'm going up to bed. 'Night, Lou, Martha." She dropped a kiss on her father's shiny forehead. "'Night, Pa."

Louisa did not even look up. "Better get some sleep while you can, Sally. It may be a long night." She smiled, keeping her gaze on the ball of ivory crochet thread in her lap.

Sally exhaled in exasperation. Oh, she didn't care what they all thought was going to happen! She wasn't going to sit around on tenterhooks all evening waiting for an angry rancher to show up. She had better things to do with her evenings. Besides, even if she was a bit nervous, she'd never let any of them see it.

And she'd never let anyone get the better of her, especially not Jake Bannister.

Long past midnight Sally awoke in the tiny upstairs bedroom to hear Shep growling. When he let out a tentative bark, her eyes snapped open, and she sat up.

The blue-flowered wallpaper shimmered in the moon's frosty light. Sally tipped her head and listened.

"Quiet, Shep," a man's voice said. It wasn't her father. Shorty? Or maybe the foreman, Hank? But what would Hank be doing up at this hour? Could Martha be ill?

The unmistakable thunk of a man's boots sounded on the gate path. Sally's breath froze. Three steps, then silence.

She opened her mouth, but before she could call out, there was a sharp ping on her windowpane. Silence, then another ping.

Stealthily she thrust her legs over the edge of the narrow bed and crept to the window.

Jake Bannister's tall, muscular shape loomed in front of the porch, his hands stuffed casually into the back pockets of his jeans. At the sight of him, a thread of apprehension wove into Sally's brain. As quietly as she could, she raised the window and leaned out.

The gray Stetson tipped back, and Jake looked up at her. "Close your mouth, Miss Sally," he drawled, parroting her statement earlier that afternoon. "It's me, Jake Bannister."

"I can see who it is," Sally snapped. "What on earth do you want at this hour?"

"Come down," Jake said, his voice quiet.

Lamplight flickered suddenly through a downstairs window, and Sally heard a muffled thump as her father pulled on his boots. Jake stepped into the pool of light.

"Go back to bed, Tom. This is between Sally and me."

Tom grunted, and Sally heard the bedsprings creak in the downstairs bedroom. *Pa was right, Jake's mad as*

a bull. And he's gone back to bed and left me here to...
Her mouth went dry.

"Sally?" Jake's deep voice unnerved her.

Oh, heavens. What was he going to do? He wouldn't dare wallop her again, would he?

"Jake, I'm—I'm sorry about the horse. She just got the bit in her teeth and—"

Jake cut her off. "One thing I always admire in a woman is honesty."

For some reason, Sally fancied a hint of laughter in the low voice. He was right, of course. She hated lying, herself.

"Oh, Mr. Bannister, I'm sor—"

"Come down here, Sally," Jake ordered. There was no hint of laughter in his tone now. His voice cut through the crickets and night rustlings like tempered steel. Another lamp glowed, this time upstairs, and Sally heard Louisa's bedroom window slide up. *Oh, for pity's sake,* Sally thought with growing trepidation. *Nobody ever wants to miss anything around here.*

"I most certainly will not come down! You can't order me around, Mr. Banni—"

"Jake."

"It's the middle of the night, Jake," she whispered down to him. "I'm not dressed."

"As a matter of fact, it's three o'clock in the morning," Jake drawled pleasantly. "But I didn't ride all the way over here just to pass the time, Miss Sally. So *get* dressed. Your lesson starts in four minutes."

"Lesson?" she gasped. Whatever could he mean?

"You heard me." The voice hardened. "Hurry it up, Sally. I haven't got all night."

Something in his voice stopped her breath. She stared down at him.

"Now," he ordered.

Dumbstruck, Sally pulled on jeans and a blue plaid outing-flannel shirt. She had no time to pin up her hair properly, but caught it at the nape of her neck with a ribbon. She stumbled down the stairs and out onto the front porch in her bare feet.

Jake lounged in the porch swing, the only sound the creak-creak of the supporting rope rubbing against the roof beam. Sally let the screen door slam behind her and confronted the lean figure, hands on her hips.

Jake surveyed her at leisure. Without the shoes and the stylish hat, she looked about sixteen. Her luscious, curved form, outlined by the tight jeans and clinging shirt, made him feel suddenly warm. It would be pure pleasure to humble her a bit.

"You got an apron?" he inquired, his voice lazy.

"Why, of course I've—" The look in his eyes made her skin prickle.

"Then put it on, Miss Sally. I missed supper on account of you."

Sally blanched. "Now? At three o'clock in the morning?"

"Now!" Jake echoed, his voice whip sharp.

Sally heard her father choke off a guffaw. *Oh, good heavens, Pa's in there glued to the window, watching all this! And Louisa, too!*

"Jake, you've got Olla Hendricks to cook for you at the Bar Y. Why—why can't you eat supper there?"

Too late she saw her mistake.

"Because, Miss Sally, Olla wasn't the cause of my missing supper in the first place!" He pushed back and forth in the swing. "Now, I admit I didn't take all this time getting back from town," he continued. "As a matter of fact, I could have stayed in town tonight. But

I didn't. I borrowed a horse from Charlie at the Silver Cup, so I didn't even have to walk out here."

"Then why—why didn't you borrow dinner from Charlie, too?"

Jake's eyes under the brim of the Stetson were calculating. "Because if you cook me supper at three in the morning, a task you brought upon yourself by your bad manners, you might take pains to learn better ones! I figure having been back East to school and all, you're smart enough not to make the same mistake twice."

Above her, Sally heard Louisa's stifled laughter. Oh, the man was insufferable. Somehow he always managed to humiliate her in front of other people! She'd be damned if she'd cook him supper, tonight or any other night.

"Look, Mr. Bannister—"

"Jake," he reminded her. He came to his feet and stood close to her, his eyes hardening. "And I like my bacon crisp, but not burned, and my eggs over easy. And stir up some flapjacks," he added. "I'm partial to them."

Sally backed away from him. "Jake, couldn't you just come to supper tomorrow night, instead?"

He smiled. "I could do that, all right." He reached out one tanned hand and closed iron fingers over her shoulder. "But where's the lesson in that, Miss Sally?" He propelled her toward the front door.

Jake lowered his frame into a chair at the round oak kitchen table, removed his Stetson and watched Sally as she moved about the room. She was a picture, all right. His eyes strayed to the provocative curve of her behind as she moved from stove to counter. Might not be too bad married to Sally, temper and all. A good meal goes a long way with a man. He liked her hair down like that—it looked thick and soft. He wondered what it would feel like laced in his fingers.

Sally tied a blue-checked gingham apron on over her jeans and wiped her hands on it as she measured out milk and flour for the pancake batter. Her fingers shook, and she spilled a half cup of flour on the floor. Why was he watching her like that, like a cat at a mouse hole? She tossed her hair back and managed to cut six thick slices of bacon from the slab in the pantry cooler without cutting herself. There was no sound save the clink of the heavy iron skillet as she lifted it from its hook over the wood stove in the corner. She added more wood to the coals Martha had carefully banked, then settled the pan on the metal. She felt like throwing it at him, but instead she laid the sliced bacon in it.

And then an idea formed in her mind. Sally stifled a smile and flicked a droplet of water onto the hot griddle, where it danced and spit.

Jake nodded approvingly. "There's nothing worse than flapjacks cooked on a lukewarm griddle," he remarked genially.

Sally curled her bare toes on the cold board floor and listened to the bacon sizzle in the pan. She cooked the meat until she was sure it was done more than he liked it, taking care to shield her handiwork from Jake's view. After she lifted the slices out, she broke three eggs into the remaining ooze of grease. She fried them rock hard, poking the yolks to make sure they were broken. While they were congealing into a yellow mass, she mixed up the pancake batter, purposely omitting both the baking powder and the eggs.

The kitchen smelled wonderful, Jake thought idly, watching her set the coffeepot on the stove. Courting Sally seemed like a pretty good idea after all.

He lifted his fork expectantly when she slid the plate before him, then slowly lowered it. The eggs swam in bacon grease, the toughened yolks showing through the shriveled whites in hard, yellow splotches.

Sally directed her sweetest smile at Jake. He bypassed the eggs and instead forked a mouthful of pancake past his lips. He tried to chew the leathery disks, but it took a long time to get the stuff past his throat. Sally watched him, smiling. In desperation he took a swig of the black coffee.

Her smile broadened. She'd made it with last night's grounds.

Jake made a choking sound and managed to swallow. She might have the sassiest little butt in the county, but she sure as hell couldn't cook. His glance flicked to the satisfied grin on her face. Or could she? Mm-hmm! Well, Miss Sultana, two can play at this game!

Jake said nothing. His face impassive, he worked his way slowly through the entire plateful of blackened bacon, rubbery eggs and flat, rawhide pancakes.

Seated across from him, Sally watched him down the last of the muddy coffee and felt vaguely disappointed. Not one complaint. Not even a reprimand on the bacon.

"Delicious!" he drawled at last. "Got any more flapjacks?"

Sally was flabbergasted. "You ate them? All of them?"

I sure as hell did, Jake thought grimly. *And she'll never know what it took to do it.* He tilted his chair away from the table, balancing precariously on the two back legs while he looked at Sally appraisingly.

Her cheeks looked flushed. Would she look like that if he kissed her? he wondered. He stared at her reddened lips.

Under his keen glance, Sally lowered her eyes to Jake's bent knees, hooked as an anchor just under the edge of the table. He had incredibly long, lean legs. They matched the rest of him—the lithe, controlled motion of his body when he walked, the lazy way he tipped back in his chair.

Her pulse leapt. She wasn't beaten yet, not by a long shot!

She stood and padded over to the stove. She tested the handle of the coffeepot. Still hot. Wrapping a dish towel around it, she picked it up.

"Is the lesson over for tonight?" she inquired, moving deliberately across the kitchen toward him.

Jake opened his mouth to reply, and Sally gently lowered the hot container onto his left knee. He jerked violently, and that was all it took. The carefully balanced chair toppled backward, spilling Jake's tensed body onto the floor. The crash was deafening.

Sally stared down at him. Peals of laughter burst from her as she studied the man who lay spread-eagled on her kitchen floor. The look on his face was worth a hundred breakfasts.

"What the hell's goin' on out there?" her father's voice thundered from the bedroom.

Sally alternately gasped for breath and laughed, one hand held to her stomach as her diaphragm labored for air. Oh, but revenge was delicious!

Wary, she looked down at Jake. His mouth tightened into a thin line, and his deep blue eyes—the bluest eyes she'd ever seen, she thought irrationally—stared up into her own. Then in one tigerlike motion he was on his feet, facing her.

She didn't stop laughing, couldn't even if she'd wanted to. And she didn't want to.

A net of fine crinkles started at the corners of his eyes, and then she heard his rich laughter blending with hers. Well, it *was* funny, she thought. But surely not to him!

"Sally," her father's voice boomed through the wall. "You all right, honey?"

Her breath came in short gasps, and for the life of her she couldn't answer. Jake, too, could not speak.

"Sally?"

"Yes, Pa, I'm fine," she managed to say. She was helpless. Her stomach ached from laughing.

Jake lifted the coffeepot out of her hand and turned away to set it back on the stove. When she saw the back of his dark blue wool shirt, splotched with an abstract design of fine white flour, she set off on another gale.

Jake's eyes glinted when he turned again to the slim, gingham-aproned girl before him. One thing for sure, he acknowledged, life with Sultana Maguire would never be dull. But if he could break mustangs, he could gentle Miss Sally.

He waited until she had calmed down, then he righted the chair and reached for the gray Stetson. "I guess that's enough lesson for one night," he said, a chuckle in his voice. "I'll see you tomorrow at the ranch. Tom said you want to look at some horses. We've got some good ones—you can take your pick." He moved to the door and tipped his hat. "*Au revoir,* Miss Sally. Thanks for the flapjacks."

His laughter echoed out the front doorway and down into the yard, fading gradually into the dark as Sally stood staring after him. Then she turned her gaze to the havoc she'd created in the kitchen.

Oh, heavens, what a mess! She'd better clean it up before Martha got up. But it was worth it. The look on his face...

Another hiccup of laughter bubbled from her throat.

In the morning Sally rode the five miles to the Bar Y with her father. She had hastily pinned up her thick, red hair and stuffed it under a wide-brimmed black Stetson, which she knotted under her chin. Her eyes felt grainy from lack of sleep.

"Pa, do we have to do this today?"

Tom looked over at his daughter. The purple shadows under her eyes accentuated her pale skin. "Honeygirl, it takes some time to get used to a new horse. Better to pick one out early, then get to know him some before you press him too hard." He resisted the impulse to add that the same was true of men.

Maybe he was right, Sally thought. School started in a week. She wanted to get used to her new mount before she had to face her pupils.

It took more than an hour of steady riding over the dusty, sun-parched land to reach the Bar Y entry gate. J. C. Bannister the carved wooden sign read. Horses And Beeves.

Tom dismounted and opened the wide, steel-hinged gate, then swung it closed after them, and they rode on to the corral. The September morning air was crisp and bore the tang of wood smoke. "Venison," Tom said, sniffing. "Jake's got his smokehouse goin' early this year."

Sally's stomach knotted. She'd slept through breakfast and had only had enough time to gulp a cup of

Martha's coffee before joining her father in the stable where he'd saddled the sorrel for her. Oh, well, they'd be home by lunchtime. She could eat then. Picking a new mare shouldn't take long. She had learned how to judge horses from her father, and even he said she was good at it.

Jake stood a short distance from the corral, running his hands over the foreleg of the most beautiful horse Sally had ever seen—black as polished metal, with a white slash on his forehead. He looked up as Tom and Sally approached, flashed a quick smile in their direction and turned his attention back to the gelding.

Tom dismounted quickly and joined the men strung along the top of the plank fence. "Cole, Nebraska." He nodded in greeting to the two men nearest him.

"Mornin', Tom. Mornin', Miss Sally. Welcome home." Blond, gangly Cole Sieversen hunched over a bit to make room for Tom.

A short, gray-bearded wrangler worked a big bay in the corral yard. Don Hendricks, Sally recalled; everybody called him Dutch. Sally dismounted and stood next to Will Boessen, the foreman at the Bar Y, who lounged against the fence. Next to Will the hired man, Slim, heaved his corpulent body onto the fence rail. Despite his girth, he had been called Slim ever since Sally could remember.

Will touched the brim of his battered tan hat. "Miss Sally," he offered quietly. "I hear you're wanting a new mare."

"Well, maybe not a mare, Will. What's that magnificent black over there, the one with Jake?"

"He's part Arabian," Will answered. "But he's not—"

"I'll try him," Sally cut in.

"Miss Sally—" Will closed his mouth after one look at Sally's face. He knew better than to contradict her. Words from him or anybody else would never deter her.

"Mr. Bannister," Will called to Jake. "Miss Sally's taken a fancy to the black."

Jake straightened and stared at Will. "He's not for sale."

Sally stiffened. Will turned to her and shrugged. "There's a nice chestnut mare, and that bay with Dutch—"

"Let me talk to Jake," Sally blurted.

Jake straightened again when he heard footsteps approaching and found himself looking into Sally's clear blue-green eyes. They were the damnedest color, he thought. He'd seen stained glass that color in France. *Bleu d'azur* they called it. Her jeans and flannel shirt clung to the trim curves of her body, and Jake's eyes lingered on her figure a moment before returning to her face. "You look pretty good this morning, considering you were up half the night making flapjacks."

Sally's cheeks burned, but she ignored the remark. "You said I could have any horse I wanted," she accused. "I want this one."

"Sorry, he's not for sale. He's green yet. Not completely broken."

She bit her lip. "What you mean is, you want him for yourself!"

Jake's eyes darkened. "No, that's not what I mean." Damn the woman. Didn't she ever say please or thank you? "What I mean is exactly what I said. This horse is not broken."

"I don't believe you," Sally answered. "*You're* handling him. I know a good horse when I see one. You won't let me have him because *you* want him."

Jake gave her a long, appraising look. No one accused Jake Bannister of lying. No one, not even Miss Sultana Maguire. He smiled grimly. Lesson number two, coming up.

"Suit yourself, Miss Salty."

"Sally," she corrected automatically.

Jake looked at her. Without taking his eyes from her face, he called to the man working the bay in the corral. "Dutch, saddle up the black for Miss Sally."

Dutch stared, and the soft buzz of talk among the men on the fence rail ceased. When Sally headed for the corral, Will Boessen walked to meet Jake.

"Jake," he remonstrated, keeping his voice low, "she could get hurt."

Jake looked at his foreman. "You ever try to talk Sally Maguire out of anything, Will? She won't even get seated right," he added in an undertone. "He'll buck her off in five seconds, and then she'll have it out of her system."

Will shook his head doubtfully. "I dunno, Jake. She rides well and all, but—"

Jake clapped his foreman on the shoulder and glanced over at Tom. "Okay with you, Tom?"

Tom grinned. "You're the boss, Jake."

"Son of a gun, Tom!" Nebraska turned incredulous brown eyes toward the older man. "You gonna let her ride that black?"

Tom drew a long breath. "Yup. Wouldn't matter if I told her not to—she hasn't listened to me since she was ten."

Perched on the other side of Tom, Cole gave a short laugh. "One of these days that girl's gonna get herself killed."

"Oh, she's pretty savvy about horses," Tom offered. He rolled a cigarette, hiding the fact that his hand shook.

"She's a damn fool," Jake muttered. He handed the black's reins over to Dutch and joined the men on the fence. He gave Tom an extra-long look.

Nebraska swore softly. "Miss Louisa'd never do such a fool thing, never."

At the mention of Louisa, Sally saw Will Boessen's head jerk up. She gave the tall foreman a quick look and smiled to herself. So, Lou had made another conquest. Sally approved. She liked Will.

Without a backward glance she strode to the center of the corral.

Dutch spread the saddle blanket on the gelding's broad back and gingerly settled a saddle on top of it. At Sally's approach, the horse stamped nervously, snorting and rolling his great black eye. The wrangler cinched up the saddle girth and leaned toward Sally.

"I t'ink iss too much horse for you, Miss Sally," the wiry Dutchman ventured.

"No horse is too much horse for me," Sally snapped. "Just hold him steady so I can mount."

Dutch shook his head and cupped his hands for Sally's booted foot.

Chapter Three

Sally looped the reins twice around her left fist and swung her leg over the saddle. Carefully she settled her weight onto the back of the huge, black beast and sat perfectly still, holding her breath. Dutch backed cautiously away.

For a moment nothing happened, and Sally exhaled slowly. She was right. Jake wanted this horse for himself. Jake was a lot of things she hated, but she never thought he'd lie about a horse.

Before she could draw a breath of relief, the animal leapt, arched his back and became a thrashing demon.

Sally grabbed the saddle horn with one hand and dug her knees into the black's plunging form. Relax, her brain hammered. Go with him. Bend in the middle. She felt her back muscles tense, and her thighs burned against the gelding's heaving sides.

Jake watched from the corral fence, a twinge of guilt stabbing his conscience. He shouldn't have let her do it, no matter how much she goaded him. He clenched damp palms into fists and watched the slim girl struggle to stay in the saddle.

Sally's hat flew off and sailed to the ground in front of Jake. As the horse bucked and pounded beneath her,

her hairpins loosened. Her hair tumbled free in a thick cascade of shiny auburn, whipping about her face and shoulders.

Jake's heart caught. She was the most untamed, wildly beautiful woman he had ever seen.

The cowhands cheered from the sidelines, shouting their encouragement. "Hell," Cole barked to Tom, "I never thought she'd last this long." Impressed, he watched the slim figure toss on the gelding's back. "Ride 'im, Miss Sally!" he hooted.

Tom tossed away the cigarette he'd pulverized in his gnarled fingers. "Hang on, honey-girl," he yelled. Pride and fear made his voice quaver; he didn't trust himself to say anything else.

Sally hung on. Her stomach heaved sickeningly with each plunge the black made, and she thought her neck would snap. But she hung on. She wasn't going to give Jake Bannister the satisfaction of seeing her whipped.

Jake ground his boot heels into the fence rail. She'd lasted maybe twenty seconds. Damn, the girl had spirit. She couldn't make flapjacks worth spit, but she could sure as hell ride.

And then the black leapt in a vicious, double-twisting roll, and Sally was airborne. She hit the ground flat on her back and lay still.

Tom sucked in his breath and started up off the fence rail.

"Great balls of..." Nebraska breathed. "Is she—?"

The wrangler, Dutch, caught the stamping horse and led it away from the prone figure.

Jake was off the fence in an instant. "I'll get her, Tom. Stay where you are," he shouted.

He moved swiftly to where Sally lay. Crazy little fool! She had no more sense than a honeybee. What if her back was broken? Or her neck? Hell's feathers, somebody should take her in hand.

Sally sprawled in the dusty corral yard like a doll carelessly tossed onto the ground. Jake knelt over the motionless form and glanced at the pale, still face. His heart lurched oddly. "Sally! Sally!" With a shaking hand he gently touched her shoulder. *"Sally!"*

What a damn fool thing to let her do! It wasn't like him to let his anger push him like that. What if she was seriously hurt? What if she—

Sally moaned but did not open her eyes, and Jake heaved a sigh of relief. Her hand twitched at her side. He enveloped it in his.

Tom, his face white, sank back onto the fence rail. Suddenly his knees felt weak. "Nah, she's not dead," he growled to Nebraska. "She's too stubborn. Probably got the wind knocked out of her, though."

He tried to roll another smoke. Nebraska finally took the paper out of his shaking hand and finished the task for him.

Sally struggled to draw breath. A great weight pressed on her chest, crushing her. She tried to edge out from under it, but she couldn't move. She couldn't even open her eyes. Oh, God, she must be dying.

Jake's low voice came to her as if from a great distance. "Lie still, Sally. You're all right. You've had the wind knocked out of you. Try to breathe now, slow and easy."

His hand on her forehead felt reassuring, heavy and warm. Sally inhaled a little bit at a time and opened her eyes. All at once she felt like throwing up. She struggled to sit up and turned her face toward the dirt.

Jake grasped her shoulders and raised her body to a semiprone position while she coughed and struggled for air.

The wave of nausea passed. She dropped her forehead against Jake's forearm and closed her eyes. Oh, how good it felt to breathe! Tears choked her throat, but she fought them back. Nobody—especially not Jake Bannister—was going to see her cry. He'd made a fool of her, but she'd die before she let him see how embarrassed she was.

She kept her head pressed down against Jake's arm, and breathed in and out slowly. The smell of dust and the sweaty, pine-soap scent of the man holding her made her dizzy. She inhaled again.

"She's startin' to look okay," Nebraska observed, watching his boss and Sally in the center of the corral yard. "Hell, Tom, what's Jake doing, anyway? How come he don't help her up?"

"Maybe he's courtin' her," Tom suggested slyly, relief lightening his voice. He figured to move things along, if he could. Letting the Bar Y hands know the lay of the land might help.

"Courtin' her!" Nebraska exploded. "You crazy? Hell, she's half-dead. And when she hasn't had the stuffing kicked out of her, she's downright—" The rangy cowboy lapsed into an embarrassed silence.

Cole glanced at the couple in the corral yard and watched as Jake bent over the prone girl. "No offense against Miss Sally," he remarked in an undertone. He studied the toes of his boots. "But Mr. Jake's been run after by purty near every girl in the county, and he's never courted a one of them. Not one. It's not likely he'd...um...take to Miss Sally."

"Besides," interjected Nebraska. "Why would any-one want to court Miss Sally when Miss Louisa's around?"

Will Boessen's head snapped up. He glared at the cowhand, then purposefully looked away.

Tom grinned and took a deep draw on his cigarette. "Care to lay down some bets on it, gents?"

Nebraska and Cole goggled at him. Cole recovered first. "Also no offense, Tom, but while Miss Sally's a real looker, she's, uh, got a tongue like a rattlesnake."

"Downright dangerous," Slim added in a low mut-ter.

"I know, I know." Tom laughed. "But look at it this way, boys. I'll lay you a bet that in the end, Jake'll get Sally to the altar. As a matter of fact, I'll lay five gold dollars on it right now."

Silence. Slim and the Bar Y hands edged nearer. Dutch, holding the gelding's reins a few yards off, strained to hear what was going on.

"I'll bet he don't," Nebraska challenged. "Miss Sal-ly's gonna be the new schoolmarm. She'll never marry Jake, or anybody else. Anyway, she's so prickly she'd have to hog-tie him and drag him to the church."

"Want to wager she'll do just that?" Tom coun-tered. "Right now, they scrap like cats and dogs, but every time Jake wins a round, he's one step closer."

"My bet's on Sally," Will Boessen said quietly. "Every time Sally bests the boss, she's one step closer to teaching school for the rest of her life."

Tom's eyes twinkled. "It'll be a real horse race, it will. How 'bout it, boys?"

The Bar Y hands looked speculatively from Tom to the corral yard where Jake still knelt beside the dusty form on the ground. In silence they waited to see what would happen next.

Sally raised her throbbing head and looked into the eyes of the man whose arms supported her. "You mangy polecat," she said through gritted teeth. She pulled her trembling arm back and hit him as hard as she could.

"One dollar on Miss Sally," Slim intoned to Tom.

Jake flinched. "What the hell—" He imprisoned Sally's wrist in an iron-handed grip. "You little hellion. You get yourself half-killed on a horse you'd no business riding in the first place, and it's *my* fault?"

Sally gasped and wrenched her hand free. Maybe he didn't do it on purpose, but she was mad as a wet hen anyway. She scrambled to her knees, then rose unsteadily to her feet. Her head reeling, she stalked as straight a path as she could manage over to the fence where Dutch stood holding the black gelding. She snatched the quirt out of the wrangler's hand, then pivoted and advanced toward Jake with murder in her eye.

"Make it two dollars," Slim amended, his avid eyes on Sally.

Unmoving, Jake watched Sally approach. The sight of her flushed cheeks and tumbled hair mesmerized him. He wondered idly if she'd be that wild in bed with a man.

When she got within a few yards of him, Sally raised her quirt.

Before she could strike, Will Boessen moved to intercept her. He caught the cord end of the whip in his gloved hand. "Don't do it, Miss Sally."

Sally stared at the Bar Y foreman. Will's quiet warning tone penetrated the haze of fury boiling inside her.

"Mr. Jake could carve his initials on your backside with a whip quicker than you could spit," Will continued in an undertone. "Don't tempt him."

Sally's eyes blazed into Will's for a long moment. Then she turned away, her shoulders sagging in defeat. Will was right, of course. She'd already made a fool of herself in front of Jake and all the Bar Y hands. Attacking him would only make it worse. She knew Jake could tan her to within an inch of her britches. What could she have been thinking of? Oh, damn the man, anyway!

She took a faltering step, and the world around her spun. Swaying, she reached out a hand and grabbed the fence rail.

Jake scooped up her hat from the corral yard and strode toward her, brushing past his foreman. "It's all right, Will—I'll handle it."

Sally's tangled hair tumbled about her face, and her eyes looked unfocused. He fought the impulse to wrap both his arms around her. Carefully he reached one hand to grip her shoulder.

Sally felt Jake's arm slide around her, steadying her, and in spite of herself, she leaned into him, the fight in her draining away. How she hated admitting defeat. She wanted to cry, but she wanted to do it in private, not here. Not in front of Jake. She didn't want those self-satisfied eyes on her when she couldn't fight back. Damn, damn, damn him!

She struggled against the rising sobs as Jake walked her slowly toward her sorrel. "Listen, Sally." The warm, resonant voice spoke near her ear. "Let me pick out a horse for you. I have a couple of beauties in mind—a good, strong bay and a chestnut mare that would be just right for you. After supper tonight, I'll bring them over so you can take a look."

Sally nodded, her mind working. She barely listened to what he was saying.

The men lounging on the corral fence assessed the couple moving slowly out of the yard. "Two dollars on the boss," Cole whispered to Tom. He watched Jake's arm tighten around Sally's shoulders, then amended his statement. "Make it three. Jake could honey-talk a porcupine out of its quills."

Oblivious to the murmur of voices behind them, Jake bent his head toward Sally. "I'm sorry about today, Sally, believe me."

She nodded again.

Tom slid off the fence rail, ground his cigarette into the dirt and headed for his horse.

Still listening to Jake's voice, Sally moved toward her father, struggling to focus her thoughts. When she reached the sorrel, she found her father already mounted and waiting.

Jake reached for her stirrup and held it steady. With a groan, Sally pulled her aching body up into the saddle.

Jake studied her pasty face. It wasn't like her to be so quiet. Maybe she was hurt worse than it seemed. "Can you ride, Sally? Will can drive you home in the buggy if you'd rather."

Sally shook her head. "I'll ride."

Jake handed up her black Stetson. "After supper," he reminded her. "I'll bring two of my best. You can choose."

Sally stared down into Jake's intense, indigo eyes for a long moment. "I want the black."

"Oh, for God's sake, Sally!" Jake exploded. "The black's not for sale."

"The black," she repeated.

Deliberately he shook his head. "No."

Tom choked down a chuckle. He stole a look at his daughter's face. To his amazement he saw her lower lip jump in a telltale quiver. She'd had more than the wind knocked out of her, he thought. Maybe he should've laid *ten* dollars on Jake. His spitfire of a daughter had finally met her match.

Jake shot a glance at the older man. "I'm sorry, Tom. She's not bad hurt, but she's plenty mad."

Tom grinned. "Never mind, son. A man who's never riled up a woman is a failure." He flicked his reins, and the big horse moved away.

Instinctively Sally nosed her mount after her father's. At the last moment she inclined her head toward Jake and spoke three words into the uneasy silence. "Bring the black."

Jake gazed at her in disbelief. Hell's back door, what a woman. Without a doubt she was the most exasperating, provocative, unpredictable female he'd ever encountered. And all rolled up into a body that... He slapped his dusty Stetson against his thigh and watched her walk her horse sedately through his open gate.

Court her! Hell, he'd have to hog-tie her just to get close enough to talk to her! He stared out across his parched rangeland. But he needed water. He hated to admit it, but he needed Sally Maguire, temper tantrums and all.

Okay, if he had to hog-tie her, he'd hog-tie her. She wouldn't like it, but with no rain the past two seasons and none in sight this summer, he didn't have a choice.

* * *

After supper that evening the entire Maguire household drifted out to the front porch. Martha and Hank Blane, the foreman, sat side by side in the porch swing holding hands, the bulky frame of the housekeeper contrasting with the lanky slimness of her husband. Hank gave the swing an occasional push with his foot to keep it moving.

His evening chores done, Shorty lounged on the bottom step, whittling a piece of oak with his jackknife and humming under his breath. Shep snoozed at his feet.

Sally perched on the top step, her knees drawn up to her chin. She felt light-headed. Louisa had spent all afternoon laying cool, damp cloths on her forehead to quell the splitting headache she'd nursed from her morning encounter with the gelding. Now she felt slow and a bit dreamy. Idly she listened for the sound of horses, puzzled at her vague disappointment when an hour passed and there was still no sign of Jake. Or the black gelding.

She breathed in the spicy, vanilla scent of the Belle of Portugal rose her mother had planted years ago. The lush pale peach blooms trailed all along the split-rail fence Shorty and her father had put up, covering the arbor at the side of the two-story frame house where Sally and Louisa had been born. The warm, still air was silent except for the screech of crickets and the creak of the porch swing. The talk, what there was of it, was mostly disjointed commentary on what her father called "nobody's business news" and the continuing dry weather, the subject of primary concern among all the ranchers in the valley.

Through the open front door Sally gazed at her sister, perched on the piano bench. The sensuous ripple of a haunting Schubert melody drifted out onto the soft night air.

Tom tipped back in the battered oak chair, his long legs propped on the porch railing, and surveyed the scene before him. He'd built this ranch, he and Marie. Lord, thank you. Those had been good years. You couldn't ask for better. Unless, of course, it was a warm summer night like this one, with Louisa playing the piano and Sally, quiet for once, sitting at his feet. He smiled into the gathering dusk and reached into his shirt pocket for his tobacco pouch.

Just as he finished rolling his cigarette, Jake and his foreman rode into the yard. "Evenin', Jake, Will," Tom called as the two men approached.

Both men touched their hat brims, dismounted outside the fence and walked through the gate.

Sally's heart gave a little skip at the sight of the tall man with the gray Stetson. She stifled the smile of satisfaction that touched her lips. She might have lost the battle, but she certainly hadn't lost the war yet.

Jake nodded in the direction of the porch. "Miz Blane, Miss Sally." He rested his gaze on Sally. "It's still light enough to ride. Want to do a little horse choosing?"

As if her body were disconnected from her mind, Sally rose and followed him outside the front fence to where a bay and a dark chestnut were tethered. "Where's the black?"

"Try the bay," Jake suggested, avoiding her question. "She's strong and steady. The chestnut is more spirited, but she can be skittish. The bay will do you better when snow comes."

Sally sniffed, but she mounted the bay. She didn't feel up to an argument tonight. Jake climbed on the chestnut, and they moved off down the road together.

Sally puzzled over how good it felt to ride beside the tall, quiet man. Part of her liked the companionable silence that fell between them. Another part of her wanted to... oh, tonight she didn't know what she wanted. Maybe she'd hit her head harder than she thought this morning.

Jake glanced over at her. She looked softer somehow. He chuckled to himself. Got some of the vinegar kicked out of her, he guessed. "You going to be riding sidesaddle?"

"What? Why would I ride sidesaddle? I've ridden astride since I was five years old."

"Well, Miss Sally, you're not five years old anymore. You're not going to teach school wearing jeans and a raggedy old shirt of Tom's, are you?"

"I—" She hadn't thought of that. As the schoolteacher, she'd have to wear the long skirts and starched, high-necked blouses Aunt Josie had insisted she buy in St. Louis. She'd have to dress like a lady, she supposed—give up her beloved jeans and boots and her father's soft, comfortable, worn-out shirts. But ride sidesaddle, like the prissy, stuck-up girls in town? Never.

"Maybe you should drive a buggy instead," Jake offered, surmising her dilemma. "This chestnut would make a good buggy horse."

"I don't want a buggy," Sally snapped. "I want a horse. And I'll ride astride, thank you, as I always have."

"In a skirt?"

"Oh, Jake, leave me alone." Her head was beginning to ache again. "I'll figure out something." She lapsed into silence.

Jake shot a quick look at the girl mounted beside him. It wasn't like Sally to give in without a tirade of sharp words and some temper. She sure was acting funny. His eyes flicked to her downcast face. She'd pinned that mass of hair up on top of her head again, but without her usual wide-brimmed black hat to block his view, he could study her face surreptitiously.

She looked calm. Gentle, even. Hell, courting her might not be so bad. That black gelding had taken all the starch out of her! Already he could see his hundred acres, knee-deep in lush green grass, could see Sally in her blue-checked gingham apron, puttering in the Bar Y kitchen. Not half-bad at all. He wondered whether Sally's fire and sparkle would return in the bedroom.

In the silence, Sally pondered Jake's question. Of course she couldn't teach school in jeans and flannel shirts. She was grown up now. A lady. She weighed the prospect of her new life as the Honey Creek schoolmistress. She desperately wanted to succeed at teaching, knew instinctively that she had a flair for it. She'd be the best teacher Klamath County ever had.

Her heart skipped a beat. But did she want to become a *lady* in the process? Join the young women's church league and drink tea on Sunday afternoons instead of ride and have picnics and go fishing and canoeing and swimming in the river?

No, she did not. Schoolmarm or no, she didn't want to change a thing.

"No!" she blurted. "I won't do it!"

"Won't do what?" Jake ventured.

Sally's hands tightened on the reins. "I won't give up fishing, or swimming in the river, or—" She took a deep breath. "And I won't ride sidesaddle!"

Jake pulled the chestnut up short. "Suit yourself, Miss Sally. But you'll show a lot of petticoat riding astride in a skirt."

"I don't wear petticoats," she retorted.

"All ladies wear petticoats," Jake remarked, his voice matter-of-fact.

"Then . . . then I won't *be* a lady!"

Jake laughed. "Grow up, Sally. You're not a four-teen-year-old tomboy anymore. You're a twenty-three-year-old schoolteacher who needs a horse."

Sally's eyes hardened into green ice. "You leave what I need out of this, Jake Bannister." She spurred the bay and drew away from him, turning her mount back to-ward the house. Oh, she was positive he was deviling her. Nothing got her hackles up faster than being teased.

Jake watched her for a moment, but he altered nei-ther his pace nor his direction. She was a lot like that black Dutch was breaking for him. Wild and proud. What she needed was a bit of gentling.

He turned his horse and caught up to her. Leaning down to catch the bay's bridle, he brought both horses to a stop. "Sally, hold on a minute." He jockeyed his mount closer. "You've seemed kind of skittish ever since you got off that train yesterday. Anything wrong?"

"Wrong? Certainly not. I—"

"Then what are you so het up about?"

"I'm not—" She broke off. Well, of course she was. Any fool could see that, and Jake Bannister was no fool. But she didn't want him probing into her private thoughts. Her concerns about being the schoolteacher, and what it meant to her, were nobody's business but hers. She didn't want to talk about it. In fact, she didn't want to think about it anymore. And she especially didn't want to think about Jake. For some reason, being close to him completely unnerved her.

Jake gave her a penetrating look. "Men have an easier job of growing up, I guess. They grow taller, get long pants, a better horse, but essentially they still do the same things. Not that much changes for them. But a woman—especially one like you—a woman has to give up all kinds of things she enjoyed as a child."

"I'm not," Sally said, her voice tightening. "I'm not going to give up anything. I'm going to have everything exactly as it was before. I'm going to ride and swim and..."

Jake nodded. "Exactly as it was before what, Sally?"

Her eyes widened.

"Why, I don't know, exactly."

"Sally, how old were you when your mother died?"

The question jarred her. Startled, she allowed herself a moment of reflection. "Mama died three days before my fifteenth birthday."

Jake nodded. "And you're afraid that if you grow up, become a full-blown woman, wear petticoats and do those other things that women do—like fall in love, have kids—you're afraid that you'll die, too? Or that someone you care about will die. Is that it?"

The color drained from her face. She'd never thought of that before, but...

Anger pulsed through her, and her head began to ache in earnest. How could this man invade the most secret part of her heart? She didn't want to think about her mother. She didn't want to remember any of it. The aching, desolate feeling of loss threatened to engulf her, and she steeled her emotions, welcoming anger to mask the pain. Jake had no right to peer into her innermost thoughts. It was none of his business.

He leaned toward her and pushed his hat up with one forefinger. "Nothing comes for free, Sally," he said close to her ear, his voice low and oddly gentle. "If you never saddle your horse, you never win the race."

She stared at him, openmouthed.

Jake's eyes held hers. "Risk it, Sally. Let it happen."

Risk it? Risk what? Wearing petticoats? Riding side-saddle? Whatever was he talking about?

Jake tugged on her bridle and they moved to the fence. Silence hung between them as they dismounted and walked toward the house, now barely discernible in the deepening dusk. Only the lilting sound of the piano and sporadic bursts of laughter from the porch broke the stillness.

Suddenly Sally wanted to cry. How beautiful and peaceful it was. She didn't want anything to change, ever. What did he mean, let it happen? Let what happen? She didn't want *anything* to happen.

Jake whistled the melody along with the piano. When Sally glared at him, he broke off with a shrug. "I have a weakness for Schubert." And, he thought to himself, he had a weakness for eyes the color of prairie grass in the spring and a spirit that disdained the conventions of petticoats. He understood her, felt sympathy for her. Liked her.

Sally stared at him. What kind of a rancher out here in the West whistled Schubert? The question rose to her lips, but she bit it back. She didn't want to know any more about him. Even though Jake Bannister had been their neighbor for most of her life, she really knew very little about him. Long ago she had decided the man inside the slim jeans and blue, high-collared shirt was a self-satisfied know-it-all, but beyond that he was a bit of a mystery. All she knew for certain was that she had hated him since her fourteenth year. She spun away from him, toward the house.

Jake reached for her, caught her arm above the elbow and swung her around to face him. He raised his other hand and held her by both shoulders. "Sally—"

Sally's eyes flashed into fire. "You take your hands off me this instant, Jake Bannister!"

The piano music ceased abruptly, and a thick quiet descended. Jake dropped his arms. "Sally," he continued in a low tone, "just listen a minute."

Her head came up defiantly, and Jake saw a wet sheen on her cheeks. His heart turned over. She was like a little banty rooster with its feathers all fluffed out. Frightened, hurt maybe, but ready to do battle. Something in his chest began to ache, and without thinking, he reached for her again.

"Don't you touch me," she blazed. The seemingly endless silence was broken only by the *scrick-scrick* of the crickets and the breathing of the man before her. She hesitated. *Why don't I move?* she thought. *Walk away from him, into the house?*

Then Tom's voice floated out on the still air. "Aw, hell, Sally, kiss the poor bastard!"

Sally froze. Laughter erupted from the front porch, and the piano resumed its cascade of arpeggios. Her own father! How could he be so crude?

Jake chuckled. What was it Tom had said? A man who never made a woman angry was a failure? He guessed he was anything but. After a moment he drew her around the corner of the house and then pulled her stiff body carefully into his arms. She felt warm and fragile, and her hair smelled so good, like roses and lilacs mixed up together. He closed his eyes, feeling her body tremble against him.

"Sally," he murmured. "Sally." He ached for her. He bent and covered her soft mouth with his.

At the touch of his lips, something within Sally leapt into flame. In spite of herself she clung to him, smelling his leathery, smoky scent, savoring his mouth for a long, delicious moment. When at last she drew away from him, she stood perfectly still, staring up at him.

A surge of panic replaced the flush of pleasure she had felt a moment before. She struggled to breathe evenly. How dare he kiss her, make her melt against him like that? It was... dangerous. The word popped unbidden into her mind. Very dangerous. She didn't know exactly what she was afraid of, but something about Jake Bannister frightened her.

Without warning, her arm snaked out and she slapped him, hard. The sound cut through the night air, and the piano halted again.

Without an instant's hesitation Jake pinned her arms behind her. He'd never struck a woman before, but right now it sure would feel good.

"I didn't deserve that," he said evenly, "and you know it." His arm ached to teach her a lesson she wouldn't forget.

A thread of pain darkened her eyes into emerald pools, and Jake groaned in frustration.

Sally said nothing. Inside she knew he was right—he hadn't deserved it. She had wanted him to kiss her, and she had liked it. In fact, the feel of his mouth on hers had been exquisite. The fact that she'd felt an inexplicable fear at her response didn't warrant slapping him. Her wrist smarted where his fingers dug into her skin.

Watching her face, Jake suddenly understood the turmoil that was raging inside her. Sally was afraid. Afraid of life, afraid she'd be hurt again, as she had been when her mother died. But she'd grow out of it— he knew she would. She had to.

His brain sang. Years from now, he thought, maybe all the rest of his life, he'd remember that kiss. Sally Maguire was warm and soft and yielding, and a little wild. She made mush out of his senses. She smelled of lilacs, and she had wanted him. She wanted him! This was the beginning of their courtship. *Kiss the poor bastard,* Tom had said. Good old Tom. What a fine father-in-law he would make! It was only a matter of time.

"Sally, I—"

Panic pushed all reason aside. All Sally knew was that she had to get away from Jake. She felt herself pulled toward him, inexorably drawn to something that terrified her. She mustn't allow this, mustn't be close to him, feeling his warmth and steadiness, smelling his male scent. It would be better if she never saw him again.

"I'll take the bay," she snapped, her voice icy. "And I believe that's the end of my business with you. There is no need for us to meet again."

"Well, now, I wouldn't say th—"

Sally's eyes flashed. "Goodbye, Mr. Bannister."

In disbelief Jake watched her stalk away from him. Dad blast it, what had got into her now? He shook his head as he heard the screen door slam behind her.

What a merry chase she was leading him! He was caught like a tenderfoot with his bootlaces tied together, pulled between an irresistible land deal and a totally incomprehensible woman. Still, he had nothing to lose by courting her. Providing things went right, he had everything to gain: land, water for his thirsty stock—and Sally. Everything.

And after that kiss, he knew in his gut that Sultana Maguire was sure as shooting going to be worth the trouble.

Chapter Four

Sally pulled open the heavy plank door of the school-house and stepped over the threshold. She inhaled deeply. Oh, it smelled so good! The pungent, piney scent of the new wood blended with the spicy perfume of white clover and purple lupine carpeting the meadow where the simple log building stood. Erected just a week ago and not yet weathered, the split-pine log walls glowed in the afternoon light.

A large oak desk, darkened with age, sat facing the row of rough pine-board benches—her pupils' seats. There hadn't been time to order desks for the students, her father had warned her. The men had barely completed raising the walls and nailing on the roof before Sally arrived on the train. Well, she'd just have to make do until spring.

Just that morning at breakfast Louisa had reminded her how hard all the ranch families in the valley had worked to get the schoolhouse ready in time for fall term. The women had baked pies and made dozens of sandwiches for the men who labored under the searing August sun. Every ranch family for miles around wanted a real school, and a trained teacher, for their children.

But would they accept *her?*

Her application, submitted in her absence by Louisa, had been turned down at first. "Too unorthodox and outspoken," the letter read.

Too unorthodox? Sally sniffed. All she wanted to do was get her pupils interested in learning. Schools back East had been doing such things for the past ten years. Surely it was time for change in Klamath County?

When no other candidates had applied, Sally got the job. It paid one hundred dollars a year.

If she lasted a year. Faced with the prospect of teaching whoever came to sit on those long, narrow benches, Sally experienced a moment of panic.

She would be responsible for the intellectual development of perhaps twenty children, some not yet five years old, some as old as fourteen or fifteen. Would they like her? More important, would they obey her? Learn from her? And what would she do if they didn't?

Her preparation was adequate; she knew that. But she also knew the ranch families in the valley, knew they would look on her methods as unusual. "Progressive," Professor Baird at the teachers' seminary had pronounced. Acceptable in St. Louis, but what about out here in the West?

And, Sally thought with a sigh, out here in Honey Creek she would not be accountable to Professor Baird, but to the nine-member school board.

She gazed about her at the bare walls, the stack of new slates in one corner, the black potbellied wood stove in the other, and her resolve stiffened. Light from the small paned window—a generous donation from Reverend Mathews's Tuesday Ladies' Club—washed over the plank floor.

She squared her shoulders. This was *her* school! She'd had to struggle to get this appointment in the first place; she'd sooner die than give it up without a fight.

A fierce sense of possession swept over her. She'd do anything she had to do to teach in this room, even wear skirts and starched lace blouses and petticoats. She'd show the school board. She'd show them all. She'd be the model of propriety on the outside, where it didn't count. But she could be as creative as she pleased in her teaching methods. No one would question them if they worked, if her pupils really learned their sums and letters.

Sally blew out a long breath and sat at her new desk. Bees hummed in the silence. Outside, a gnarled pine tree, its lower branches drooping almost to the ground, shaded the water pump. Someone had hung a shiny new bucket over the iron pump handle.

In an instant she was out the door, filling the bucket to the brim. Then she rambled through the meadow picking armloads of blue lupine and stuffing them into the bucket.

She stepped over the threshold, set the container on her desk and stood back to admire it. Perfect. How proud Mama would have been to see her doing something so ladylike.

At the thought of her mother, a cloud settled over her heart. Her chest squeezed as Jake's words echoed in her brain. *You're afraid...someone you care about will die?* Her throat ached.

It wasn't your fault, Mama. I know that. The buggy overturned and... It was an accident. You didn't die on purpose.

But it hurt, just the same. It hurt, and kept on hurting, for all these years. When she was younger, the pain was so keen she had wanted to die, too. Now that she was older, the knife blade of grief had dulled somewhat, but still Sally knew she never again wanted to experience anything as devastating as that loss. Never.

She gave herself a good shake and cast one last glance at the bucketful of flowers on her desk, then moved toward the door. She'd plant a cutting from one of Mama's roses right outside the schoolhouse door—a Harison's Yellow, maybe. Or a climbing Cecile Brunner that would twine over the wooden lintel. That way, Mama would always be close.

Sally's heart caught. *Oh, Mama, I miss you so much! It still hurts.*

"*A* is for..." Eleven-year-old Jacob Hendricks chewed his lower lip and frowned. "Aw, gosh, Miss Maguire," the dark-haired boy blurted, "I can't think of any countries that start with *A*."

Sally sighed and moved on to the next child. "What about you, Elsa? Can you think of a country that starts with the first letter of the alphabet?" At seven years of age, frail, blond Elsa Baker could not yet read or write, but once she heard something spoken, she never forgot it.

"Argentina!" she shouted, triumph making her blue eyes sparkle.

"And where is Argentina located?" Sally asked Billy Peterman, seated next to Elsa. Billy was nine, with orangey red hair that flopped over his eyebrows. Remembering the cruel gibes about her own red hair when she was a child, Sally never allowed the other children to tease Billy. As a consequence, his transparent adoration of Sally shone on his thin face. Billy blushed to his hairline and stared at his boots.

"Billy?" Sally prompted from her desk. The boy shook his head.

"Can anyone give him a hint?" She glanced at the nineteen rapt faces and waited expectantly. She had been teaching for only a month, but already she found herself in love with a whole roomful of children. Her students, ranging in age from six to seventeen, learned quickly, and their pride in their accomplishments warmed Sally's heart. She tried to make the school lessons fun, but she brooked no nonsense. The children basked in her praise, cringed at her displeasure. But underneath, she knew they worshiped her.

"It's south of Oregon," twelve-year-old Bobby Wolnowsky offered.

"It's bigger than...than...Idaho Territory," blurted out another boy.

"It is not!" countered a girl's voice from the back. "It's—"

The voices broke off as the heavy plank door swung open and Jake Bannister ducked under the low doorframe.

Sally started. What was *he* doing here? She felt the heat rise in her cheeks.

It had been a month since she'd seen Jake. Though she rode the fine bay he'd picked out for her, she purposely steered her thoughts away from its former owner. And, she thought triumphantly, she rode astride, not sidesaddle, as Jake had suggested. She admitted she did show a bit of petticoat, but she didn't care one whit. She arrived at the schoolhouse an hour before anyone else. Besides, no one in Klamath County cared about her petticoats.

A tremor of unease rippled through her as she recalled her last encounter with Jake, how she had waited for him to kiss her and then slapped him when he had. In a rush of anger she remembered the iron grip of his hand on her wrist and how foolish she had felt for letting her temper get the better of her. That was the third time Jake had made a fool of her—first with Tommy Pearson, that night behind the barn, and then when she had tried to ride that black gelding. She hadn't realized she'd been keeping score, but... She would get even with him for that if it was the last thing she ever did.

"That's enough geography for today," she announced. "It's time for spelling. Slates up, please."

The children rustled with slates and chalk, and Sally rose from her desk and moved toward Jake.

Jake nodded at her and removed his gray Stetson. "Miss Sally." He noted the form-fitting, high-necked blouse, its myriad tucks swelling over her breasts, and the handsome navy blue skirt that swung gracefully when she moved. He found himself wondering if she was wearing a petticoat.

"Mr. Bannister?" Sally gave him her sweetest smile. "What brings you out to the schoolhouse?"

Jake stood just inside the door. "Actually, this is an official visit of sorts. Last night I was elected head of the school board, Miss Sally, and I'm supposed to...uh...visit you four times a year, just to see how you're getting along."

"You? You're head of the— Why, you aren't even married!"

A titter ran around the schoolroom. Sally quelled it with a glance, then turned her gaze on Jake. "You haven't even got any children!"

Jake shrugged. "They didn't figure I needed any to be head of the board, I guess." He glanced at the quiet line of students seated on the double row of wooden benches. He had heard Sally was a demanding but unorthodox schoolmistress. Dutch and Olla Hendricks's boy trudged home from school every day, and after his evening chores around the ranch he put in extra time painstakingly copying his letters over and over on his slate. "He learn to read," Dutch exclaimed proudly at dinner each night. "And write, too! I t'ink dat Miss Sally know what she's doin'."

But other parents weren't so sure. Tales of acting out scenes from the stories in their readers, impromptu picnics, spelling bees including words the parents had never heard of and—worse—youngsters caught reading poetry instead of attending to their chores had been aired at the last school board meeting in Jake's front parlor. He wanted to see for himself what magic it was Sally cast over her schoolroom. He shouldn't have let her know his visit was official—she'd get herself all riled up, and that he could do without.

"So," Jake repeated, "how are you getting along?"

Sally resisted an impulse to laugh. "Just splendidly, Mr. Bannister." He looked so hugely out of place in the tiny room, his tall frame blocking her view of the blackboard. She relished seeing his sudden awkwardness.

"You got enough firewood?" The Blane twins, Rob and Richie, were to keep the wood box near the small potbellied stove full. Jake, as head of the board, was responsible for all aspects of school life, and he intended to do his duty. The firewood was the only excuse he could think of on the spur of the moment.

Sally struggled to keep her face straight. "We have plenty of wood, Mr. Bannister." She knew perfectly well why Jake was here. He was checking up on her, reporting to the parents how she was managing their offspring through the long school days. He didn't care a fig about her wood supply. "It's early October, Mr. Bannister. We're not using a lot of wood yet. The weather's quite warm still." Oh, it was such fun to devil him.

Jake shifted position and lounged against the doorjamb. "Mind if I watch a bit?"

"Why, not at all, Mr. Bannister," Sally said, her voice silky. In fact, it gave her a positively wicked idea. She didn't want him, or anyone else, spying on her in her schoolroom. She'd teach him a lesson that would put a stop to such visits.

She turned to the assembled students. "Now, class, we're going to spell the words we've been studying for Mr. Bannister." She paused to be sure Jake's attention was focused on the proceedings. "The first word is *gentleman.*" She paused. "Definition, a man of honor. Used in a sentence, a gentleman never hits a lady." Sally always supplied the definition from the dictionary on the corner of her desk, then used the word in a sentence. The older children wrote the words out on their slates; the young ones, like Elsa Baker, learned them by rote.

A chorus of voices began. "G-e-n-t…" Sally glanced at Jake as the children finished the word. He looked interested.

"Good. The next word is *scoundrel.* A cheat, a dishonest man. That man with the black horse is a scoundrel."

Dutifully the children began to spell. "S-c-o-u-n…"

Jake's expression grew wary. Sally could barely suppress her glee. Now she'd go for the jugular.

"Fine, children. The next word is *jackanapes.* An arrogant fellow. A man who thinks he knows everything is a jackanapes."

"J-a-c. . ."

All at once Jake caught on. He wanted to laugh, but he managed to stifle the twitch in his lips. He turned a bland face toward Sally, and their eyes met. He smiled carefully. "Very impressive, Miss Sally. Mind if I choose a word just for fun?"

Sally stepped back to her desk, and Jake took her place in front of the benches.

"Virago," he pronounced carefully. "The lady is a virago."

The children looked blank. Even Sally looked nonplussed.

Jake seized his advantage and addressed the students. "This word may be new to you, so you'll have to sound out the letters," Jake supplied helpfully. "Give it a try."

He waited. Slowly he shifted his attention to Sally. Her face was a study in conflicting emotions—puzzlement and annoyance predominating. While the children stared, and Sally sat speechless at her desk, Jake ambled toward the door. "Look it up," he whispered to her as he passed.

The door creaked shut behind him. Automatically Sally reached her hand to her dictionary. She ruffled through the leaves and quickly scanned down a page. "Virago," she read out loud. "A sharp-tongued, complaining—"

She broke off as the children's voices began to spell in singsong rhythm. "V-i-r-a. . ."

Sally snapped the dictionary shut. No smooth-talking know-it-all was going to get the best of her! *Just you wait, Jake Bannister.* A slow smile curved her lips. *Hell hath no fury like a virago.*

* * *

"Sally, tote this pitcher of lemonade out to the front porch, would you?" Martha bustled about the kitchen, clattering more wood into the stove. "There's two thirsty ranch hands out there courtin' Miss Louisa. I'll bring some of my ginger crisps out in a minute." She slid a pan of unbaked cookies into the oven.

It must be Sunday afternoon again, Sally mused. Courting day. A beribboned Louisa sat demurely in the porch swing. Inside, Martha baked dozens of cookies and sliced lemons for lemonade as the steady stream of eligible males presented their compliments to her younger sister.

As usual, Sally looked on with interest. Louisa did not seem attracted to any of the young men. Why in the world did they keep coming around?

She kicked open the screen door and set the brimming pitcher down on the top step. Plopping down beside it, she drew her jean-clad legs up to her chin and prepared to watch the show.

Slim, dark Ned Barker, foreman at the Peterman place, and Cole Sieversen from the Bar Y lounged on the steps below her. Both men looked recently scrubbed, their hair slicked down and shiny. Scented with bay rum, too, Sally noted. She dipped her head toward Cole's rangy form and sniffed unobtrusively. His revolver, strapped around his hips, clanked against the steps as he reached for the lemonade pitcher. Sally smiled. He only wore the gun to impress Louisa when he came to call; she knew Jake didn't allow his hands to carry sidearms on his ranch. Cole had been coming around all summer, Martha told her. Louisa didn't seem much interested, but he kept coming, anyway.

For the next hour Sally watched Ned and Cole spar verbally, vying for Louisa's meandering attention. "Hell—er, heck," Cole corrected at one point, his eye on Louisa. "Ranchin' ain't so hard. The only thing you have to know is that a cow will have a calf. Any greenhorn knows that."

He shot a glance at Louisa, who pushed back and forth in the swing in silence, a preoccupied smile on her lips.

"Now a foreman, he's got a *real* job," Ned responded, his brown eyes sliding from Cole to Louisa. Ned had worn his Sunday spurs and jingle-bobs and a vest that Sally swore smelled of mothballs.

"Bein' a cowhand's too easy," Ned continued, prodding Cole's long leg with one booted toe. "A cowboy's just a plain bowlegged human being who smells like a horse and sleeps in his under—" He blushed suddenly and glanced upward. "Beggin' your pardon, Miss Louisa."

Louisa made no reply. In the momentary silence Sally heard the unmistakable sound of hoofbeats. Ned frowned in annoyance as Louisa lifted her head.

Will Boessen walked his mount to the front gate. Ned groaned, then shifted over to make room for the Bar Y foreman.

Sally smiled to herself, enjoying the competition. There was something about Will she'd always liked. Maybe it was his quietness. Will never raised his voice, and, she noted, he never wore his gun. Never had to. His steady gray eyes were calm, and his movements, even when roping or branding, always seemed relaxed and unhurried. He was respected by everyone in the valley.

Will nodded at them. "Miss Louisa, Miss Sally." He grinned at Ned and Cole. "You settled who's got the leakiest mouth this afternoon?"

Ned laughed, and Will clapped him on the shoulder and seated himself at Louisa's feet.

"We're about even, I guess," Cole offered.

Sally stole a glance at her sister while the men bantered. Louisa's dress of yellow cotton was trimmed at the throat in white lace, which fluttered slightly with each pulse beat. With her gold blond hair arranged in shiny ringlets about her delicate face, she made an absolute picture, Sally thought with a rush of pride. And, she saw, the effect was not lost on Will.

Why, he's in love with her! she realized suddenly. Well, they all were, really. But there was something else in Will's eyes, something quiet and sure, almost sacred. A little tremor of joy bubbled up in her throat. She wondered if Louisa knew. Her sister's face exhibited the same pink-and-white serenity it always did, but her eyes . . . Good heavens, she was positively glowing!

Sally let a slow smile shape her mouth. "Here, Will," she said warmly. "Have one of Martha's ginger cookies."

When the afternoon edged into dusk and talk of ranching and the continuing drought had dwindled, Ned and Cole mounted their horses and cantered off down the road. Will also rose to leave, but Tom's voice rang out from inside the house.

"Why don't you come on over to supper tonight, Will? Martha's cooking up some of her chile stew—there's always plenty. And bring Jake along with you."

Sally stiffened. "Oh, Pa!"

"Please, Sally," Louisa whispered, her eyes imploring.

Sally shut her mouth over the protest that rose to her lips. She guessed it wouldn't hurt her to tolerate that overeducated popinjay Jake Bannister for her sister's sake. Besides, it might give her a chance to get even with him for making a fool of her in her own schoolroom.

Will nodded to Louisa and moved toward his horse, tied up outside the front fence.

"Around seven," Tom called.

Sally yanked open the screen door and let it slam behind her. "I'll help Martha with dinner."

In the kitchen Martha bustled between countertop and stove, alternately humming and muttering to herself. She put Sally to work peeling carrots and potatoes for the stew. "Cut 'em up small, honey," the housekeeper cautioned. "Just bite-size. It don't help a tired, hungry man to have to work his jaws too much."

Sally peeled and chopped and sliced with a vengeance while the bulky woman stirred and sniffed and tasted. "Mmm-mmm," she crowed, rolling her eyes. "Kissin' don't last, but cookery sure do! Now, for my 'piece of resistance.'"

Sally watched her raise her knife to the braid of chile peppers hanging from the ceiling near the pantry door. She sliced off one red pepper and smelled it, handling the small dried fruit gingerly. "Just one will do it, I think," she muttered to herself. She made one deft incision along the length of the pepper, carefully raked out the seeds and dropped it in the stewpot, whole.

Sally watched her, fascinated. "Just one chile?"

"Just one. These are terrific hot. More than one of these little devils would burn your mouth good."

An odd, expectant feeling settled in Sally's midsection. "Martha," she blurted, "shall I set out the bowls before I go upstairs and change?"

Preoccupied, the housekeeper nodded. Sally collected the china bowls and spoons from the pantry, and when she'd arranged them to Martha's satisfaction, she flew upstairs to change.

She could hardly get dressed fast enough. Opportunities like this didn't come along every day. Hurriedly she pulled the pale blue muslin dress over her head and down over her shoulders. With its low neck and full, puffed sleeves, she knew it would catch Jake's eye. And tonight that's exactly what she wanted to do—distract him.

As she came downstairs she heard Jake's voice in the sitting room. "In Texas it got so hot we had to cool the bit in water to keep it from blistering that gelding's mouth."

Her father's laughter rolled to greet her, and for a moment her resolve wavered. Her father loved a practical joke as well as anyone, but she didn't know for sure how Jake would react. Should she carry out her plan?

When she entered the room, both Will and Jake rose.

The light in Jake's eyes when he looked at her flushed her with an uneasy warmth. She would have ignored him but for her father.

"Daughter," he prompted, "welcome our guests. Then we'll go in to supper. I can smell Martha's stew from here."

Sally smiled at Will, then turned her gaze to Jake. Welcome him? The words stuck in Sally's throat. She'd like to throw him off the front porch. At last she managed a faint "Hello, Mr. Bannister," followed by an unenthusiastic "We're so glad you could join us."

Jake offered his arm. "It's always a pleasure to visit you, Miss Sally."

Sally hated lies, even for social reasons. She was most certainly *not* glad he could join them. "Is my nose getting longer?" she whispered to him as they followed Will and Louisa into the dining room.

Jake didn't bat an eye. "No. Is mine?"

His wit caught her by surprise, and she choked down a laugh. Jake hated lies, too. One thing she'd say for him, he was quick! But, she mused smugly, not as quick as *she* was.

"Excuse me, won't you, Mr. Bannister—" she began.

"Jake," he reminded her.

"Jake. I have to help Martha serve supper." She ducked into the kitchen as Louisa and the men trailed into the dining room. Out of the corner of her eye Sally watched her father seat himself at the head of the oblong walnut table. Louisa and Will took chairs across from each other, Martha's husband, Hank, sat next to her and their twins, Rob and Richie, scrambled onto the two chairs next to Jake.

In the kitchen Martha lifted a pan of biscuits from the oven and dumped them into a straw basket. "Ladle the stew into those bowls, honey," she puffed. "I'll fetch the butter from the pantry."

The instant Martha's back was turned, Sally seized the butcher knife and sliced two more red chile peppers off the braided strand. Hurriedly she chopped them up and scooped them, seeds and all, into one of the blue pottery bowls. Her fingers burned from the contact with the chile skins. She ladled the hot stew into the bowls and carried them, two at a time, through the swinging door into the dining room.

She served Will first, then Jake, making sure he got the right bowl.

"You're in for a treat, boys," Tom exulted. "Martha's famous for her hot chile stew and biscuits."

After everyone else had been served and Martha emerged from the kitchen, Sally sank into the chair across from Jake.

"Miss Sally, how are you liking that bay you're riding?" Jake asked, his voice pleasant.

Sally watched his hand pause over his spoon. "Just fine, Mr. Bann—Jake."

"What do you call him?" He reached for the biscuits, lifted one out and passed the basket on to Louisa on his left.

"Flapjack." She watched Jake slather butter onto a biscuit half. Oh, would the man never pick up his spoon?

He chuckled. "Flapjack," he repeated. His eyes sought hers as he bit into the biscuit. "Very appropriate." Still chewing, he reached for his spoon, then hesitated.

Pick it up, she willed him silently. *Take a bite.* Mesmerized, she watched the owner of the Bar Y ranch spoon the first mouthful of Martha's stew past his lips.

"Jake," she murmured, her voice honeyed, "I know your family comes from Philadelphia, originally. Tell me again, how did you end up ranching in Oregon?" She watched his jaw move up and down.

Jake swallowed and opened his mouth to speak. Son of a gun, that mouthful was hot—and getting hotter! What the— He shot a glance at Sally, but she gazed intently at the bowl in front of her, her head bent.

He groaned inwardly. Something was definitely wrong. He glanced at Will, then at Tom and Louisa and the twins. All ate with gusto and no apparent discomfort. Either they had mouths of iron or...

He looked again at Sally. Her eyes were downcast, but a telltale stain suffused her cheeks. That hellcat! She's poisoned me!

Jake lowered his spoon, looked directly into Sally's clear, turquoise eyes and smiled. *Oh, Lord, help me! My tongue feels like a cactus, but please help me to talk, anyway.*

"My father," Jake began in an even, controlled voice, "came west to Texas before the War Between the States. He rounded up a bunch of longhorns that had been running loose and drove them north to Kansas. He 'learned cow,' as they say down in that part of the country, and sold them off at a good price. Then he packed a mule with twelve thousand dollars in gold and came on to Oregon to stake out his claim. Bought all the land he could see, and the Bar Y grew from there."

He smiled again at Sally. *Thank you, Lord,* he breathed. Her eyes widened in innocent anticipation.

Sally stared at him. Any minute now, he's going to explode, she thought. She couldn't take her eyes off his lips.

Again Jake's hand crept toward his spoon. Sally's eyes followed avidly. The others ate and talked, occasionally sipping the wine Tom had poured into their glasses.

"Then," Jake continued, purposely dabbling his spoon in the fiery mixture, "my father went back to Philadelphia and married my mother. After a while I came along, and when I was about two or three, we all came out to Oregon. I grew up here, on the Bar Y."

Jake took a deep, steadying breath and shoveled in another mouthful of stew.

Sally watched the silver spoon rim slide between his lips.

Jake pressed his lips together. *One more time, Lord, if you're willing.* He swallowed, tested his tongue and spoke again. "When I was about twenty-one, Dad left the ranch in my charge and took my mother back to Philadelphia for her health. A couple of years later he sent for me—wanted me to go to college. To please him, and my mother, who was still alive then, I did. Princeton. And after college, they sent me abroad. Guess they hoped I'd marry an heiress!"

Sally's entire attention was riveted on his mouth. Why, he must be burning up inside!

Jake smiled at her. "I missed the ranch, though," he continued. "And after a few years, Dad agreed to my settling here. It was hard on him. Mother was gone by then. I was all he had left."

Jake's mouth was on fire, but he steeled himself to take just one small sip of the wine in his glass. He knew now what Dante's *Inferno* was all about.

Sally stared at him, spellbound. Her own mouth burned from Martha's stew, and *that* had only one chile for the whole batch. She felt a small twinge of guilt. How can he talk—and eat—as if nothing was wrong? Puzzled, she rose to bring more biscuits.

The instant Sally disappeared through the kitchen door, Jake's hand snaked across the table and captured Will's wineglass. He drained it in one gulp while Will gaped at him.

"Must have bit down on a chile pepper," Jake rasped. "I thought my teeth would melt." He eyed his own, almost full glass of wine. He didn't want to drink any more of it; he wanted to let Sally think he was unaffected by the fiery mess she'd fed him. Hell, he should have known something was up the minute she said she'd named that mare Flapjack. What a name for a horse.

"You couldn't have eaten a chile," Martha said defensively. "I put just one whole chile in the stew, and I found it on my first bite—it's right here in my own bowl." She held up the pepper's gravy-soaked remains.

"Maybe," Tom offered slowly, "Sally added . . ."

All heads swiveled toward Jake. "I thought maybe she did, but I don't want to let on just yet," he said, his voice hoarse.

The twins gaped, their eyes riveted on Jake. Louisa slid her wineglass toward him, and he guzzled the contents gratefully. Tom did the same with his glass, then Hank and Martha offered theirs. By the time Sally returned bearing the biscuits, Jake was calmly discussing the fall roundup with Hank.

Tom rose to replenish the wineglasses.

Jake held up a restraining hand. "None for me, Tom. Guess I'm just not thirsty tonight."

The twins squirmed with delight.

"That was mighty good stew, Martha," Jake continued, his voice bland. "Think maybe you could give me the recipe for Olla?"

Sally blinked. Then she caught the glint in Jake's blue eyes. *He knows!* Their glances locked for an instant. *And he knows that I know,* she acknowledged in rising alarm.

Her appetite evaporated. She watched Martha disappear into the kitchen and bring out the apple pie she'd retrieved from the oven. The housekeeper sliced it into thick wedges and passed around the plates.

Nervous, Sally gulped more wine as the conversation rolled around her. Her fantasy of revenge had stopped at the look on his face she had expected after his first mouthful. Now, two—or was it three?—mouthfuls later, he was still apparently unaffected. But he knew! If he knew, he must be feeling *something,* and if he . . .

Her stomach flipped. He did know, and he was at this very moment planning his revenge. A cadre of butterflies swirled inside her belly.

The twins fidgeted and giggled, punching each other under the table until Hank silenced them with a look. Apparently unperturbed, Jake munched his apple pie.

"I'll get the coffee," Sally blurted. She escaped into the kitchen. She hadn't counted on Jake's surviving the chiles. She hadn't thought beyond that first mouthful.

She took a long time assembling the cups and saucers. It really was an awfully mean trick, she admitted to herself. Her hands shook as she skimmed off the thick cream that had risen to the top of the milk pan she lifted from the cooler. She wondered why her triumph over Jake brought her no pleasure. Fiercely she suppressed a seed of guilt and busied herself with the coffee tray. When she couldn't think of one more thing to occupy herself in the kitchen, she took a deep, fortifying breath and reentered the dining room.

In growing dread she poured coffee, passed out cups and saucers, added cream and tried to breathe normally past the tight knot in her throat. Jake's hard, cobalt blue eyes followed her every motion. Oh, if she could just drop through the floor rather than face those eyes.

Finally she could stand it no longer. "I'll help Martha with the dishes." She nearly choked getting the words out. In rising terror she fled through the kitchen door to safety.

Martha pushed back her chair and started to rise, but Tom held up a restraining hand. "Mighty nice evening for porch sittin'," he said, his voice amiable. He directed a pregnant look at Jake. "We'll just leave Sally to the . . . dishes."

Amid the scraping of chairs and the smothered giggles of the twins, all the diners drifted toward the front porch.

All except Jake. When the dining room was empty, he deliberately pushed back his chair, stretched his long legs and headed straight for the kitchen.

Chapter Five

Jake advanced toward Sally, his darkened eyes menacing. "What the hell are you trying to do, kill me?"

Sally's gaze darted behind him, searching for Martha.

"Don't bother looking for her," Jake said softly. "She's not coming. She's gone out to the front porch with the others. It's just you and me, Sally," he added, his voice quiet. "You and me."

Sally gave a little squeak of fear.

Jake's eyes bored into hers. "There's an old story around the cow camps," he began, his voice steel hard, "about the fellow who rides out to the range from the city to buy himself a herd." He took a step toward Sally. "Seems the man inspected the herd . . ." Jake took another step toward Sally. Sally backed away. Her gaze lit on her blue-checked apron hanging on the wall near the stove. She snatched it off the hook with hands that shook like aspen leaves.

Jake moved closer. "And when he paid the drover, the fellow asked if there was another herd for sale."

Sally edged away, but the tall, lean man advanced closer. Cornered, she fumbled behind her back with the apron ties. At last she managed to fashion a floppy knot at her waist. Her breath fluttered in and out in shallow gasps, and her mouth felt stuffed full of dry thistles. She quailed as Jake took another step toward her. He looked mad enough to—

"The drover said, 'Sure, I got another herd. I'll just drive these to the pen and...'"

Sally retreated until she felt the stove at her back, the still-warm oven door pressing into her buttocks. She was trapped.

"'Bring the other herd for you to look at.'" Jake edged closer. "So the cowhand drove those same damn cows around a little hill—"

Sally stared at the tan V of skin where Jake's shirt opened at the neck. The pearl button at his collar drew nearer and nearer, then halted right in front of her chin.

Jake drew in a long breath. "And so the damn fool bought his own herd again." He locked Sally's wrist in an iron grip and brought his face close to hers. "Nobody likes to be made a fool of, Miss Sally," he breathed. "That's the second time you've driven that herd around *your* hill. Try it again and I'll—"

"You'll what?" Fear pushed her voice up an octave above normal. "You think you're some kind of high-and-mighty rangeland rajah who can order me around?"

Before Sally knew what was happening, Jake hooked his fingers inside her apron waistband and tugged. Helpless, she took a reluctant step toward him.

"Miss Sultana," he said, staring at her mouth as she opened it to protest. "You have a ravishing body, a dangerous mind and a tongue that could mow hay. You've had your fun—again—at my expense, and now I'm mad as a bull. I expect an apology."

"Well, you're not going to get one!" Fear made her reckless.

"Yes," he said, his voice deliberate, "I will." Holding her eyes, he reached behind her. In one quick jerk he untied her apron and tossed it onto a chair.

A thread of panic spiraled into her chest. "You get out of this kitchen, Jake Bannister!"

"I'll leave this kitchen when I'm damn good and ready," he said quietly. "And I'm not ready... yet."

Sally lunged for the door, but Jake's hand whipped out and fingers like five steel bands closed on her forearm. He pulled her backward, toward him, until she felt his breath ruffle the tendrils of hair on the back of her neck. Without thinking, she grabbed the heavy iron skillet on the stove and whirled.

He was ready for her. He caught her arm as she raised it and yanked the pan away, then with one hand pinned both her wrists behind her.

Immobilized, Sally stared into his face. His eyes looked odd. Calm, like a dark river sliding silently over shiny black stone. A muscle in his jaw twitched. Was that glint in his eyes fury? Or... A thought popped into her brain. She wet her lips. For one heart-stopping moment she didn't know whether to laugh or scream. She inhaled a careful breath and opened her mouth to scream.

"Shut up, Sally," Jake said evenly. "No one will hear you."

A thrill of apprehension knifed through her belly. Jake tightened his fingers on her wrists and raised his other hand to tip up her chin. "I'm going to teach you a lesson you won't forget."

Sally felt his lips graze hers, then return and press hers into reluctant response. She closed her eyes. His mouth was like dark velvet. A thread of flame pulsed through her, and she felt her breasts swell, the nipples begin to tingle.

His kiss deepened as he slid his fingers from her chin to her neck and moved them purposefully along the length of her collarbone. His thumb grazed the underside of her jaw.

Her knees turned to jelly, and the tips of her breasts burned where they pressed against his chest. And still his mouth moved over hers. It was magic.

"Can you feel me?" he whispered against her lips. "Can you? Because to tell you the honest-to-God truth, you little vixen, my mouth's so numb I can't feel a damn thing."

"What a waste," Sally murmured without thinking. Reason fled and in its place a slow warmth built in her midsection. She raised her lips to his, and he kissed her again.

"Don't stop," she breathed at last. "Don't—"

His mouth smothered her words. She felt his body tremble against hers, and she freed her wrists and wound her hands around his neck. She parted her lips under his. She wondered idly why she did it, but a voice in a far corner of her mind told her to stop analyzing and just enjoy it. She knew only that she needed to feel his body hard against hers, needed to taste his mouth again. Inexplicably she felt like weeping. "Jake." Her breath caught. "Jake . . ."

"Don't talk, Sally."

She made a little moan of hunger as his breath warmed her neck. His lips traced her jawbone, circled into the shell of her ear, then again sought her mouth. She felt his tongue, warm and smooth, trail lightly over her lips, traveling slowly, inexorably around the perimeter of her mouth. His breath gusted gently against her skin.

"My tongue's numb, too," he whispered hoarsely.

"I'm so sorry, Jake...about your tongue," Sally breathed. "But it—it feels wonderful. Don't—don't change a thing."

Jake forced himself to slow down, to look at her. "Sally, what are you saying? Don't you want me to stop?"

She thought about it for a split second. "No." He made her crazy, wanton. But for some reason it didn't matter. Only this moment—and Jake—mattered.

He bent to her again. "Sally. *Sally.*"

Her heart fluttered at the sound of his voice speaking her name. "You're right," she whispered lazily against his mouth. "This is a lesson I'm never going to forget."

Jake's arms tightened around her. "I think," he said into her ear, "I've been hoisted on my own petard. I wanted to... Hell, I don't know what I wanted to do." He drew in a shaky breath. "But I sure as shooting do now."

"You do?" She felt a bit giddy. What *she* wanted to do was strip off all her clothes and go swimming in the river. With Jake. What in heaven's name was the matter with her? She must have drunk more wine than she thought.

In the next instant she felt his mouth, hot and silky on hers, and all she could think about was how inviting it felt, how it made her ache.

"Sally, Sally," he murmured. "I—"

"Jake?" Her voice shook. "Jake, could we..."

"Could we what?"

She hesitated. It was madness. She wanted to be naked. She wanted to feel his skin, his body, touching hers all the way down to her... "Could we go swimming? Down at the river?"

"Now?" His tongue curled into her ear.

"Yes, now."

There was a long, long pause. "No," he said at last.

"Jake, I want—"

Jake groaned. "I know what you want, Sally. I want it, too. And that's why we're not going swimming."

"But we'd just swim and—" She faltered. "Cool off."

He set her away from him, and when he spoke his voice was husky. "I'm shaking like a leaf I want you so much, Sally. I don't trust myself."

Her eyes flew open. "But nothing would happen, Jake. Our families have shared that swimming hole ever since I can remember."

"Everything would happen."

To avoid his eyes, she let her lids flutter shut. He was right. Ten minutes ago she'd hated him, and now... Well, she still hated him, but suddenly she felt other things, too. Things she'd never felt before. Hate him or not, she felt pulled toward him. Her physical response to him stunned her. Life could be so unpredictable! It wasn't that she didn't trust Jake. It was herself she didn't trust.

Oh, Lordy. Who's hoisted on whose petard? She'd made a fool of herself again. She glanced up to find him studying her, an odd, hungry look on his face.

What was he feeling? Was it anything like what she was experiencing—a hot, restless yearning deep inside? He must be feeling it! His darkened eyes probed hers with a question in their depths.

Suddenly she was sorry for what she'd done. Sorry about the chile peppers, at any rate. She was most definitely not sorry he had kissed her. "I guess I shouldn't have done that," she admitted in a low voice.

"Which—poison me? Or kiss me?" A hint of laughter warmed his tone.

"Pois—the chile pep—"

He stopped her words with a quick, hard kiss. *"C'est la vie."* He worked to keep his voice light.

Sally felt herself begin to float, and then suddenly he lifted his mouth from hers. Damn the man, anyway. She felt let down, edgy. She longed for him to touch her again, anywhere. Just touch her. And he claimed his mouth couldn't feel a thing. What a waste! *C'est la guerre* was more like it!

Before she could move, he kissed her again, hard and very thoroughly, then released her as if her body burned him where it brushed his hand. "Damn!" he swore.

Jake stuffed both hands in his pockets and strode toward the back door. "That's twice I've risked my life in your kitchen, Miss Sally. Next time, *I'll* do the cooking." His jaw muscle twitched. "You can do the kissing."

Whistling, he strode out the kitchen door.

Chapter Six

Sally awoke to the whine of the sewing machine in the downstairs hallway. She lay in bed, listening as the treadle machine sporadically whirred and fell silent. At last her curiosity overcame her sluggishness, and she threw off the lavender-and-blue-patterned quilt.

Her toes curled when they touched the cold wood flooring, and she shivered in the early-morning chill. After a long, dry Indian summer, the weather had turned nippy. Frost sparkled on the road in the mornings when Sally rode the five miles to the schoolhouse, and in the meadow the maple and alder trees were splashed with patches of scarlet and gold. Winter was coming.

She shivered again as she pulled on her jeans and an oversize wool flannel shirt. Unexpectedly, she thought of Jake. She hadn't seen him since he'd come to supper with Will. And, she told herself, she didn't want to, ever again. She'd made a complete fool of herself, throwing herself at him like that.

What had come over her that night? Too much wine? At any rate, she resolved, Jake was never, ever, going to touch her again. Something about being close to him caused an inexplicable ripple of hot joy to course through her. But along with it came the old panic, the nameless, choking fear she had fought ever since Mama had died. It threatened to engulf her every time Jake came anywhere near her. And that she could do without, thank you. She pulled her hair back and tied it with an old blue bandanna, then headed downstairs.

Louisa bent over the humming black metal machine, feeding material through the presser foot as she rhythmically pumped the treadle up and down.

"What on earth are you doing up at this hour, Lou?"

"Making a dress." Louisa tipped her head toward the dining room. "The pattern's laid out on the table. When you've finished breakfast, could you pin some pieces down for me?"

Sally stared at her sister, then peeked into the dining room. Yards of ivory silk taffeta covered the walnut table and spilled off the end onto the floor. She ran her hand appreciatively over the smooth material and frowned. It was elegant. Too elegant for the barn dance at Peterman's that night.

"Lou, what are you making this dress for?"

"It's my wedding dress," Louisa replied evenly.

"Wedding dress!" Sally was thunderstruck. "Are you and Will . . ."

"Yes, eventually." Louisa did not even glance up. "But," she added in the same calm tone, "Will doesn't know it yet." She pressed her foot down on the treadle and the machine purred again.

Sally stared at the back of Louisa's blond head. "What do you mean, he doesn't know?"

Louisa's voice rose over the whir of the Singer. "He hasn't asked me yet."

"Hasn't . . . Then how in the world do you know you'll be getting married?"

"Oh, I know." The calm blue eyes looked into Sally's. "Will loves me," Louisa said simply. "He hasn't asked me because he hasn't realized it yet. But he will." She raised the needle and deftly turned the piece of ivory fabric, then lowered the needle again. "And I love him."

Sally was flabbergasted. "How do you know he loves you?"

Louisa smiled down at the length of silk slipping beneath the presser foot. "I just know. Sally, do you think this silk will be too hot?"

"Too hot? Too hot for what?" Sally exploded. Sally adored her younger sister, but she had never been able to fathom her. Louisa seemed to understand, and accept, all the mysteries of life that to Sally, for all of her skill in mathematics and horsemanship, were...mysteries.

"Too hot for summer, silly! The wedding will be next June."

Sally gaped at her. "June!" Then, on impulse, she bent to hug her sister. "Oh, Lou, I want you to be happy. You remember how we talked when Mama died? About what we both wanted out of life? I said I wanted to do something important. You said you wanted to love someone. You were only eleven, but you knew, even then." She shook her head in amazement. Nothing was beyond Louisa.

"June," Louisa repeated, her voice muffled against Sally's shirt. "In the garden. Mama's Belle of Portugal will be in bloom."

Mama's roses. Sally's eyes misted. "No, honey, it won't be too hot. It will be just right. It will be the most beautiful wedding—" Her throat closed.

Louisa glanced up and caught Sally's hand against her cheek. "Sally, don't you ever want to get married someday?"

"No," she said quickly. "I don't. Nothing against Will, but men are..."

"Men," her younger sister finished for her. She eyed Sally with keen intelligence. "Sally, you're my sister, my dearest friend." She hesitated a fraction of a second. "Now don't take this wrong, honey, but when are you going to grow up?"

Sally jerked her hand away. "Why, whatever do you mean? I am grown up. I'm older than you!"

Louisa gazed up at her sister and shook her head. "That's not what I meant, honey," she said, her voice quiet. "And you know it."

Sally frowned. Grow up? Wasn't she grown up? She filled out her father's shirts in a way no man ever could. She had creditable table manners and a flair for conversation when she felt like talking. What's more, she had been kissed, and she had to admit she'd enjoyed it thoroughly. In one mad moment she'd even wanted it to go a bit further. And if *that* wasn't grown up, she didn't know what was. And anyway, what did Louisa know? Her head was in the clouds over Will Boessen.

Sally sniffed. She'd show her. At the barn dance tonight at Peterman's, she'd be the most grown-up lady on the floor.

The sound of fiddles carried clearly on the crisp November air as the wagon pulled past the gate and rattled up to George Peterman's barn. Sally sat in the front between her father and Louisa. Hank and Martha sat in back with Rob and Richie. The twins tumbled out and were off in a flash to inspect the tables of food the ranch families had brought for the evening.

Sally watched Martha make a stiff-legged descent; her rheumatism was bothering her again. Heavens, it must be awful to get old.

Tom handed Louisa down. Luminous in a yellow cotton print, her pale hair a cloud of spun silk around her fragile face, Louisa looked so beautiful tears rose in Sally's eyes.

"Coming, daughter?" her father asked.

Sally sat immobile, unwilling to move despite the siren call of the fiddle and the thump of boots on the Petermans' barn floor. She loved to dance. She hadn't missed a one except for the two years she'd spent in St. Louis. Despite her fiery tongue, Sally was easily partnered at such affairs, partly because she was Louisa's sister. Proximity to Sally eventually led to proximity to Louisa. Also, Sally didn't talk much at dances—she danced! Indefatigable, her father said. Sally was good company, as long as she kept her mouth shut.

"Go on ahead, Pa. I'll be along in a minute." She couldn't explain her hesitancy. She wondered if Jake Bannister would be here. At the thought of him, a tiny finger of trepidation paused on her heart. Jake made her feel wary, as if she were on the brink of something. And Sally liked to keep both feet firmly on the ground—no brinks for her. If Jake was here, she'd stay away from him.

Peterman's barn overflowed with clean-shaven ranch hands, aproned women, children, bewhiskered old men, squalling babies. Everyone in the valley came to the last social gathering before winter set in. Couples of all ages and sizes and shapes circled the clean swept plank floor in each other's arms. The Bar Y hands, sought after for their prowess on the dance floor after Jake started his now-famous "Friday night, back East dancing lessons," never sat out a reel or a waltz, but claimed grateful partners from among the town girls as well as those from neighboring ranches.

Sally deposited Martha's still-warm rhubarb pies on the plank table already groaning with food. Relieved that Jake was nowhere in sight, she turned to watch the dancers. Instantly she found herself whirled away in the arms of Cole Sieversen. Her mind on the polka and the lanky cowboy's hard leather boots, which more than once narrowly missed the soft toes of her buttoned leather shoes, Sally forgot all about Jake.

Or thought she did. When she spotted him, her heart lurched. He stood off to one side with Judge Randall and his daughter, Paula. A town girl. She'd heard the elegant young woman had a beau back East somewhere, but watching her move close to Jake and smile up at him like that, she didn't believe a word of it. It was Jake she fancied.

Oh! She glanced away quickly and tried to smile at Cole. Paula looked stunning. Her deep burgundy dress was low necked, with flounces from waist to hemline. She looked citified, Sally thought. Fragile and helpless. She'd bet Paula Randall couldn't ride worth a damn. Or shoot rabbits, or catch fish. Or have any fun at all!

But she certainly looked as if she was enjoying herself now. Jake, too, looked engrossed. Well, let him, Sally fumed. What did she care?

She looked down at her simple, full-skirted blue gingham with the high white lace collar, then shot another glance at Paula.

Her fine, white skin contrasted with the dark hair that hung down past her shoulders in tight corkscrew ringlets. Sally had piled her own unruly mass of deep red curls on top of her head and secured it with her mother's tortoiseshell hairpins. All at once she felt dowdy and old-fashioned.

Closing her ears to Paula's high, trilling laughter floating over the music, Sally concentrated on the fiddles and tried to anticipate the dance calls.

"Gents to the center and four hands 'round..."

She moved automatically as the ladies circled outside the men. Out of the corner of her eye she glimpsed Jake still standing on the sidelines. Paula clung to his arm.

"Swing your partners off the ground..."

As Sally watched, Paula reached her hand to Jake's chest and tugged playfully at the fringe of his dark buckskin jacket. Well, he certainly preferred his women to be forward! Then, remembering how her own arms had reached up almost in spite of themselves to twine around Jake's neck, she felt her cheeks burn. Damn him, anyway.

"Next set!" the caller directed. The couples shuffled and reformed with new partners.

Halfway into a "bow to your left, swing your corner," Sally found herself in Jake's arms.

"Hello, Miss Salty," he managed to say as he turned her around him.

Before she could open her mouth to correct him, he had returned to Paula, and the women gathered in the center for a ladies' star.

On the next swing, Jake again smiled down into Sally's eyes. "Cooked any flapjacks lately?" His lids crinkled at the corners.

His eyes held hers through the "gents' star in the center" and into the allemande left. When his hand gripped hers in the right and left grand, he added in an undertone, "Or any hot chile stew?" Then he swung off to Paula again, his lips twitching in amusement. Oh, the man could be exasperating!

"Mr. Bannister," Sally hissed at her next opportunity. She had to wait through the next few calls to deliver her next sentence. Then she smiled her sweetest smile and intoned for his ears only, "Beware the sleeping tiger."

Jake's eyebrows rose. "Is that a warning?"

Sally made no answer, and the allemande left took them apart again. She didn't know herself why she felt compelled to devil Jake tonight. Each time she looked at him with his arms around Paula Randall, her nerves jumped.

What was the matter with her? She'd seen the man dance before. Jake had been at every barn social she could ever remember. And she'd seen those town girls mooning over him, always fluttering their eyelashes and chattering a mile a minute about nothing. Paula was just prettier than most of them.

And the way Jake was holding her! For some reason it made her mad. She wanted to talk to him, insult him. Anything to draw his attention away from Paula.

On the next do-si-do, Sally managed to kick Paula's flounced skirt into Jake's path, forcing them to step out of the set while she readjusted her dress. *Serves him right,* she thought. No country-bred girl would come to a barn dance in all those flounces. This was Oregon, not Philadelphia or...or Paris. She squashed down a quiver of guilt, and at the next allemande she was ready for him again.

Keeping her voice as bland as she could manage, Sally sent off her arrow. "You're a college graduate..." she began innocently. On the next "swing your corners," she continued. "How many flapjacks and chile peppers..." She whirled away from him in Cole's arms, and then passed him in another do-si-do. "Can a jackanapes eat at one sitting?"

Jake swung her hard and sent her back to Cole, his laughter echoing in her ear all through the next figure. Oh, to best Jake was joy unequaled.

When the set ended, Jake drifted off to the punch bowl with Paula hanging on his arm. Nettled, Sally watched them with narrowed eyes.

"Next dance is ladies' choice," the caller shouted. "Choose your partners now, while they're still sober!"

Jake sent Sally an expectant glance. She smiled pointedly and moved toward him. Now she had him.

Jake shook himself free of Paula and faced in Sally's direction. Still smiling, Sally glided past him and laid her hand on her father's broad shoulder. Resisting a backward glance at Jake, she moved out onto the floor and curled her hand in her father's callused palm.

"Well, honey-girl," Tom said when the fiddle started, "you havin' a good time?"

Her smile faded. "I... Oh, Pa, I don't know. I don't know anything about anything anymore. Maybe I'm getting old and dowdy like Aunt Josephine?"

To her relief, her father didn't laugh. He just tightened his arm about her waist. "You'll never be like Josephine," he soothed. "You've got too much vinegar in you. And you'll never get old, honey. You're like a young colt sometimes, you've got so much life and spirit. But maybe your problem is you haven't been broke yet, Sally-girl. You're still buckin' everybody off."

"I don't want to be 'broke,' Pa. I want to be happy, like we were before Mama died. Remember? Things changed so much when Mama died."

"I remember," her father murmured. "But, daughter, you can't hold on to what's past. You got to look forward. Any good horse trader knows that. The ones with spirit give you the best they got in 'em. They don't hold anything back."

Sally gazed up into the wise blue eyes. "Pa, is that what's wrong? Am I holding back?"

"You are if there's something you're wantin', or needin', and you don't go after it. You got to reach out a little, honey. Nothin' comes for free."

Sally sighed. "Funny, that's what Jake Bannister said once."

"Did he, now?" Tom said evenly. "Well, next time he says somethin' smart like that, maybe you oughta listen to him." His eyes twinkled.

"There won't be a next time, Pa. Jake and I don't get along."

Tom struggled to keep from smiling. "Well, maybe not, honey-girl, but there's something you should know now. He's headin' across the floor toward us right this minute."

Sally gasped and glanced sideways. Sure enough, Jake was moving across the hall. She stiffened.

"The next one's a waltz," Jake said. Expertly he disengaged Sally from her father's arms and pulled her into his own.

"And how would you know that?" Sally asked.

Jake chuckled as he spun her away from Tom. "I bribed the fiddle player."

Sally stumbled. "You what?"

"You know how to waltz, don't you, Miss Sally?" Jake inquired, his tone bland.

"Of course I know—"

"Then shut up and dance with me, Sally. I've been waiting all evening."

"You have not!" she exploded. "You've been busy flirting with Paula Randall!"

Jake's rich laughter rolled over her. "And you've been busy all evening watching me?"

"I have not! I—well, maybe I have, just for a minute here and there. I admired her dress, her being a town girl. It looks so fashionable and sophisticated. I guess I felt a bit..." She drew in a long breath.

Jake said nothing. Paula! He had barely noticed Paula all evening. Dammit, it was Sally who did something to a man's insides. Just looking at her in that blue dress sent waves of heat through his loins.

When the music began again, Jake's arm tightened around Sally, and she forgot everything except the fluid movement of his hard, muscular body close to hers.

Tom watched his daughter from the sidelines for a few moments, a thoughtful look on his face. Then he moved toward the knot of Bar Y hands at the punch bowl. "Gents," he announced, "I'm puttin' ten solid dollars on Jake."

The crowd around the Irishman swelled instantly.

Chapter Seven

Sally avoided Jake's eyes as he pulled her close and guided her about the heavy plank floor of Peterman's barn. The fiddle alternately sang and sobbed the melodies of "Over the Waves" and "Clementine" against the background of guitars tirelessly strummed by two of George's ranch hands. Lulled by the music, couples moved quietly together in varsoviennes and waltzes, foregoing the raucous "yeows" of the earlier square dances and reels.

Jake's arms, thinly covered by the blue wool flannel of his shirtsleeves, enveloped Sally's tense form, his body heat soothing her like a sleep-inducing draft. He waltzed with the same lithe grace she noticed when he rode or worked a mustang. He had removed his dress buckskin jacket, and her throat tightened as she felt his hard body moving so close to hers. With his arm tight about her waist, she felt a little dizzy.

He held her just far enough from himself to avoid contact between her dress and his shirtfront. She longed to close the distance and press her breasts against him.

"Your hair smells like roses," he murmured.

"I washed it today in the rain barrel. You smell like . . . wood smoke, I guess."

Jake laughed. "I've been hanging so much meat in the smokehouse lately, Will says I smell like a walking hunk of beef jerky!"

Sally laughed. The knot of tension in her belly began to dissolve, and she took a mock sniff of him. "No, not jerky. Sausage maybe."

Jake chuckled, a low, growly sound that made her pulse quicken. Before she could stop herself, the words at the back of her mind just tumbled out. "Jake, could you—could you hold me a little closer?"

For the first time all evening, Jake missed a step. *A little closer,* he groaned inwardly. It was very, very hard to hold her at all without wanting to button her up inside his skin. He rolled his eyes. "Who's leading who in this dance?" he queried, keeping his voice light.

"Oh," Sally blurted, aghast at her temerity. "I don't know why I said that!" She knew color was flooding into her cheeks, and she tipped her head down.

"A waltz is a pretty formal dance, Sally," he teased. "In Europe you wouldn't even hold a lady *this* close. You'd..."

He demonstrated by withdrawing his arm from around her waist and resting it lightly at her side, separating them even farther. He raised his other arm, her hand encased in his, higher than his shoulder. "Catch your skirt up in your other hand."

"And show my petticoat?"

"Yes, if you've got one on," he said with a grin.

She sniffed. Before she could reply, Jake spun her into a dazzling series of swoops and dips. Oh, it was heaven, gliding around the floor like this with him. She anticipated each move his body signaled, and she let herself go, following him instinctively around and around the hall until she grew light-headed. When the fiddle picked up the tempo, conversation on the side-lines died.

"Jake, people are watching!"

"Let them. You dance well. And you're quite a beautiful woman. Why shouldn't they watch?"

Sally's heart thumped. She was beautiful? Suddenly she wanted to be more beautiful than any girl Jake had ever danced with. More beautiful especially than Paula Randall. She straightened her back imperceptibly and glanced over Jake's shoulder at the now-silent crowd, watching them.

The Bar Y hands gathered around Tom at the punch bowl. Over the scraping of the fiddle, Sally heard Dutch Hendricks' voice. "T'ree dollar on Mr. Jake."

"Donald!" his wife exclaimed. "Vat are you think-ing of!"

"Olla, I t'ink Mr. Jake, he vin Miss Sally." The stocky wrangler patted his wife's hand and smiled into her lined face. "I t'ink I bet on Mr. Jake, and ve get rich!"

Bet on Jake? Whatever was Dutch talking about? One of the Bar Y horse races, she guessed. She concen-trated on the music and Jake's voice humming snatches of the melody. When the music slowed, Jake slid his arm around her waist.

"Lesson's over." He pulled her closer, brushing his shirt buttons against the front of her dress.

"Do you like her?" Sally heard herself say.

The humming ceased. "Who?"

"Paula."

"Paula," he repeated. "You mean Nate Randall's daughter?"

Sally nodded, mute with embarrassment. Had she really asked him that? What in the world had gotten into her?

"Yes," Jake said simply, "I do."

Sally fell silent as a weight descended on her heart. *What's the matter with me? I don't care if he likes the Randall girl. Jake can like anyone he pleases.* She just wanted this waltz to last a little longer. It felt so wonderful to be in his arms, breathing in that faint smoky, spicy scent. She closed her eyes. When she opened them again, Jake's dark blue gaze pinned her.

"Sally, there'll be a slow dance coming up later, after the supper break. Would you save it for me?"

For an instant her heart stopped beating. "Why ask me now, so far ahead?"

"Because," he replied softly, "I may not have another chance. I'm eating supper with Judge Randall."

Anger pricked her. He was eating supper with Judge Randall? And Paula? Well, let him. She didn't give a fig who he ate supper with. "I'll have to wait and see," she snapped.

Jake chuckled. He let the arm against her back slide away for just a second. "Okay, Miss Salty, I'll take my chances. But just remember that I asked first. I want you to."

"I have such a bad memory, Mr. Bannister," she blurted in annoyance. "Want me to what?" She flashed him an innocent smile.

Jake felt his body throb to life. Hellfire, what a tease she could be. *Want me to what?* What he wanted to do was tug out those hairpins and lace his fingers in that sweet-smelling hair of hers, watch it spill down over her shoulders, over her... He groaned.

But he'd settle for a dance. A slow one. "Want you to dance with me," he managed to say in an almost normal voice. "Slow," he added in an undertone.

Sally's heart pumped so furiously she was certain he could hear it. For the first time she could ever remember, she could think of absolutely nothing to say. The only word that presented itself in her brain was *yes,* and she bit her tongue to keep that incriminating syllable inside. After all, he *had* chosen to eat supper with Paula Randall. Even if Paula had done the asking, it didn't matter. She tried to control her erratic breathing. It didn't matter one whit. Jake was his own man, and she didn't care who he ate—or danced—with. Not one fig.

When the dance ended, Sally disengaged herself from Jake's arms and fled toward the supper table. After loading up her plate with ham and beans and potato salad and coleslaw, she found a seat next to Will and Louisa. Restless and fidgety, she picked at her plate of food. Try as she might, she could see no sign of either Jake or Judge Randall.

"Stop craning your neck," Louisa said quietly. "Jake's outside, with Paula Randall."

"Outside! But it must be freezing out there by now!"

Louisa shrugged and dug her fork into her scalloped corn.

A vision of Jake and Paula out behind the barn assailed Sally. Pooh! She didn't care what Jake Bannister did behind the barn. That was his business. She pushed Jake out of her mind and attacked Olla Hendricks' potato salad.

After supper the dancing continued with more reels and polkas and schottisches. Except for the breaks taken by the fiddler and the two guitar players, Sally was never off her feet. She danced with Ned Barker and with Cole and Nebraska, with wiry, spirited Dutch Hendricks from the Bar Y, with nine-year-old Billy Peterman and even with Tommy Pearson, grown now into a great hulk of a man with a drooping, straw-colored mustache. His tiny, very pregnant wife sat on the sidelines chatting with Martha.

Toward the end of the evening Sally and her father headed up the Grand Virginia Reel. Amid yells and riotous hoots and clapping hands, Sally proudly led the line of couples down the length of the hall. So absorbed was she in helping her father keep the reel lines straight, she forgot all about Jake.

When George's fiddle lapsed into a slow, nostalgic tune for the last dance of the evening, Sally suddenly found herself in Jake's arms.

"Miss Salty," he said, his voice rising slightly on the last syllable.

She shivered at the tone in his voice. "Jake, why do you call me that?"

He laughed softly. "You know how they take their liquor in Texas?"

"No, but what's that got to do—"

"Texans take their drink neat. Learned it from the vaqueros. They cut a lime in half, and pour a little salt into their fist. Then they toss down the shot, lick the salt, and suck on the lime. The salt gives it an extra kick."

Sally stiffened. "You mean I'm 'an extra kick,' is that it?"

"I mean you're—" Jake held her carefully away from him, struggling with himself. *Oh, Sally, Sally. You're making me ache from wanting you.* "That, yes," he breathed at last. "And more."

"What more, Jake? Tell me."

No. He wouldn't. Couldn't.

He pulled her closer. "How about a little less talk and a little more dance, Sally?"

She felt the front of her dress brush his shirt. Instantly a current shot through her. She closed her eyes, inhaling his wood-smoky, male scent. Her pulse hammered, and she began to feel giddy, the way she had that night in the kitchen.

"Jake, did you...did you kiss Paula Randall behind the barn?"

For the second time that night, Jake missed a step. "Sally, that's not a proper question to ask a man. It's like asking a stranger at your campfire for his last name."

"Did you?" she pursued.

He waited half a heartbeat before answering. "Yes. Or rather, she kissed me. But not behind the barn."

Unexpected pain stabbed through her midsection. "Did you like it?"

There was a long pause. "Yes," he said finally.

Sally's heart plummeted. *Oh, why did it even matter! Let him kiss her. Let him do anything he wanted!* But deep inside a tiny voice nagged, *But let him do it with me....*

"Sally," Jake murmured, his voice very low. "Miss Salty. Look at me."

Sally clamped her lips together and stared at the topmost shiny pearl button of his blue shirt. She *wouldn't* look at him.

But she did. His gentian eyes held hers for a moment, then he pulled her tight against him and settled his chin against her hair. Through the soft fabric of his shirt she felt his heart pump erratically against her breast.

"Your body's all grown up, Sally," he whispered into her ear, "but your emotions are kind of stuck back on the road somewhere."

She started to twist away from him, but he tightened his arms around her. "Now, hold on a minute while I think of how to tell you something."

"Whatever it is, I don't want to hear it!"

Jake ignored her remark and danced with her in silence. Then he bent his head until his lips grazed her temple. "Dammit, Sally," he breathed in her ear, "can't you ever just shut up and let yourself be courted?"

"You're not courting me if you're kissing Paula out behind the barn!"

"I told you it wasn't behind the barn. And she kissed me. Once. I didn't," he added significantly, "go down to the river and go swimming with her."

"You didn't with me, either."

Jake stopped dancing and stood still for a moment. "No, but I sure as hell wanted to. There's been nights since then, Sally, when I lie awake wondering what the hell stopped me. I wanted you bad enough. I wanted you enough to do something damned foolish."

Something in Sally made her close her eyes and slide her hand from his shoulder to the back of his neck. She longed to wind both her arms around his neck. "And now?"

Jake said nothing. He danced her to the most crowded section of the floor, away from the onlookers seated around the perimeter of the room. Her breath whispered against his neck and her heart fluttered, birdlike, against his chest. He put his lips to her ear. "I want you like I've never wanted any woman before, Sally. And I've been wanting to tell you that from the first minute I saw you at the train station in that green dress. But if you don't stop moving your hand on my neck that way, you're liable to make a public spectacle of us both.''

Her eyes opened wide, and she looked up into his face. "Show me.''

He gave a low laugh. "Right here? You wouldn't rather go swimming in the river?''

"Too chilly this time of year,'' she said, her voice lazy.

"Damnation,'' he whispered. "You sure do blow hot and cold.''

"I just want you to kiss me, Jake,'' she said shakily. "And you won't, and I want to know why.''

He held her at arm's length. "You know why, Sally. You're not ready. You're just playing games. You're like that black gelding you tried to ride—all wild spirit and no sense.''

"I am not!''

"You are. And more. A man can get hurt on a horse like that. A man with good sense will wait till a horse like that has gentled some.''

"I've changed, Jake. You haven't seen me for years and years. I'm different now.''

Jake sighed. "Not enough. That black was too much horse for you. In a sense, real life is too much horse for you, too. Right now, at least. You need to grow up some. That's what birthdays are all about—to mark growth. You need to have a birthday, Miss Salty. Soon.''

"Why, of all the—!'' Just who did he think he was, telling her she needed to... Cold fury swept over her.

She hit him hard across his cheek with all the strength she could muster. The sound carried over the music, and the fiddle broke off.

A sudden flurry of activity broke out around the punch bowl. In the silence a voice sang out. "Four dollars on Miss Sally!"

Jake's fingers closed around Sally's wrist. "That's three times around that particular hill," he said evenly, his voice so low she could barely hear him. "And that's enough."

Sally glared at him.

"Fi' dollar on Mr. Jake," another voice called.

Tears pushed at the back of her throat. They were betting on them! Her face flooded with heat. She'd kill him!

Before she could think further, the fiddle started up again, and Jake put both his arms around her and pulled her close.

"Don't you touch me," she gritted.

"Don't give me orders," he said, his voice soft and menacing. He pressed her head down against his chest. "I can't take much more of this, Sally. When you want me to touch you, I don't trust myself. When you don't want me to, I lie awake nights thinking about it."

She struggled against his grasp, but he tightened his arms around her and kept dancing.

"Jake, let me go."

"I can't. Not yet."

"You can, and you will," she demanded.

He stopped and stood still. "Oh, the hell with it." He scooped her up in his arms and headed for the barn door.

In a blur Sally saw Dutch Hendricks' jaw drop open. He punched Cole Sieversen on the arm, and the two of them broke into grins. Heads swiveled as people moved out of Jake's path. The barn door swung shut behind them as a voice called out, "Make that six dollars on Jake!"

"Where are you taking me?" she protested, her voice muffled against his chest.

"Where do you think? Out behind the barn. I'm either going to kiss you until you say uncle or beat the living hell out of you. I haven't decided which."

He set her down with a thump. Before she could draw breath, he grabbed her shoulders and shook her once, hard. Then he tightened his fingers and drew her toward him.

Sally lifted both hands inside the circle of his arms and tried to break his hold. "Let me go!"

"Like hell." He pulled her close, catching her doubled-up fists against his chest, and lowered his mouth to hers.

Sally tried to wrench away, but his arms pinned her fast. After his initial assault, his lips softened, then teased and invited until her senses swam. For one mad, delicious moment she gave herself up to the sensations he evoked.

Then reason returned. This was ludicrous! She'd overreacted, of course, and he... She pulled back and studied him for a moment. He was acting like a man on a hot griddle. Suddenly the whole situation struck her as funny. She suppressed a gasp of laughter.

Through his haze of anger and desire, Jake felt her shoulders jerk. Oh, God, she was crying! Quickly he released her.

Sally clasped one hand against her mouth and looked up at him, shaking with laughter.

"What the—" Jake's eyes hardened into blue-black coals, and an odd light flared in his pupils. "Well, that just about does it."

He grabbed her shoulders, dragged her over to a hay bale and sat her down on it.

Sally turned away from him, but he reached for her and pulled her to face him. Tears glistened on her cheeks, and her mouth twisted. His gut wrenched. "Sally, Sally—I'm sorry. I'm—"

Before he knew what he was doing, he was rocking her in his arms, kissing her temples, her hair, her wet, closed eyelids. "Oh, Sally, I'm sorry. I shouldn't have got mad. But you're awful hard on a man, and I—"

She looked up at him and his heart stopped.

"Shut up, Jake," she said unsteadily. "I deserved it." She watched his face. "Now," she continued with a little hiccup, "stop apologizing and kiss me again. I've earned it."

Jake stared at her. Earned it? What kind of game was she playing, anyway? But then, what kind of game was *he* playing? He'd talked Tom into letting him court her in exchange for a piece of land. What did that make him? He'd agreed to marry someone he hadn't laid eyes on in almost ten years, someone he hadn't even liked very much when he *had* known her.

But, he acknowledged, that was before. Now he wasn't sure how he felt about Sally. Or how she felt about him. And, most puzzling of all, why it even mattered in the first place. If all he wanted was water for his stock, he'd make any sacrifice—even marry Sally—to get what he needed to save his ranch. So, why the pangs of conscience? God knew he had to save the Bar Y; he'd die before he'd watch it go belly-up. So what the hell did it matter what Sally felt about him? Or what he felt about her? If he asked her to marry him now, would she say yes? Isn't that what he wanted? Sally Maguire and one hundred acres of grassland?

To be honest, yes, he wanted it. At least in the beginning. But in the beginning he had just wanted the land. Now he wanted—really wanted—Sally herself. She was the most intriguing, exasperating woman he'd ever had the misfortune to know, and somehow that changed things. If you didn't care about a woman, nothing she said or did mattered. But if you *did* care—God help you.

What was at stake here was a hell of a lot more than a few acres of grass, and a lot more dangerous. A woman like Sally could whittle away your manhood.

All his horse-breaking instincts told him to forget about her. Forget about the land, the ranch. Sally Maguire would never be anything but wild and careless. Heartless. Marrying him would just be another notch in her whip handle, another game to get the better of him. While to him . . .

Carefully, Jake cupped Sally's upturned face between his hands and bent to her mouth. When he felt his loins tighten and swell into the familiar ache, and her name rise unbidden in his brain, he steeled his emotions and dropped his arms.

Deliberately he rose and walked away.

Sally thought about that kiss for a week. Jake's lips had moved on hers so carefully, so gently. And then all of a sudden she had felt his breathing catch, and he had released her. But as he had kissed her in that long, slow moment, she'd felt herself fill with a warm, drowsy light, and a rough joy had surged through her. It hadn't been exactly desire she'd felt as he had held her, but a strange kind of distilled happiness, hot and sweet, like the taste of the sloe gin she had sneaked once from her father's liquor cabinet.

So she wasn't grown-up enough, was she? A sob rose to her throat, followed by swift, instinctive comprehension. She didn't want Jake to just kiss her. She wanted more. Her mind reeled as she realized how much more.

She wanted all of him. Just once, but all of him.

Chapter Eight

Jake dropped the reins of the chestnut mare and settled back in his saddle. From the hilltop he could see the broad sweep of his land spreading below him in an endless sea of sparse brown grass. Hell's fire, it was dry. And hot. Even the cottonwoods drooped for lack of water. He wiped the sweat from his forehead with a red bandanna.

A buzzard circled high against the cerulean sky, and Jake swore. Another dead cow out in the brush somewhere. Probably a heifer—the young ones seemed to suffer most from the drought. Three years and not a drop of water except for winter snow runoff into the small streams that fed into the river. If it didn't rain soon, he'd go bankrupt.

Damnation! He'd die before he'd lose this land. His father had fought to build up the Bar Y holdings. It broke his mother, and in the end it took his father, too. But it wouldn't break him.

Only the hardiest souls survived the inexorable cycle of eastern Oregon's harsh winters and searing summers. Lately Jake had begun to wonder if he had what it took to survive out here in the West. Since his return after college and his years abroad, he'd felt like an outsider.

Oh, his hands respected him. And the townsfolk were friendly enough. But he felt different. Alone.

Was it just his education? Once Cole had teased him by asking, "How come you always talk like book talk, boss?" He'd meant it as a joke, but at bottom, the cowhand was right. He didn't really fit in. There was no one he could really talk to. Even Judge Randall, for all his university legal training, had a mind as straight and narrow as a stagecoach trail. Sometimes Jake felt like a giraffe in a Louisiana swamp.

Then again, what the hell difference did it make whether he fit in or not? He had a three-year drought on his hands, and all the education in the world couldn't save his ranch if it didn't rain. He squinted into the sun.

Or if he didn't marry Sally Maguire. He sure had to do something soon, but right now he didn't know if he could stand either prospect.

The first snow fell in mid-November. Early in the morning Sally mounted the bay mare and struggled over the white-encrusted road to the schoolhouse, noting how the pine and fir trees had disappeared under mounds of white, powdery residue. Cooped up inside with her pupils, she felt the day drag to a close.

Four days later another storm hit. The older students rode to school on horseback as they always did, but the younger ones could no longer walk on the snow-laden roadway and they were too small to ride. Their fathers brought them in on horseback or loaded them into a neighbor's wagon and drove over the drift-clogged road with a team of horses.

Despite the weather, Sally's classes went on as usual. Rob and Richie Blane kept the wood box piled high, so the schoolroom was always toasty. Billy Peterman's grasp of geography continued to be abysmal, but Elsa Baker could now read a few simple words. Today, sitting behind the oak desk listening to her pupils recite their lessons, Sally let her thoughts wander. To her consternation, she ended up thinking about Jake.

She remembered the rush of heat, the feel of his arms around her, holding her close and warm while George Peterman fiddled a slow, lazy waltz. Weeks had passed without her seeing him. For some reason this made her more testy than usual. She didn't know why his absence nettled her so much, but it did. She had to work not to snap at the children.

That evening at supper, Louisa reported that Will and all the Bar Y hands had gone with Jake on the fall roundup.

"They won't be back until late November. Then Will is riding on to Montana with Jake for the Stock Growers Association meeting in Miles City," Louisa added between dainty bites of Martha's stewed chicken and dumplings. "Now, with all the snow, who knows when they'll be back."

Sally shrugged and helped herself to another dumpling. It was the same way every year. All the ranchers in the valley pitched in for the fall roundup, each working his assigned area until all the cows and their calves had been gathered, sorted, tallied and branded. Her father had taken Hank and the rest of the Circle L hands except for Shorty, who stayed behind each year to see to the chores around the ranch. When roundup was over, the weary men would head home for the winter.

She probably wouldn't see Jake until close to Christmas. Just as well, she reasoned. Whenever she was with him, she felt upset and off-balance. Let him go to Montana. Let him go to the devil, for all she cared! She hoped he froze his backside to his saddle.

After supper Louisa stitched on her ivory silk wedding dress while Sally planned primer lessons and corrected papers. A notebook propped on her drawn-up knees, she fiddled with her pen, then gazed pensively at her sister.

"Lou, has Will asked you to marry him yet?" The question had been niggling at her for the past month.

Louisa smiled down at the ivory folds in her lap and pushed her needle into the silk. "Not officially. He wants to speak to Pa first."

"But if he's going on to Montana with Jake after roundup, that could be weeks from now!"

"It won't matter, Sally." Louisa stitched in silence, then spoke again, her voice calm. "You should be thinking about a bridesmaid's dress."

"Bridesmaid's dress! For a wedding that's not even an engagement yet?"

Unperturbed, Louisa smiled at her sister. "A pale peach, I think." She cast Sally an appraising glance. "Few redheads can wear peach, but your hair's so dark, I think you would look stunning."

"Peach is a summer color, Lou. It's almost Christmas! Or are you too much in love to notice?"

Louisa smiled and sewed. "There's some new yard goods in at Baker's. Next time Shorty goes to town, let's go with him and pick something out?"

Sally shook her head at her sister's single-minded perseverance. Once Louisa had her mind made up, there was no use arguing. She swallowed her retort and went back to her papers.

The following week Tom and the hands from the Hope Valley ranches returned. On Sunday Olla Hendricks, the cook at the Bar Y, came to help Martha put up applesauce.

Sally and Louisa tied aprons on over their cotton day dresses and peeled apples until their fingers ached. The overheated kitchen was redolent with the scent of cinnamon and cloves, and Sally fought to stay awake as Olla chattered while the golden apple-skin spirals dropped from her paring knife.

"Most ranches lay off their hands each winter," the buxom cook observed, her face ruddy from working next to the stove. "But not Mr. B. He keeps the men on year-round. Dutch says they get a bit stir-crazy from settin' in the bunkhouse, so the boss keeps 'em busy choppin' firewood and mendin' the roof. They allus complain about it, but me and my Dutch, we're grateful to have a place all year long."

Martha nodded. "Shorty's out now, sprucing up the chuckwagon for spring roundup. I been chopping all my own kindling for a week."

"He's lucky." Olla laughed. "If they were at the Bar Y, Mr. B'd have 'em out ridin' fence or chasing wolves. Slim and Nebraska are up at them line shacks right now. Won't be back till spring. Nobody much to cook for 'cept Dutch and Sonny. And Mr. B, of course. Say, these apples cook up nice, don't they?"

Sally fumed in silence. Mr. B this. Mr. B that. Didn't anyone ever tire of Jake Bannister as a subject of conversation?

Before Martha could answer, someone rode in the front gate and a few moments later clumped up the front steps.

"It's Ned Barker and Cole!" Louisa whispered as she peered out the kitchen window. After a quick glance at each other, Sally and Louisa tore off their aprons and escaped to greet their guests.

It was too cold for porch sitting, so Louisa's callers sat in the front parlor and Martha served hot cocoa instead of lemonade with her ginger cookies.

"Looks like a hell, er, heckuva storm blowin' up," Cole observed as he reached for another cookie. "Sky's blacker'n a stove lid." Louisa smiled at the lanky cowhand and poured out the cocoa.

"Nothin' a top hand in a good buffalo coat can't handle," Ned countered, his dark eyes snapping. "Unless his brain ain't big enough to sew a button on. What about it, Miss Sally? You gonna close the school tomorrow?"

Sally considered before replying. "I can't do that without Jake's—without permission from the school board. I think school will be held as usual."

But it did look like a big storm brewing, she admitted, glancing out the lace-curtained window. The slate-colored sky pressed down on the surrounding hills, and the wind moaned about the eaves.

The Petermans' foreman shrugged. "Jake's not back from Montana yet. Guess the school board meetin' will just have to wait."

The following morning when Sally saddled the bay and rode to school, the sky looked black and threatening. But to her relief, no more snow had fallen during the night. It looked as if the storm had blown over. The road was easier to travel than it had been a week ago, when the drifts were up to Flapjack's knees. But even so, at each step the bay sank in up to its forelegs.

When Sally finally arrived at the schoolhouse, she made sure the fire in the blackened potbellied stove in the corner was roaring by the time the first pupils arrived.

Late that morning it began to snow. The silent, white flakes drifted slowly past the window, covering the tracks made by the horses and the buckboard that had brought the younger children. By noon the wind had picked up. Sally looked up from the book she was reading aloud and gazed out the window. Without a doubt they were in for a blizzard.

Lordy, what should she do? She could be marooned out here, responsible for seventeen children, with no way to get them home! They would just have to wait it out, she decided. Eventually one of the fathers would come for them with a wagon and a team of horses.

She was determined she would not let her uneasiness show. To keep her pupils' attention off the howling wind, she doggedly continued reading. "'For the first time, Hawkeye was seen to stir. He crawled along the rock, and shook Duncan from his heavy slumbers.'"

Sally read on until her throat was raspy. When dusk fell and still there was no letup in the storm, the younger children began to whimper.

"Rob, put some more wood on the fire, please," Sally ordered. She rose from her desk, walked to the center of the room and sat down on the floor. "Sit in a circle around me, near the stove. And Elsa, you and Rachel come here to me. Sit close, now, and watch my finger point to the words as I read them."

The girls huddled close to Sally as she continued. "'You know not the nature of a Maqua, if you think he is so easily beaten back without a scalp!' he answered. 'Keep close! Or the hair will be off your crown in the turning of a knife!'"

She read for another hour, and suddenly the door burst open.

A snow-covered giant clumped into the room. The gray Stetson was white with snow, the calf-length fur coat covered with powdery flakes. "Miss Sally," a cracked voice said.

"Jake! Oh, Jake, thank heaven you're here! All the children—"

"I know." He pulled off his leather gloves and held his palms to the fire. "Since my ranch is the closest, I came with a wagon to take them out. We'll bunk them at the Bar Y tonight, then tomorrow morning my hands will take them home on horseback." He turned his back to the stove and faced her. "I'm going to have to borrow your horse, Sally. The wagon won't hold all of them."

"Yes, of course. Take it!" Oh, she was so glad to see him, and . . . Good heavens, he looked so cold!

Jake turned to one of the older boys. "Jim Eckloff, isn't it?"

The boy nodded, flushing with pride at being remembered by the owner of the Bar Y. "Yessir?"

"Jim, take Miss Sally's bay tied up outside. Mount two of the smaller children with you—one in front and one behind."

The boy leapt up from the floor and began to pull on his woolen jacket and gloves.

"You others, get into your things and climb into that wagon outside, the smaller ones in the front. You, Elsa, and you," Jake said, gesturing to Rachel, "I'll take you with me on the wagon seat. Quick, now! We don't have any time to waste."

Sally caught at Jake's sleeve. "I'll stay behind, Jake. That way you can fit all the little ones in the wagon."

Jake turned to her and spoke in an undertone. "I'll come back for you later, Sally. You're right, there's not enough room for all of you in the wagon. If we overload it, it'll bog down in a drift, and I'll never get them out."

Sally nodded. She turned away to quell the bedlam of excited voices and sort out the forest of coats and mittens. When the children were ready, Jake carried them one by one to the waiting wagon and covered them up with thick buffalo robes. When the last child had been safely ensconced, and Jim Eckloff was mounted on Sally's bay with two of the smaller boys, Jake made one last trip into the schoolhouse.

"Don't worry," he said, laying one hand on her shoulder. "That bay is a fine snow horse. With the wagon breaking trail for him, the Eckloff boy won't have any trouble. I'll ride that black gelding back for you tonight—Dutch finally got him broke. There's a lot of horse there. He's got stamina, and he has heart."

"So do you," Sally heard herself whisper in an unsteady voice. "But be careful, anyway."

He gripped her shoulders. "Do you have plenty of firewood?"

"Yes. It's stacked up outside the door. You can't see it under the snow."

"Don't let the stove go out," he admonished. "And be sure to keep yourself warm."

In a quick movement he unholstered his revolver and laid it on her desk. "I've got my rifle" was the only explanation he offered.

"I'll be back." He plunged out the door into the swirling snow.

Sally ran to watch through the window.

The team of horses strained forward against the load, steam puffing out of their nostrils. When the wagon finally inched forward, her breath expelled in a rush. Thank God. She watched until all trace of the wagon and her bay following close behind was obliterated by the driving wall of white.

Hours passed. The wind howled around the schoolhouse, the gusts buffeting the small log building until Sally thought surely the window would blow in. When she dashed out for another armload of wood, the wind wrenched the heavy door out of her hands. Once back inside, she had to use her entire body weight to pull it shut.

The snow piled up to the windowsill. The little potbellied stove popped and crackled each time Sally added more of the wet wood, but once the logs ignited, they burned steadily, and she was surprised at how warm the room was.

Close to midnight Sally found herself growing more and more nervous. She lit the kerosene lamp, and the flickering flame cast a soft glow about the room.

They would have made it to the Bar Y by now, she thought. Was the snow so heavy Jake wouldn't be able to ride back through the storm tonight? She didn't see how any horse—even the black gelding—could break trail through the deepening drifts. Well, there was nothing to do but wait it out. At least she was safe and warm.

To pass the time she opened the book she had been reading, found her place and squinted at the words in the lamplight. The wind tore at the roof, and she shivered. Dear God, let him not try to get through tonight—it was too risky.

She read for what seemed like hours, and then stopped abruptly. She heard something. Or thought she did. A gunshot. No, two. A signal, asking direction!

Jake was out there somewhere, maybe lost. She knew he wouldn't be able to see the schoolhouse through the swirling snow. He probably couldn't even tell which direction to head.

Sally reached for the gun on her desk, cocked it with shaking fingers and went to the door. She fired once through the crack she made in the doorway and listened.

Nothing. Then, far off, she heard the crack of another gunshot. She fired again.

A long silence, and then through the whine of the wind she heard his voice a long way off. "Sall-e-e... Sall-e-e?"

"Jake!" she screamed. "Over here." She ran for her heavy coat.

He was on foot, leading the black gelding step by halting step through the mounded pale drifts, his head down against the wind, the gray Stetson tied onto his head with a wool scarf. His entire figure was white with powdered snow.

She labored through the drifts toward him, the wind whipping the full gores of her dark blue wool dress. Her icy-wet petticoat ruffle slapped against her ankles.

"Sally, for God's sake, you'll freeze to death out here. Get back inside. I'm all right, just cold."

She grabbed the lapel of his thick fur coat and pulled him toward the schoolhouse.

"Wait," he shouted. He reached back and lifted his saddle off the horse, then unfolded the saddle blanket and spread it over the gelding's broad back. He led the horse close to the log wall and turned him away from the wind. Then he laid his arm heavily across Sally's shoulders and floundered with her toward the doorway where the firelight beckoned.

He was stiff with cold. Even his eyelashes were encrusted with snow. He dropped his saddle and the bulky bedroll, wrapped tight in a thick buffalo robe, onto the floor and clunked his Winchester down on her desk.

Sally struggled to pull the door shut against the wind.

Using his teeth, Jake pulled off the stiffened leather gloves and stretched his hands toward the fire. "I didn't stop to pack up much. The way the storm was, I was afraid I wouldn't get back at all. As it is, I damn near froze my feet off!"

Sally looked at him questioningly.

"The kids are okay," he said before she could speak. "They're all at the ranch. Olla's cooking them some supper."

"All the children? Elsa? She's so frail, Jake. . . ."

Jake laughed. "She's fine. Told me about Hawkeye and the Mohicans all the way to the ranch. Never stopped talking for a minute. Sort of reminded me of you."

Sally sighed with relief.

"But," he continued, a frown drawing his dark brows together, "there's no way we can get back to the ranch tonight, with the wind like it is. The snow's blowing so thick you can't see your hand in front of your face. I'm afraid we're stuck here for the night.''

Sally stiffened. ''You mean together? Here?'' Her voice rose an octave. *''All night?''*

Jake avoided her eyes. ''All night.''

Chapter Nine

Sally stared into Jake's somber face, her heart slamming against her ribs. "We're going to spend the night here, in the schoolhouse? Just the two of us?"

Jake gestured with his hands, palms up. "You want me to go back out there?"

"Oh, of course not, Jake, but—"

"I only brought the one horse, Sally. The snow's too deep for the black to carry us both at night. It's blowing so hard you can barely see. Safer to stay put."

"But what about—"

"No need to worry," he offered, anticipating her question. "If we can't get out, no one can get in. Your father thinks you're at the Bar Y, and the Bar Y hands will think you're at Tom's."

She frowned, and he swung away from the stove to face her. "I'm sorry, Sally, but it can't be helped. Under the circumstances, that's the least of our worries. I'm starving, and you must be, too. What have you got to eat?"

"Just my lunch," she said slowly. "I wasn't hungry, so I didn't even open it at noon. I've had a little since. Martha always puts in more than I can eat."

"Describe it," Jake ordered. "I'll bet it's not more than *I* can eat."

Sally peered into the square metal lunch box. "There's an apple and a meat-loaf sandwich. And—" she searched through the contents of the box "—a slice of Martha's mince pie."

Jake chuckled. "Well, I guess we won't starve. And we won't freeze to death with this buffalo robe. My supplies are pretty meager, I'm afraid. I've got some jerky, some whiskey and my bedroll. And me," he added with a smile. "Take your pick."

Sally laughed in spite of herself. "Dinner," she announced.

Jake sliced the jerky into pieces with his jackknife and cut the apple into quarters, flipping the core into the belly of the stove. He divided the sandwich and the wedge of pie into two portions and uncorked the small bottle of whiskey. He looked at it a moment, tipped it up and took a healthy swig. Then he passed the bottle to Sally. At the first gulp, she coughed and gasped for breath. Tears came to her eyes. "Tastes awful," she rasped when she could talk.

Jake laughed and took the bottle from her. "It's the Silver Cup's finest, but you're supposed to sip it, not swill it!"

"*You* didn't!"

"I'm used to it. You're not. Anyway, tonight it's for medicinal purposes. You're warm, but I'm still bloody cold. I need it more than you."

He took another swallow from the bottle, corked it and set it on the floor. He spread the buffalo robe in front of the stove, laid out the food on sheets of Sally's lesson paper and lowered his lean frame onto the fur. Then he leaned back on one elbow and casually stretched his long legs out in front of him. "I guess our picnic's about ready."

Sally sat across from him on the thick robe and tucked her full skirt around her drawn-up knees. Jake handed her half of the sandwich, and she took a small bite in silence.

After a few moments Jake looked up at her. "How have you been?"

The question surprised her; it was so polite, almost formal.

"Fine." She searched for something else to say. "Elsa Baker can read a little now," she added. "And Rachel, the other little girl you took with you on the wagon, will be reading soon, too." She hesitated, then continued in a rush. "Richie Blane fell out of that big pine tree at the edge of the school yard and broke his arm. Martha set it for him, as Doc Varner was out at the Pearson place, delivering Miranda's baby. She had a baby girl. And Louisa's sewing on her—"

She caught herself in time.

Jake chuckled, watching her face. "Her wedding dress, I'll bet."

"How on earth did you know that?"

"A cowhand—even a top hand or a foreman the likes of Will Boessen—is worthless when he's in love. Lately Will's been acting like a sick calf."

Sally giggled. "It's funny, but Louisa isn't the least bit ruffled. She loves Will, I know she does. And she's waiting for him to ask her. But she's so—I don't know—calm. Steady."

"Love is like that sometimes, I guess. One shows it, the other doesn't." He glanced at her face.

"You won't let on you know, will you, Jake? Louisa would never forgive me."

"I won't. I'm a good keeper of secrets."

Jake noticed how the firelight shone on that thick roll of red hair she'd piled on top of her head, how her high-necked blue dress stretched over the swell of her breasts. He licked his lips, his mouth suddenly dry. He wanted to kiss her. He didn't need to remind himself that the last time he had kissed her he'd had to keep himself under tight control. Now he felt the same overwhelming urge to dig his fingers deep into that mass of thick hair, tip her head back, and feel her mouth under his. *Careful, old son,* he cautioned himself. *Take a long, deep breath. Think of something else... anything else.*

Sally glanced up to find him staring at her, an odd, hungry expression in the dark blue eyes.

He coughed abruptly and reached for the whiskey bottle. "Would you like to hear about the Montana Stock Growers' meeting? Will and I just got back yesterday." He concentrated on slicing off more jerky.

Sally nodded, watching his hands work the knife through the dried meat. He had wonderful hands—lean, strong, no-nonsense hands, the fingers long and slim. They looked capable. Sensitive. She shivered suddenly.

He handed her the whiskey. "Cold?"

"No, not really." But she took a sip anyway. And then she took another.

"Well," Jake continued, "ranchers all the way from Texas to Wyoming—the big ones, anyway—are trying to figure out a way to avoid rustling each other's cows during roundup. With thousands of square miles of rangeland now, we've got everybody's stock all mixed up together. Sorting it out can be a real pain in the..."

"Posterior," Sally supplied, laughing. She re-wrapped her skirt about her knees.

Jake caught a whiff of the rose-lilac scent she always wore. He'd thought about her smell, her softness, all the way to Miles City and back. He wondered if she'd thought about him while he'd been gone. *Ask her! No, don't ask her,* an instinct warned. *She'd probably bite your head off. Or maybe... No, don't ask her.*

"Anyway," he continued, keeping his voice light, "the stockmen hashed this over for the better part of one day and finally decided... Oh, hell, Sally, you don't want to hear about this."

"Yes, I do!"

"Now, why would the schoolteacher in Honey Creek, Oregon, who's reading—" he craned his head to see the book on the corner of her desk "—Fenimore Cooper, want to know what ranchers in Montana are doing about their unbranded calves?"

"I—Jake, we're going to be here all night. We have to talk about *something.*"

"Do we?" He stood suddenly and slid another log into the belly of the wood stove. "Why do we?"

"Because..." She faltered. "If we talk about something interesting, something... neutral, maybe we won't... fight," she finished.

Jake sucked in a long breath. "We fight because of what happens when we're *not* talking, Sally." *We fight because we want each other,* he thought. Lord, it was going to be a long, long night.

"I think," said Sally after a pause, "that we should be sensible and practical and decide how best to spend this night... uh... togcther."

He laughed, the warmth in his voice soothing her oddly. "Miss Salty, let me tell you about the Montana Stockmen's Association ball."

Sally nodded quickly and bit into an apple quarter.

She chewed for a full minute before Jake wrenched his eyes away from her mouth and continued. "It was a big military affair, with a six-piece orchestra and lots of starch and sparkle, pretty women dressed to their hairlines. Granville Stuart's daughters were there. They're half-Indian, you know, very good-looking women. You got any Indian blood?" he asked suddenly.

Sally swallowed. "Great-Uncle Matthew always claimed he was half Sioux. Does that count?"

Jake chuckled softly. "Anyway, there was dancing until almost four in the morning and—" He broke off. "Dammit, Sally, I don't want to talk about this." He reached for the whiskey bottle.

She watched him tip the bottle to his lips, and she waited. When he had downed another swig, their eyes met.

He hesitated a long moment before he spoke. "I want to tell you how beautiful your hair is in the firelight," he said slowly, his voice throaty. "And how much I thought about you. And how I'd like to—"

"Then why don't you?"

He stared at her, his pupils dilating. "Sally, you are the most unpredictable..."

He recorked the bottle and carefully set it down beside him.

"I thought about you, too, Jake. I guess I like having somebody around once in a while who can...speak French."

Jake threw back his head and laughed. Sally stared at him. She liked it when he laughed, his voice low and rich and caressing. But she didn't like it so much when he laughed at *her,* she decided. She shifted her knees uneasily.

Jake sobered, and in one quick motion he was on his feet, pulling her up to him. "As I was saying, Sally," he continued, his voice soft and urgent, "I wanted to tell you how much I'd like to..." His voice trailed into silence. "Kiss you," he breathed at last.

Sally's heart jumped. "How much?" she asked softly.

"More than I'd care to admit." His hands tightened on her shoulders, the full, gathered sleeves crushing softly under his fingers. He looked at her for a long moment, then lowered his mouth to hers.

He kissed her slowly, thoroughly, his brain screaming for him to stop, his mouth hungering for more of her. Without half trying, he could lose his head completely.

Sally gave a little moan and moved in his arms. He smelled of horses and leather and pine trees, and she felt again the rush of inexplicable happiness she always did when he touched her.

Jake lifted his mouth from hers. Her breath fanned his lips. Her eyes were closed, and a little pulse fluttered at her temple.

Sally raised her hands to his upper arms. She needed to hold him still, away from her, needed to keep him from moving so that her breasts brushed his chest. She wanted to touch him, to feel him against her, but she knew it was dangerous. She wanted it too much. She should open her eyes, break the spell, but somehow she couldn't. Something inside her didn't want to. What she really wanted was...

He kissed her again. His lips tasted sweet, his mouth dark and inviting, like warm, black silk. She opened her lips under his. He hesitated for an instant, then gently moved his mouth against hers, opening her to his tongue. A shimmer of exquisite tension swam into her belly, and she moved against him. The tip of his tongue gently outlined her upper lip, then deepened into her mouth.

Sally raised her arms to his neck. Her mind slowed. She felt her body open to him, ache for him. She smiled under his mouth, and he lifted his head. Lazily she drew him to her again. She wanted him to touch her, kiss her, all over. The thought made her breath stop.

"Jake . . . Jake," she whispered. "I'm frightened."

"Of me?" he said against her lips.

"No. Of me. What's frightening me is . . ."

"Is . . . ?" he echoed.

"That I feel so wonderful when you kiss me," she breathed. "When you touch me. I don't want you to stop."

Jake smiled down into her eyes. "You want to go swimming in the river?"

"Yes," she whispered. "Yes! In some crazy way, I do." Her voice trembled. "And I'm scared."

He gathered her against the full length of his body, one hand pressing her buttocks against his thighs. "Sally, Sally," he groaned. "If you want me to stop, you'd better tell me now, because in another minute—"

She reached both hands behind his head and pulled his mouth down to hers.

Jake struggled to breathe evenly. She was so warm and soft in his arms.

"Don't stop, Jake. Don't. You said once to be alive, really alive, you have to risk things. I want to try out a little of life. Now. Here. With you."

His body tensed into stillness. "Sally," he said softly, his voice grainy, "are you sure, really sure, you want this?"

She ignored his words, feeling her breasts press against the hardness of his torso. The backs of her knees were weak and hot. "Jake, I—yes. Yes!"

He groaned again. "Sally, you're going to make an old man of me. Are you absolutely certain?" he repeated.

"I want you," she breathed. "Of that I'm very, very certain." She moved in his arms, pushing her aching nipples into his chest, her face close to his.

"Jake," she whispered. "How big is your bedroll?"

His arms tightened. "Big enough."

"I'm still frightened, Jake, but..."

Her body trembled against his, and he pressed her head against his shoulder, holding the back of her head with one hand. "You remember the day you tried to ride that gelding, Sally?"

She nodded against his chest.

"That took a lot of courage. Or maybe foolhardiness. But anyway, with all of us watching, you climbed up on him, and you held on. But Sally..." He held her away from him and looked into her face. "The most courageous acts in life—getting born, making love the first time, bearing your own child, maybe dying—all these things happen in small rooms, with nobody watching."

He ran both his hands down her rib cage to her waist, then to her hips, and spread his fingers against the soft wool. Her heat burned his fingertips.

"And this," he whispered raggedly into her ear, "is one hell of a small room. And there's nobody watching, Sally. Nobody."

An ache flared from her belly. "I want this," she whispered. "You."

In the silence the fire flickered and popped. They stood still, listening to each other's breathing. Very slowly Jake reached up and withdrew one of her hairpins. His hand shook slightly as he drew out another. A strand of loosened hair trailed down to her shoulder.

Carefully, deliberately, he removed all the pins, one by one, until her hair tumbled free in a mass of waves. He gathered it up in both his hands, closing his fingers upon the silky warmth, inhaling the elusive lilac scent.

He looked at her for a long moment in the flickering light. "Sally," he said at last, his voice low and hoarse. "Take off your dress."

She held his eyes as she slipped the buttons free, one by one, working slowly from the neck down across her breast, then below her waist. She let the soft wool garment slide down over her undergarments to the floor and stepped out of it. Then she untied the drawstring of her petticoat, and it drifted to the floor around her ankles.

Jake watched her, not moving, while she slipped the straps of her camisole off her shoulders. Last, she unbuttoned the lacy pantalets, slid them off her hips and stepped out of them.

She stood before him, naked, and his breath caught. She was exquisite.

He turned away from her and bent to pull off his boots, then stripped off his jeans and underwear and unbuttoned his vest, then his heavy wool shirt and pulled it over his head. When he was finished, he leaned to blow out the lamp, then knelt on the soft robe before the fire. Gently he drew Sally down beside him.

He stroked her shoulders, her breasts with gentle, sure hands, and she sighed and lay back. Jake looked at her slim body and shook his head. She was the most beautiful woman he had ever seen, and she was here, with him, offering herself. Her eyes looked like smoky green jewels in the firelight.

He roused her slowly, deliberately, moving his hands, his tongue over her body, feeling her tense and then relax, listening to her breathing, hearing her begin to moan as he touched her. He wanted it to be good for her. Slow. Sweet. He wanted her so much, wanted to hold her, bury himself inside her. And he could tell she wanted it, too. He shook his head again. He could not believe she was his.

Sally thought she had never known anything as rich, as exultant, as the soaring in her body when Jake touched her. She was floating, a sweet, hot ache spiraling upward inside her. She raised her arms over her head and arched her body to meet his hands. A splendor built inside her, making her want to scream, to weep, and she reveled in it. It was like the first time she had sat up high on a horse, all by herself, and made it move under her, the first time she swam the river, terrified, all the way to the sand bar.

She moaned, whispered his name, cried out, her voice rising and falling, passion-blurred and inarticulate.

Softly Jake spoke into her ear. "Let go, Sally. Let go. No one can hear you." He kissed her swollen mouth, the taut nipples of her breasts, circling his tongue over them as if he were licking honey, listening to her voice. The sound of her cries made him ache. He smoothed his hands over her entire body, slowly, his thumbs pressing, his fingers gentle, teasing. Inexorably he moved lower, below her belly, below the triangular growth of soft, curled hair between her thighs. He felt her heat, her movement against his hand, and something stirred inside him. He felt savage, and then suddenly he felt like crying. In all his experience with a woman, it had never been like this.

When she was ready, the slick, silky wetness between her thighs opening to him, Jake positioned himself over her and lowered his body slowly into hers. Sally gasped and cried out, and he withdrew partway. He entered her again, moving deeper, then at her sharp intake of breath, he again pulled back.

She moaned and reached out for him, pulling him down to her, into her, and with a hoarse cry he drove all the way to her core.

Sally arched her body to meet his, sobbing brokenly, rising with his rhythm until she cried out with pleasure, and cried out again. She soared, spinning into a fathomless black space where time stopped. Shudders washed through her like rippling velvet.

Her response triggered his. He buried his body deep within hers, and lost himself. Crying out her name, he moved beyond himself into a place he'd never known existed. And in that place Jake acknowledged with a desperate certainty what he had known all along. He was hopelessly, dangerously in love with her.

Sally heard a man's racking sobs. After a moment she realized it was Jake. Stunned, she held him to her, smoothing her hands languorously up and down his bare, muscled back, listening to his ragged breathing. His heart pounded erratically against her flesh.

Shaken, Jake clung to her, his eyes closed, his face pressed against her breast. Then, still sheathed inside her, he turned them both to one side and cradled her body against him.

After a long time Sally spoke softly. "Is it always like this?"

"It's never like this."

"Was it the whiskey?"

"No," he said, his voice unsteady. "It wasn't the whiskey. It was you and me."

She smiled into his eyes, a fierce joy bubbling within her. She sighed and moved languidly in his arms. "Then, before morning comes, will you make love to me again?"

Jake brought her out the next morning, riding double on the black gelding. He wrapped the buffalo robe around her and set her on the saddle in front of him, and she pressed her back against his chest.

She felt no need to talk; the movement of his body against hers was conversation enough. She leaned her head back under his chin and closed her eyes.

The wind had died, and a hushed stillness lay over the white-shrouded landscape. The drifts were shoulder high, white and silent as statues.

Jake thought he had never felt as content as he did now, riding somewhere, it didn't matter where, with Sally in his arms. After last night he knew he was not the same man who had ridden out to her the night before. He would never be the same.

It took the entire day to get to her father's ranch.

Chapter Ten

Sally curled her body up in the narrow bed and reluctantly opened her eyes. She groaned, watching the white flakes drift past her window. She knew her father and the other ranchers would be relieved that it was still snowing—the runoff in the spring would replenish the dried-up creeks, and the hills would be green with grass for the cattle. But it had been snowing off and on for the past month, and it seemed to her that all life in the valley had stopped.

School would be closed until spring. She missed the children, missed teaching, watching her pupils grow and learn. And with the bad weather, neither Will nor Cole from the Bar Y had come calling on Sundays. Ned Barker, too, had stayed away, busy with winter chores at the Peterman spread. And Jake...

She had not seen Jake since the blizzard, but the thought of him, and of the night she had spent with him at the schoolhouse, stopped her breath. She had wanted it to happen, wanted him. The ecstasy, the feeling of shattering vulnerability that had swept over her, had shaken her. Making love with Jake had been the most profoundly moving experience of her life. She knew she would never forget the splendor of those hours with him. She had been more frightened than she could ever remember, but somehow, in the end, it had not mattered.

She gazed up at the blue-wallpapered ceiling and sighed. She was still frightened. Of what, she didn't know exactly. But every time she thought of Jake, her unease built until her heart skipped at the mere thought of him. She raised her head and looked out the window.

Outside, a carpet of snow blanketed the landscape. White-swathed bushes drooped under the weight of snow-laden branches, and her mother's Belle of Portugal rose lay buried under a shroud of white velvet. The only sound was the soft sighing of the wind through the pine trees. Other than that, everything was still. Expectant.

A corresponding expectancy lay in Sally's heart. With the ranches isolated from each other by the snow, and trips into town hazardous, she had busied herself these past weeks sewing on Louisa's wedding dress and helping Martha bake mince and apple pies for Christmas.

On Christmas Eve she unpacked the ornaments stored in the attic and helped Martha and the twins decorate the huge Douglas fir her father and Hank hauled into the front parlor.

The holidays dragged by, filled with endless lists of keep-busy tasks as the snow drifted ceaselessly past the windows and Sally waited for her classes to resume. She'd thought up all kinds of creative games as a way to teach geography—even Billy Peterman would master the subject.

Now, the day after New Year's, Sally decided she'd had enough of winter. She kicked back the quilted coverlet and stepped onto the braided rug beside her bed.

She was ready for spring. Anything to avoid thinking about Jake.

Halfway through her morning task of packing up the ornaments and lugging them up to the attic, she glimpsed two riders through the window in the upstairs hallway. Her heart lurched. "It's Will!" she called to Louisa. "And Jake is with him!"

Louisa deliberately laid her sewing on the dining table, went into the kitchen and set the blue enamelware coffeepot on the stove.

Sally raced down the stairs to the front door. With her hand on the doorknob, she drew a double deep breath, then swung the door wide, admitting a blast of icy air.

Will tramped in, followed by Jake. Sally gave Will a warm smile, then transferred her gaze to the tall man at his side.

Jake stood motionless in the front hallway, his gray Stetson in his hand, as Louisa drew Will away into the parlor. Hypnotized by his gaze, Sally could think of nothing to say.

"Will's come to ask for Louisa," Jake intoned when his foreman disappeared into the study with Tom. "I never saw a man more scared. He says it's worse than breaking horses."

Sally nodded. She could imagine his fear. Irrevocable commitment to one person, for the rest of one's life, would frighten anyone in their right mind.

Jake hesitated a moment, then spoke, his voice low and urgent. "Get your coat, Sally, and walk out with me a ways. We've got to talk."

A thread of fear laced through her chest. What did he want to talk about—that night in the schoolhouse? In silence she lifted her wool wrap from the coatrack. Despite her unease, she was glad for the chance to be out of the house, glad also just to be near him. Already a sweet ache began below her belly. She hungered for him, longed for him to touch her. Lord, she was wanton!

They trudged through the still, white world, the only sounds the crunch of snow under their boots. Tree branches drooped under mantles of snow, and pale sunshine shone through the arbor lattice. They walked for a while in silence, then Jake turned to her.

"I was kind of thinking of talking to Tom myself," he said quietly.

"Oh?" Sally widened her eyes. "What about? We've got all the horses we need till spring, and—"

Jake winced. "You know something, Sally? You are exasperating. I haven't seen you for over a month, not since . . . and you talk about horses! I came over with Will because there's something I have to know. Are you . . . all right?"

"Of course, Jake. I'm fine."

"Don't fool with me, Sally. I mean after that night—" He swallowed. "I have to know, Sally. Did you . . . conceive?"

Conceive! The thought had never occurred to her. An irrational flash of disappointment flickered into her consciousness. "No, I didn't."

"Are you sorry?" His voice was careful, almost noncommittal.

"About being with you, or not conceiving?"

"Either." He kept his tone light. "Both."

"No."

Jake groaned. "Dammit, Sally, no *what?*"

She looked up into his stern face, surprised at seeing him off-balance for the first time she could ever remember. "No, I'm not sorry, Jake, not the least bit sorry. I want you every time I look at you."

Great blazes! Jake thought. Her forthright honesty jarred him, but he kept his expression guarded.

"And, yes," she continued, "I am sorry, too. If I did ever want a child, I'd want it to be yours, I suppose. But I don't—"

He gripped her shoulders. "Sally, look at me. This isn't a game now. Do you think..." He took a deep breath. "Do you think you'd want to get married?"

She was silent such a long time, Jake found himself holding his breath.

"No," she said at last. Her clear eyes gazed into his with unnerving candor. "I don't think so, Jake. When I'm near you, I want you, but..."

"But that's not enough," he finished for her. "Almighty crawfish, Sally, you're really hell on a man. First you take him to heights he's never dreamed of, then you kick the stuffing out of him. Just once I'd like to see someone tie your spurs together and ring the dinner bell."

"Oh, Jake, I'm sorry, I really am. It's just that I get...scared." She felt the old panic clench her belly into a knot, then close her throat like choking fingers. "I'm glad about that night. I'll always remember it. But I don't think I'll ever want to give up teaching and settle down...."

Jake groaned. "Sally, nobody will ever settle you down. You'll be just as crazy as you are now, but in somebody else's kitchen, not Tom's." He gave her a little shake and took a deep breath. "It must be obvious that I love you, Sally. I want you to marry me."

Sally said nothing for a long time. A new need battled an old fear buried deep within her. "I can't, Jake."

"Can't or won't? You want to teach school for the rest of your days? Have a secondhand kind of life, loving other people's kids instead of your own?"

"Teaching school isn't a secondhand life—it's my whole life. I love it. I'm good at it. It means everything to me, doing something I'm good at. It makes me count in life. It makes me want to get up in the morning, want to live."

"It's still secondhand, Sally. All those kids are other people's families, not your own."

Sally hesitated. "A secondhand life is less threatening somehow. There's less to lose, less chance of getting hurt."

They walked on without speaking. Jake knew how frightened she was, and all at once he knew why. He caught her arm and pulled her to face him. "Sally, your mother didn't die *because* you loved her," he said softly. "She was killed because the buggy turned over on her and broke her neck. It was an accident, Sally. An accident. Dammit, don't you see—just because you love somebody doesn't mean they're going to die and leave you alone."

Sally flinched and her face paled. "How do you know?"

"Because my mother died, too," he said simply. "She had a tumor, in her brain. It took a long time. It wasn't sudden, like an accident. I had time to get used to it. And afterward, I had time to grow past it."

Sally thought about the day of her mother's accident. She remembered running barefoot over the lush grass and down the road, the powdery dust puffing up between her toes, running blindly because she had heard a horse scream. Later, after the men had carried her mother's body up to the house, she had saddled her horse and ridden into town to the barbershop next to Baker's store. She'd clung to the arms of the tall swivel chair, tears streaming down her face, and ordered Chang to cut off her waist-length hair.

"It won't bring her back, missy," he'd said.

"Cut it, I tell you! All of it!"

The barber had begun to hum to calm her down. "Okay, missy. Whatever you say." His voice had cracked as the fine hair fell away in his hand.

That night, after the funeral, she had lain awake listening to the rain on the roof. When everyone else had gathered in the parlor downstairs, she had dragged herself out of bed and crept down the hall to her mother's room.

She found her jewelry box on the dresser. Sally gathered up all her mother's things, her hatpins, the tortoiseshell hairpins, rings, brooches, everything, and shut them into a velvet-lined box she kept locked in the bottom drawer of her chiffonier. Months later, when her hair had grown out, she dug out the hairpins and used them to pin up her thick tresses. Her own hair was the exact shade of her mother's.

Now tears trembled at the edge of her lashes as she faced Jake, tilting her face up to his, her eyes shut tight.

"Sally, listen to me. I know you're scared, that you don't want to be hurt again. And you can try to protect yourself from life. But you know what? If you're careful enough, maybe nothing bad *will* happen to you all the rest of your life. But nothing good will, either. We all die sometime, Sally. It's what goes on between getting born and getting buried that matters."

He was right, of course. Bone deep she knew it. She took a step forward and walked into his arms, turning her face into his chest.

Jake held her carefully, smelling the lilac scent of her hair, afraid to acknowledge to himself how desperate he felt. It wasn't Tom's land he wanted—it was her. *Sally, Sally! What do I do now? You're just like that damn gelding. If I try to put a halter on you, you'll bolt like a green pony.* He rocked her slowly from side to side and cleared his throat. "Sally, I need to say something to you."

She lifted her head and looked up into his eyes.

"I told you once you needed to grow up some." He worked to keep his tone light. "Well, Miss Salty, that's still true. You need that birthday I was talking about. When that day comes, if it ever does, there's something I'll want to give you."

"Another lesson, Jake?" Her voice was muffled against his buckskin jacket.

His smile was lopsided. "No man could live long enough to give you all the lessons you need," he said softly.

"Jake, I'm trying, really I am. But I feel all tangled up inside."

"Maybe that's because your spurs are too big for your boots, honey."

"Well, tell me, then," she said in a very small voice, "how does a person get bigger boots?"

He laughed. "Marry me, Miss Salty." He tightened his arms around her. "Marry me!"

He waited, half holding his breath, but she didn't answer. "But if you won't—can't—marry me, then for God's sake, Sally, don't let me get too close to you. Because to tell you the truth, after that night with you, I don't think I can stand not having it all."

He held her for a long time, his eyes closed. Then he turned away and moved quickly to the gelding. Without looking at her, he pulled his lean body up into the saddle and walked the horse out of the yard.

By March, yellow crocuses poked up through the snow-encrusted yard, and the frozen streams in the lower pasture gushed and bubbled into the duck pond. The spring thaw had begun. Sally thought she would go mad with nothing but Louisa's trousseau and Jake to occupy her mind before school started.

As soon as the road was passable, she rode out to the schoolhouse, swept it from top to bottom and then scrubbed off her desk. She could hardly wait for school to open again. She'd sent away to Chicago for more books, planned lessons and made endless revisions and refinements in her teaching methods. Her students—most of whom had never had any formal schooling—had been making commendable progress before winter set in. Her heart swelled with a deep sense of satisfaction and pride. Secondhand life, indeed! Jake just didn't understand.

By May, when Sally's primers arrived, the air had softened into a soft, promising spring. Apples and wild cherry trees bloomed throughout the valley, and when the breeze came up in the late afternoon, the road over which she rode to and from school each day was dusted with tiny pink and white blossoms. There was no need for the fire in the potbellied stove. Each morning Sally smiled when Rob and Richie Blane forgot about filling the wood box and concentrated instead on kites and games of marbles or mumblety-peg in the school yard.

And then one hot, still afternoon Jake rode up to the schoolhouse. He dismounted and lounged against the doorframe for a few moments, then motioned Sally outside. "There's a box social at the river next Sunday."

Sally looked into eyes so dark they looked like pools of blue-black oil and shook her head.

"You have to come," he pressed. "The money raised from auctioning off the ladies' lunches will pay for those new desks you need. And besides—" he grinned at her "—as the schoolmistress, you're the guest of honor."

Sally accepted this information with a short nod. She'd do almost anything to get those desks. Already Billy Peterman had to fold his lengthening legs under the low wooden bench. She might even make up a picnic lunch to auction off. But she wouldn't eat it with Jake. Being near him unnerved her, made her say and do things that brought a sweet, jittery feeling to the pit of her stomach. And that frightened her. If you cared about something and lost it . . .

She could not complete the thought.

Jake waited a moment, then touched his Stetson and moved away toward his horse. Sally watched him mount, a queer ache in her chest. *If you don't want it all,* he had cautioned, *don't let me get too close.*

It hadn't been too difficult. Weeks went by when she didn't lay eyes on him except for a fleeting glance of his rangy form disappearing into the barn to talk to her father about some horse or other. On the rare occasions when she heard Jake's deep voice in the parlor, she went upstairs to read or plan geometry exercises for the advanced students.

She *didn't* want it all, she acknowledged. But in the still hours of the night when she lay sleepless under the blue quilt on her narrow bed, she admitted to herself that she did want *him.* Her longing to have Jake touch her, hold her, flowed in her body like an underground spring. It was always there, just at the edge of her consciousness. Always.

The morning of the box social, Shorty killed and cleaned two fat hens. Louisa dredged the pieces in flour and handed them to Sally, who stood with one arm poised over a deep skillet of hot bacon fat. She plopped each piece in the sizzling oil and forked it over and over, frying it to a crisp golden color. Louisa packed up identical lunch boxes with containers of potato salad and generous slabs of Martha's cherry pie, then tied a yellow ribbon around her box, a blue ribbon around Sally's. They stood together at the sink washing up the dishes.

Sally drew in a deep breath of the fresh, fragrant air wafting in the window over the sink, which they'd left open for the heat to escape. The air smelled of green grass and honeysuckle, the scent so evocative Sally found herself unable to concentrate on the plate she was rinsing. Her hands stilled in the dishwater.

For the past few days she had been feeling odd, as if something inside her was stretching, swelling into a vague yearning ache, a restlessness that never quite went away. It was a strange combination of joy and sadness mixed up together. When she didn't feel like crying, she felt like hitting something—the carpets Martha had hung out on the old clothesline were perfect. The old red rooster who lorded it over the hens pecking in the chicken yard steered clear of her at feeding time because she threw the grain with such a vengeance. Lately she'd even volunteered to split the kindling for Martha just to ease her tension.

Suddenly Louisa let a plate slip out of her dish towel. It shattered on the floor, and she swore under her breath.

"Louisa!" Sally stared at her sister. In all her life, she could never remember Lou ever uttering such a word. Why, Louisa rarely even raised her voice!

Louisa picked up another blue china plate and looked back at Sally in silence, her blue eyes distant. "You know, Sally," she said softly, her normally controlled voice vague and a bit dreamy. "All of a sudden I feel like . . . like tossing this plate right out the window!"

"Lou! What's come over you?" And then Sally understood. Her sister, too, needed something to break the tension. Lou was waiting for Will to propose. Now that her father had given his permission, Louisa was itching to fry chicken and wash dishes in her own kitchen!

Well, why not? Sally thought. She snatched up a soapy plate and heaved it through the window. It clunked satisfyingly in the thick grass and rolled to a stop under the apple tree.

Louisa gaped at her for a split second, then impulsively tossed her own plate after it. A look of complete, unspoken understanding passed between the two sisters.

Sally sailed a bowl out, then two more plates and some cups in rapid succession. Suddenly the air was full of flying china and peals of laughter.

"Oh, that feels so good!" Sally cried. She heaved the last of the cups through the open window onto the grass outside. The two girls flung their arms around each other, screaming with laughter. Not even their father's gruff "What the hell's goin' on in there?" quelled their paroxysms.

"N-nothing, Pa," Sally gasped. "It's just—"

Louisa picked up the last plate with a questioning gesture, and Sally dissolved into giggles again. "Come on, Lou," she choked at last. "Let's get dressed for the social. I feel like wearing something frivolous, something with lots of ruffles and lace!"

Still laughing, they disappeared up the hall stairs. Sally felt better than she had in days.

In the late spring the river flowed lazily, no longer swollen by snow melt from the mountains or engorged by spring rains. Now it formed a smooth, broad ribbon of blue-green water. The grassy banks sloped gently down to meet the water, and at the river's edge small wavelets lapped on a narrow strip of sandy beach. Vine maples and alders shaded the area from the sun, and the balmy, green-smelling air made Sally think of springs in years past.

Her father had taught her to swim in the shallow area of the river, near the bank. Farther out, the deeper water was a rich dark green, broken by a small sand bar. Even before she could ride, Sally had learned to swim. Her goal had been to make it to the sand bar and back. After her mother's death, she had spent hours under the spreading willow at the bank's edge, staring across the dark water.

The green meadow bordering the river was the perfect setting for the picnic social, and as they drove up in their father's wagon, it seemed to Sally that everyone in the valley had turned out. Ranch owners Tom Pearson and boisterous, outspoken George Peterman stood at the crude pine platform that would serve as the auctioneer's podium, arguing about a horse. Billy Peterman squatted near his father. At the sight of Sally, the boy bolted up and blushed to the roots of his red-orange hair.

Slim, handsome Ned Barker and most of the hands from Peterman's Lazy J ranch spread blankets out on the grass and rolled cigarettes while they swapped stories. Occasional bursts of laughter emanated from the knots of cowhands as one or another got in a good punch line.

Townspeople drove out in buggies and wagons. Mr. Baker and his willowy wife, Nora, and tiny, blond Elsa, with one of Sally's reading primers clutched under one arm, staked out a spot near the beach so Elsa could wade in the river.

Hank and Shorty dutifully carried the ladies' decorated lunch boxes to the auction block, then joined the Bar Y hands who had settled within heckling distance of Ned Barker's boys. Cole stretched out his long legs on the grass and shared his cigarette papers with Nebraska. Both men traded friendly gibes with Ned while Dutch Hendricks made sure Olla's lunch basket was plainly marked before he added it to the pile. Olla's cooking was famous throughout the valley. Bidding for her basket always ran high, and some years Dutch had a hard time coming up with enough cash to share his own wife's lunch.

Louisa disappeared with Will, her pale yellow dimity visible briefly between clumps of trees as they moved off together. Sally watched her father spread blankets on the grass, making sure there would be room enough when Hank and Martha and the twins joined them later.

Surreptitiously, Sally searched for Jake. After a few moments she spied him lounging against a thick cedar tree, deep in conversation with Judge Randall. Jake's gray Stetson angled back from his face, and he had thrust both hands casually into his jean pockets. He glanced once in Sally's direction but gave no sign he noticed her.

Paula Randall sat at her father's feet, twirling a frilly pink-and-white-striped parasol that matched her ruffled, elegantly cut dress. Her long, dark hair, curled in tight ringlets, hung down her back. She looked smooth and self-possessed, and she smiled up at Jake with a confidence Sally found annoying.

Why was it she felt as if she had two left feet when Paula was around? Sally knew she could outride Paula, could outswim her and outthink her. She could probably even cook better than Paula, too. She averted her gaze and settled herself beside her father, adjusting the shawl around her soft white Valenciennes lace blouse and arranging the folds of her gored navy blue skirt about her knees.

To distract herself, she looked around at the assembled picnickers. The two older Eckloff boys wrestled a bark canoe into the river, then argued over who was going to get to paddle first. Billy Peterman edged his skinny body closer, obviously hoping for a turn. Miranda and Tommy Pearson and their new baby girl sat with wrinkled, gray-headed Doc Varner and his stick-thin maiden sister, Nellie, who smiled and cooed at the bundle in Miranda's arms. Children raced through the scattered groups of picnickers in wild games of red rover, their shouts all but drowning out the booming voice of George Peterman, self-appointed auctioneer for the social.

"Bidding will start in one minute, gents. No loans, and no credit. Get your silver out and whet your appetites."

A flurry of activity followed, and then silence dropped over the crowd as George stepped up to the block and raised Miranda Pearson's gaily wrapped box over his head. Her slightly potbellied husband promptly garnered it with an unchallenged bid of four dollars, and a ripple of applause followed. Someone from the crowd called out to Tommy. "Think there's enough in there for the three of you, Tom? Or is it goin' on four now?"

Tommy blushed and honked into his bandanna.

"You gotta get that nose of yours repaired, Tom," someone joked. "One of these days that blast'll stampede my herd!" Tommy waved to more laughter.

Dutch Hendricks struggled to outbid four other parties for Olla's redolent straw basket. "Chock-full of her special pickles," the auctioneer shouted, shaking the contents. "I can hear 'em slosh." The purchase cost Dutch six dollars, and he won it only because the other four bidders ran out of money. Everyone was feeling flush and in high spirits now that summer was coming.

Sally found herself wondering which lunch Paula Randall had brought. She scanned the pile of decorated baskets and boxes for one that looked especially stylish; maybe that square wicker basket done up with an elaborate pink bow on top? She wondered whether Jake would bid for it.

George held up Louisa's yellow-ribboned box next and pretended to sniff the contents. "Ah, Miss Louisa's fried chicken. Come and get it, boys!" He rolled his eyes.

An expectant hush descended.

"Four dollars," a man's voice called.

Cole Sieversen unkinked his legs and sat up abruptly. "I'd bid five, but Will'd probably dock my pay," he yelled.

"Dock you!" Ned Barker shouted. "Hell, he'd probably fire you! But he can't fire *me,* so I bid six dollars!"

Louisa joined Sally on the grass and looked on, unperturbed, as Will's quiet voice cut through the guffaws. "Seven dollars."

Silence. Then, "Hell, she ain't married to him yet," a deep voice shouted. "Seven and a half."

"Who's gonna pay Doc Varner's bill for your broken bones if you outbid Will?" another voice yelled.

"Eight dollars," Ned Barker shouted.

"Ten dollars," Will's calm voice countered.

A voice floated from the gathering of Lazy J hands. "Sure you can afford that?"

"No." Will laughed. "Might have to ask Jake for a raise."

Ned opened his mouth, but before he could utter a word, the auctioneer cut him off. "Sold for ten dollars to the lucky foreman of the Bar Y."

Applause and a few whistles accompanied Will as he claimed the lunch, pulled Louisa to her feet and headed for the meadow at the bend of the river, away from the crowd. Deep in thought, Sally watched them go until she noticed George reaching for her own box lunch.

"And here's the succulent offering of Miss Sally Maguire," George boomed. "Same chicken, folks. Different gal."

"Can a fellow just eat it, or is she gonna talk, too?" a voice shouted.

Sally felt her face flame, and she clenched her hands tight in her lap.

"Okay, gents, what am I bid for the privilege of picnicking with Miss Sally?"

A long, embarrassing silence descended. Near the riverbank Billy Peterman turned his pockets inside out, scooped out the assorted coins from the other debris and counted it hurriedly. "One dollar," he piped. "And a half."

"Oooh," the crowd sang. "Billy's sweet on Miss Maguire," the Eckloff brothers chanted. Billy turned scarlet.

George's voice rose above the noise. "Come on, gents. She's just as good in the kitchen as Miss Louisa, and you've got to admit, she's mighty pretty!"

"She's good-looking as hell, George," someone called, "but oh, Miz Perkins's prayers, when she opens her mouth, it don't matter."

Sally was glad she could not identify the voice.

"Four silver dollars," Tom Maguire finally sang out. "She knows her way around a frying pan. Sure, and I taught her myself!"

Laughter, then another long silence. Tears pricked at the edge of Sally's lids. She pressed her lips together to keep them from trembling and gazed out across the river where the Eckloff boys were paddling the canoe.

Jake watched Sally from across the park. Her face was flushed, her eyes distant. His heart turned over, and a dull ache spread into his chest. He'd purposely not bid on her basket. Today she looked soft and fragile, somehow. The white lace ruffles at her throat made her look pristine and proper, but Jake knew that underneath the prim-looking blouse her skin was warm and sweet smelling, her breasts sensitive. Responsive.

His groin began to ache. Now that the drought was over—at least for this season—he wasn't desperate for that land of Tom's. But he *was* desperate for Sally. He knew he should stay away from her, but, damnation, he could not stand to see her suffer.

Before he was fully conscious of what he was doing, he had straightened his Stetson and was striding across the grass toward the auctioneer. "Twenty-five dollars," he called to George, his voice like ringing steel. "And I'll shoot the first man who says twenty-six!"

"Sold!" George shouted into the sudden quiet. "Sold to Jackson Bannister, owner of the Bar Y Ranch."

Amid cheers and clapping, Jake advanced to the stand and lifted Sally's blue-ribboned box out of George's hands.

A buzz of voices arose among the Bar Y hands. "Fi' dollar on Mr. Jake," Dutch Hendricks said to no one in particular.

Tom made a little sign in the air with his forefinger.

"Make it six dollars," sang a voice from Ned Barker's crew.

Sally sat transfixed as Jake made his way toward her. She closed her ears to the buzz of voices. She didn't need his pity. No force on earth would make her share that lunch with him. She wasn't *that* desperate!

"Come on, Miss Sally," Jake said when he was within speaking distance. "I've had two of your meals, and I'm not dead yet. I'm sort of curious about this one...."

"I'm not hungry, thank you."

"Seven big silver ones on Miss Sally," someone called to Tom.

Jake waited. "Oh, I think you are, Miss Sally."

"I'm not about to accept your charity, or anybody else's," Sally hissed at him.

"Really?" In one clean motion Jake reached out his hand and closed it around her wrist. He yanked her upright, caught her around the waist and propelled her along beside him. "Excuse us, won't you, Tom?"

"Seven on Jake," Cole Sieversen shouted. "He don't break mustangs for nuthin'!"

The laughter faded behind them as Jake pulled Sally away from the crowd, crossed the shaded meadow where Will sat with Louisa and headed for a sun-dappled patch of grass at the top of a small rise. He dropped to the ground, his back to the river, and stretched out his long legs.

Stony faced, Sally stared over his head at the river beyond. What right did he have to come barging back into her life? Just when she thought she'd gotten him out of her system and could once again give her whole attention to her classroom activities. "I don't need your charity," Sally blurted. "And I don't need your company, either!"

Jake laughed, the tanned skin around the gentian blue eyes crinkling into fine lines. "Well, suit yourself. But I'm damned hungry, and I paid for your lunch. Besides, the charity isn't for you—it's for the school-house. Your students need those desks."

"I'm not hungry."

Unperturbed, Jake looked up at her. "Sit down, Sally," he said evenly, "and shut up. You don't have to eat with me if you don't want to. But I'm not going to waste a good meal with a lot of jawing. What have you got in here, anyway—any hot chile peppers?"

In spite of herself, Sally laughed. Jake was right. He had done her a kindness. Slowly she lowered herself to the grass and drew her knees up, tucking the navy poplin skirt in behind her calves.

"That's better." Jake untied the blue ribbon on top of her picnic box. "Now, look. As long as we're stuck here together, we might as well make the best of it. *Faire beau,* as they say." He lifted the box lid. "You know, I don't know whether you can really cook anything. Besides flapjacks, that is."

"I can cook," she said slowly. "I can cook better than—"

Oh-ho, Jake thought. Blazes, she was delicious when she got mad. He watched the rapid rise and fall of her breasts under the white lace. "Better than who?" he prompted. He handed her a drumstick.

"Oh, Jake, for heaven's sake. Better than Paula, who do you think? She's always looking at you like . . . well, you know. Like she's spinning a web, hoping you'll fall into it."

He shot her an incredulous look. "Son of a . . . Sally, you're so honest you're dangerous."

"Why shouldn't I be? Anyway, you're smart enough to see what's going on, aren't you?"

Oh, I see what's going on, all right, Jake thought warily. *It's you who fails to see things, Sally. You just feel something and you open your mouth and out it comes. Lord, what a menace.* "So you think I'm smart, do you?" He opened the container of potato salad. "Got a fork for this?"

"Oh, you know you're smart, Jake. You're the only rancher I've ever known who's been to Harvard."

"Princeton," he corrected.

"Whatever. There's a fork under the napkins. Honestly, Jake, I don't know what riles me up so much about her."

"About who?" His voice was innocent.

She threw the fork at him. He caught it adroitly before it stabbed him, and shot her a quick glance. "You trying to kill me again?"

"Oh, heavens, I don't know!" She sighed in exasperation at herself. "Jake, why do we fight all the time?"

Jake took a big bite of salad. "We fight because we're alike." He chewed a moment, swallowed and looked up at her. "We fight because I want you," he said quietly. "And you want me. And we haven't figured out what to do about it yet."

Sally lowered her drumstick to the napkin spread in her lap and looked at him in amazement. Unable to meet his eyes, she let her gaze drift over his head to the river, where Elsa Baker and red-haired Billy Peterman paddled the canoe in a ragged zigzag pattern toward the sand bar. Was that true? she wondered. Jake wanted her, and she... Heat flowed through her body.

Jake stopped chewing and stared at the color rising on Sally's smooth skin. *Careful, old son,* he cautioned himself. *Breathe in. Breathe out. Change the subject. But don't reach for her. And don't look at her mouth.*

"Will's been building a house on some land I sold him a while back," he remarked, his voice careful.

"A house? What for?"

"For Louisa."

"Louisa! But he hasn't even asked her yet!"

Jake bit into his chicken. "Well, then, he better hurry up. He's sent away for a brand-new Beckwith piano for a wedding present. It's coming all the way from Chicago next month."

"A piano! Oh, how lovely." Sally's eyes softened. "Louisa will die of happiness having her own piano."

Absently she watched Jake's lips move as he gnawed on another drumstick. "Jake, do we really fight because we... Don't you think it might be because underneath we *don't* like each other?"

Jake groaned. What kind of game was she playing? It must be perfectly obvious to her how he felt about her. The woman was impossible. Not having her was hell. But living with her would be hell, too. And, he acknowledged, no sane man would trade one hell for another.

Jake took a long, slow breath. "You know something, Miss Salty?" He looked directly into her eyes. "You are the most beautiful, and the most undisciplined, spoiled, unnerving woman I've ever known."

Sally jerked as a twinge of guilt jabbed her. She had hurt him. Part of her wanted to twist the knife; another part of her wanted to unbutton her blouse and watch his eyes. She wrenched her gaze from his hands and looked out across the river.

Jake watched her a full minute, then drew her attention back with a question. "Did I ever tell you about the fancy dinner we had up in Montana last fall?" He kept his voice casual.

Sally pulled her gaze from the river and looked at him. "Is this one of your 'neutral' conversations, Jake?"

He gave a low, rumbly chuckle. "It is. Want me to go on, or want me to stop talking? Or—"

"Go on," she said quickly.

He reached for another drumstick. "Well, Granville Stuart—I told you about him, remember? He's the biggest rancher in Montana Territory. He invited us all to the Macqueen Hotel in Miles City for dinner. Will and I sat next to some ranchers from Texas, and when dinner came, it turned out to be steaks—steaks so big they covered the plate. Well, this one old Texan poked at his meat with his fork, and when the red juices ran out, he grabbed the waiter by his lapel and yelled, 'Hell, where I come from I've seen cows hurt worse than that get well!' "

Sally giggled. "You like going to the stock growers' meeting, don't you, Jake?"

He nodded, watching her face. "I like going. And I like coming back."

She looked up. "Jake, I—"

Jake saw her expression alter suddenly, heard the sharp intake of her breath. She stared at something over his head.

"Sally, what's the—"

She half rose, her face white, her hand arrested on its way to her mouth. "Elsa's fallen out of the canoe, in the river. Oh, my God, Jake! She can't swim!"

Sally was halfway to the river, running, when she heard the scream. Billy Peterman clung to the overturned canoe, his mouth open in helpless terror. Elsa's blond head disappeared beneath the surface, reappeared, then sank out of sight.

At the riverbank Sally hesitated for a split second, then with shaking hands she unbuttoned her skirt, untied her petticoat and stepped out of them. Dimly she heard a woman cry out. She tore off her shoes, stripped her stockings down and plunged into the river, stroking cleanly toward the overturned canoe.

Jake headed for the black gelding and a rope.

Chapter Eleven

Just as Sally reached Elsa, the girl's thrashing ceased, and the tiny form sank slowly beneath the surface. Sally dived into the cold green water, searching for her.

The water was icy. Her legs and arms numbing, she began to pray. *Dear God, let me find her. Please, God. Please.*

She bobbed to the surface empty-handed.

Desperation drove her, and she plunged down again. This time, as she groped near the river bottom, she felt something feathery brush her hand. Her fingers closed over something soft. She jerked on it. Clothing of some sort, with a weight attached. Her lungs aching, Sally pulled upward with all her strength.

After a moment she felt the weight begin to rise. She sculled frantically toward the light above her, pulling the frail body along with her to the surface.

Only when she broke into the sunlight and gulped air into her bursting lungs did she become aware of sounds other than the pounding of her heart—Billy, clinging to the canoe and screaming, someone to her left shouting, splashing toward the terror-stricken boy. It was Ned Barker.

Elsa's mouth gaped open, and her closed eyelids were a purplish blue against her pale skin. Sally grabbed her around the waist and lifted the child's head above the water, paddling one-handed toward the bank. Oh, God, she was cold, so cold.

At the riverbank Jake stepped the black gelding carefully into the shallow water, calculated the distance and swung his lariat once around his head. "Catch the rope, Sally," he yelled. "Pull it under your arms."

The rope sailed out in a smooth arc and dropped around Sally's shoulders. She shrugged it into place, dog-paddling desperately to keep Elsa's head above water. With shaking fingers she pulled the hemp line taut around the girl's limp form.

Jake looped the rope around his saddle horn and backed his horse out of the river, step by slow step.

A hush fell over the crowd gathered at the river's edge. In the silence Sally could hear a woman wailing. The other swimmer, Ned, splashed rhythmically past her toward Billy.

The rope tugged under her arms. She clasped Elsa close to her body and felt herself move forward.

Jake's voice rang out. "Keep the line tight, Sally! Don't let it go slack."

She tried to focus on his words. Water gushed into her mouth and nose, and she coughed. Blindly she held on to the rope.

"Just relax, Sally. Don't swim. I'll tow you in."

Elsa lay unmoving in the crook of Sally's arm. The girl's sodden weight pulled Sally down, and she gulped another mouthful of water. Her arm began to cramp. She concentrated on keeping the rope taut, on Jake's calm voice somewhere ahead of her. *Keep talking to me, Jake. Please, please, keep talking.*

"Just a little farther, Sally. You're doing fine. You're almost there."

Sally turned her face toward the sound and prayed.

When she was a few yards from the bank, Jake secured the rope to his saddle horn and dismounted. Wading into the water, he reached for Sally as she struggled to gain a foothold on the uneven river bottom. He stretched one arm around the still form in Sally's arms and propelled them both to shore.

Sally's legs trembled uncontrollably, and her breath wheezed in and out in jerky gasps. She couldn't talk, couldn't seem to get enough air. Her hair had come unpinned, and sopping strands straggled about her shoulders. The white lace blouse and her underdrawers clung to her slim frame. Her entire body shook with exhaustion.

"Somebody get a blanket," Jake ordered.

Sally felt hands lift Elsa away, out of her arms. The girl was dead, she knew it. Over her own labored breathing, she could hear Mrs. Baker's high keening.

Sally doubled over at the waist, her arms folded over her belly, and rocked back and forth in anguish. "She's dead," she sobbed. "Oh, my God, my God, she's dead!"

Jake wrapped a blanket around her and turned her into his arms. She struck out at him wildly, her arms flailing. "She's dead...dead!" Her voice rose to a scream.

Jake pinioned her arms and pulled her roughly into his chest. "She's not dead, Sally," he shouted in her ear. "She's all right." He grasped her shoulders and shook her, hard. "Sally, listen to me, listen! Elsa's all right! She's crying. Can you hear her? She's okay."

Sally clung to him. At her side she heard Ned and Billy splash to shore, heard a woman's broken weeping and her own voice choking in hoarse, wrenching sobs that she could not stop.

Jake rocked her back and forth in his arms. "Will." He spoke over her head. "Get my horse." He tightened his arms around her. "It's all right, Sally," he said into her ear. "It's all over now. Elsa's fine, just scared. She's all right." He pulled her more tightly against him. "But you're not, that's for sure. You're chilled through!"

Will walked the black gelding to the river's edge, and Jake lifted Sally into his foreman's arms, then mounted and reached down for her. He lifted her into the saddle in front of him. Someone laid her skirt and petticoat across her lap, and Jake turned the horse away from the river.

"I'm taking her to the Bar Y, Tom," he said as he passed the older man. "She's cold and exhausted, and my place is the closest."

Tom nodded agreement. "Here's her shoes, Jake. Couldn't find her stockings."

Sally opened her eyes long enough to see Louisa comforting Mrs. Baker, then she let her head sink against Jake's hard chest. Her father spoke as they passed, but she couldn't understand his words. A sleepy numbness overtook her as Jake wheeled the gelding and walked it carefully through the quiet crowd.

Tom watched them pass, choked with pride for the bravery of his older daughter. His gaze followed the gelding's progress across the grass and into the stand of pine trees at the edge of the meadow.

"Ten dollars, hell," he muttered to himself. "I'd stake my life on old Jake!" He nodded his head and smiled, his eyes bright with unshed tears.

Jake chunked three pieces of firewood into the wood stove in the Bar Y kitchen and bent to blow gently on the embers remaining after Olla had cooked breakfast that morning.

"I-I'm g-getting your floor all w-wet," Sally stammered. Her tongue wouldn't work right and her teeth chattered uncontrollably. Embarrassed, she clamped her jaw shut.

Jake didn't answer. He dipped water into the enamel coffeepot, threw in a handful of ground coffee and set the pot on the stove.

"J-Jake, your f-floor," Sally moaned.

"Forget it. Olla mops every morning." He moved behind her and rubbed the blanket briskly up and down on her bare arms and back. "You've got to get out of those wet clothes, Sally."

She nodded, shivering. The blanket was wet, too. It hung around her shoulders like a damp shroud.

Abruptly Jake stopped rubbing. "I'll look in Olla's wardrobe and see if I can find you a dressing gown or something. Take off your things and wrap up good in the blanket. The fire'll be hot in a minute. The coffee, too," he added.

He turned to go, then hesitated. "And Sally..."

She looked up at him, shaking with cold.

He gave her a long look, a smile shadowing his mouth. "Do me a favor. Don't take anything off until I get out of the kitchen."

He swung out of the room, and she unbuttoned her sodden blouse, then untied and peeled off her underdrawers. When Jake returned, she was standing wrapped in the blanket, her back to the stove.

He held out a coarse wool robe. "This was all I could find," he apologized. "I think it's Dutch's, but at least it's warm."

Sally extended one hand from the protective folds of blanket and drew the robe toward her. "I can't put it on unless you turn around, Jake."

He gave her an unfathomable look and bent to scoop up her dripping garments from the floor. He moved to the sink and twisted the fine cambric underdrawers and the lacy blouse in his hands, wringing the water out. Then he shook the garments out and spread them flat on the warm stovetop. "Should be dry in an hour or so," he remarked, keeping his voice matter-of-fact.

"An hour! What am I supposed to do for an hour?"

Jake chuckled. "Ah, a sign of life! You must be getting warm." He moved to the stove and touched the coffeepot gingerly with one finger. "Never mind what *you're* going to do for this hour. What am *I* going to do with you here in my kitchen without a stitch on underneath that blanket, and no one in the house but us?"

Uneasy, he cocked his ear for the sound of boiling coffee.

Silence.

"Sally, you'd better put that robe on."

"I will when you turn your back."

Jake pivoted away from her and resolutely stared at the wall. He heard the blanket drop softly to the floor, and he knew Sally stood naked not three feet from him. Desperately, he studied the dingy spot over the pantry doorway.

"It's all right now, Jake. I'm dressed. Or as dressed as I can get at the moment."

He turned around. Dutch's blue woolen robe hung loosely on her slim figure, the belt wrapped twice around her waist, the sleeves drooping far below her fingertips. He wanted to slip his hands inside the rough wool and touch her skin.

She began to roll up the sleeves. "Where are the rest of my clothes?"

"On my saddle."

"I'll need them," she said. "But what I need most right now is a comb to untangle my hair. Would Olla—"

"I'll look," he said hurriedly. He returned in a few moments with a boar-bristle brush and a comb. He held them out to her, then turned away and busied himself with the coffee.

Sally pulled the remaining hairpins from her hair and let it tumble down past her shoulders in a thick, wavy mass.

Jake tried not to watch what she was doing. For the first time he could ever recall, he wished she would pin her hair up on top of her head in her usual spinsterish style. He found it disturbingly arousing when she let it hang loose like that.

"Black?" He indicated the cup in his hand.

Sally tugged the comb through her wet hair.

"Cream, please."

He went to the pantry for the cream jug, watching how his hand shook when he skimmed off a thick spoonful for her coffee. "You know," he said, keeping his back to her, his voice careful, "if you'd let it dry first, it'd comb through easier."

The remark nettled her. "And how would you know that?" The sudden image of Paula Randall's dark ringlets flashed into her mind. She took a sip of the coffee and studied Jake over the rim of her cup. After a long moment, she set the brew down on the kitchen table and bent her body over until her head hung almost upside down near the hot stove. With her fingers she fluffed the long mop of auburn hair.

The gesture stopped Jake's heart. He took a gulp of the scalding coffee, felt it burn his tongue and his throat.

Sally drew her fingers through the wavy tangle again. "Jake," she said after a moment. Her voice sounded odd from her reversed position. "Why did you bid twenty-five dollars for my box lunch? Because you felt sorry for me?"

The question caught him unaware. "Because I wanted to," he said simply.

"But why? Paula was right there, waiting for you." She shot him a quick look through the veil of hair. "With her web all woven."

Jake laughed. "Yeah, well, a smart fly avoids the webs if he can see them coming." But a man, he acknowledged silently, is sometimes not as smart as a fly. He watched as Sally picked up the hairbrush and pulled it lazily through the thick russet waves. She remained bent over, brushing from the exposed nape of her neck out to the ends in slow, graceful strokes.

Jake felt his muscles tense, his groin begin to ache. *Don't watch,* he cautioned himself.

But he did. He couldn't help himself. When he could stand it no longer, he took another gulp of the hot coffee and strode to her side. He caught her hand just as she was starting another stroke, and without a word he lifted the brush out of her fingers.

Sally straightened and tossed her hair back, her eyes questioning. Her hair tumbled forward in an unruly mass of curls. For a moment he was unable to breathe.

"I can't watch you do that and not want you," he said.

A tiny light flickered in her dark pupils.

Jake laid the brush carefully beside his coffee cup and moved to within a few inches of her. She didn't move, just stared at him with that odd light in her eyes.

"Sally," he breathed. *Don't touch her, old son. Just...don't.*

But in spite of himself, he reached out and laced his fingers through her damp, silky hair. When he felt its warmth spill across his knuckles, he knew he was lost. His hands closed against the back of her neck, and he pulled her head toward him, tipping her mouth up to his.

She made a little sound in her throat, then reached both her arms up around his neck and closed her eyes.

His heart hammered. The soft wool robe tickled the skin of his forearms. Suddenly he wanted to untie the belt, unwind it slowly from around her waist and spread the material open. He wanted to look at her.

Shaking, he stepped away. "Sally, we can't do this." In the silence he could hear her soft, unsteady breathing.

"Speak for yourself, Jake."

"Sally—" His voice was low, insistent. "We can't, Sally. Not after...and not here."

"Jake. Please, Jake. I need to be close to you."

"No."

"But why?"

Jake drew a long breath before he answered. "Because you don't know what you're doing, really. At least, you don't know what you're doing to me. For you, this is some kind of a chess game. It doesn't mean the same thing to you as it does to me."

He thought about confessing his land deal with Tom. But ever since that night at the schoolhouse he had known he wanted Sally not because of Tom's land, but because of Sally herself. He was courting her for all he was worth because he had to have her. It was Sally he wanted with all his heart; to hell with Tom's hundred acres.

"I'm not going to play games with your life," he said at last. "Or with mine, either. I—"

"But I *do* know what I want," she insisted.

"No," he said, his voice steady, "you don't."

Puzzled, Sally searched his face. He wanted her. And she wanted him. Just this afternoon at the picnic he'd said as much. Now, here she was, alone with him in his kitchen, needing him, and he didn't want her. Why?

"It's because I'm a nice girl, and the schoolteacher, is that it?"

Her eyes looked into his with a candor that made his knees weak. "You're a nice girl and the schoolteacher, Sally. But that's not it."

"What, then? I was a nice girl and the schoolteacher before, the night of the blizzard, when we... And it didn't matter then."

"It did matter, Sally, but—" Oh, the hell with it.

He bent his head and kissed her slowly, savoring her scent, her sweetness, hunger for her pushing him toward the edge.

Sally felt Jake's mouth open into velvet against her tongue, his lips warm and inviting. It was a long, long kiss, and a throbbing began deep inside her. Her knees trembled. At last he lifted his head.

"But?" she breathed against his mouth. "But?"

"Oh, dammit, Sally..." His voice shook. *Yes, I want you,* he wanted to shout. *Oh how, I want you. And I've got just so much willpower. My whole body is burning to be with you. I ache to be inside you.* "Just wait a little while, Sally. Wait."

She moved closer to him and stood on tiptoe. "Wait for what? Kiss me again, Jake," she murmured. "Please."

He raised his chin away from her face and closed his eyes. She had absolutely no idea what she did to him. One thing for certain, she certainly had an unorthodox approach to life. And love. She would fit in perfectly in the art colonies on the Left Bank in Paris. The problem was they weren't in Paris. They were here, alone together in his ranch house, in Klamath County, Oregon.

"We can't, Sally."

"But I want—"

Jake put his finger over her mouth to stop the words. "Shh. I know. I want you, too."

"Well, then?"

Jake shook his head in frustration. "Seems I'm having a hard time explaining this."

"I do understand, Jake. I really do." She hesitated a fraction of a second. "At least, I think I do. I'm all grown up now, and I... want you. And now you don't know what to do about it."

Jake sighed. "No, Sally. You don't understand. I want more than this, more than a night stolen in your schoolhouse or an afternoon in my..." He drew in a long breath and let it out as slowly as he could manage. "You're right, I want you. But not the way you think. I want you in my bed, in my house. In my life."

Sally stiffened as understanding glimmered. "Jake, are you asking me to marry you?"

He was quiet a long time. "No," he said finally. "I'm not. I love you, but I want a commitment. For life. You can't give that. I'd be ten ways a fool if I married you now. You'd kick the hell out of me."

He watched her face blanch, and his belly twisted. "Sally, listen. This is a hardscrabble way to put it, but you don't love me. Half the time you don't even like me. And I want all of you," he said, his voice unsteady. "Heart and soul and body. And not for just an hour, for a lifetime. Are you able to give me that?"

She was silent, staring into his face, her eyes wide, frightened.

"My life's on the line here, Sally. I won't die if I can't have you, but I can be hurt pretty bad if I tie myself up to you and you throw me away."

Her head came up sharply.

"Hell, Sally." He plunged on. "You don't know the first thing about love."

Her eyes shone like polished jade. "I know enough. I know that I want you to . . . to . . ."

"And afterward you think you can just pull on your petticoat and go home? Well, it doesn't work like that, honey. Not with me, anyway."

He was angry now. And good and hungry for her. He wanted her, wanted her more than anything he'd ever wanted in his entire life. Damnation, he'd never met a woman like her—all fire one minute and all business the next. To tell the truth, he was afraid of her, afraid of what she could do to him.

He knew now that if he married her, put himself in the hands of that half-grown spitfire, she'd tear the soul out of him. If he married Sally, he would lose himself, and there wouldn't be a damn thing he could do about it.

He only hoped he wasn't in so deep already that he wouldn't be able to get her out of his system and get on with his life.

He lent her a horse to ride home. It wasn't very heroic, he admitted, but he didn't trust himself to be near her in the soft gathering darkness of an achingly lonely spring night.

Jake pushed his gray Stetson off his forehead and accepted the shot of the Silver Cup's best bourbon Tom Maguire slid across the oak table toward him. He took a healthy swallow. "The deal's off, Tom."

To Jake's surprise, the older man seemed unruffled. "That so?" Tom said.

"I can't do it. I can't marry Sally, land or no land."

"That so?" Tom echoed. "Looks to me like you're scared to marry her."

Jake nodded. "Maybe. It's more than the land, Tom. There's other things, too, things between Sally and me. Some things are beyond price."

A wily look crept across the Irishman's face. "Rawhide and whang leather, Jake. The way I figure it, maybe you should just, uh, lay back and enjoy it."

Jake slapped his empty glass onto the tabletop. "Hell, Tom, you know I can't do that. It would ruin her. This is a small ranching community. Everybody around here knows everything about everybody else. I don't want to compromise Sally."

Tom coughed. "I know this sounds daft, man, but I'd kinda hoped you would."

Jake jerked, sloshing bourbon over the rim of the glass as he poured another shot. "What the— Tom, you know I can't play fast with a girl like Sally. She's not loose. She thinks she, um, fancies me, but..." His voice died.

Tom sipped his drink and thought a moment. "But? Marry her, my boy! She'll have you, I'm thinkin'."

"Ah, Tom." Jake sighed in frustration. "Sally doesn't mind dipping her toe in the water, but she's not ready to stay there. I am. I'm ready to settle down. Your daughter doesn't even know what that means. She doesn't want to know."

Tom inspected the tired face before him. "What about you, my boy?"

Jake groaned. "I'll be honest with you, Tom. Six months ago it didn't matter a hoot to me one way or the other. Now it matters. I'm ready to start a family."

"And it's my daughter Sally that's made the difference?"

Jake nodded and sucked some of the bourbon to the back of his throat. "I'm in love with her, Tom. I'm almost to the point where I don't think I can live without her."

"That so?" Tom repeated for the third time.

Jake looked at the older man intently for a long minute. "Almost, but not quite."

Unperturbed, Tom chuckled. "You're not a man who gives up easy, Jake. Let it ride a while."

"Ride a while! Hell, I—" Jake gave the Irishman a black look.

Tom Maguire smiled a secretive smile into his glass. "People ain't gonna talk too much. Anyway, I'm not worried about our Sally's reputation. Half the county's layin' bets she'll die an old maid schoolteacher. A little gossip to the contrary might do her some good, joggle her up a mite."

He peered into Jake's face. "She's a good girl, Jake. You're not gonna harm her by your courtin'. By the time somebody spins a yarn about you two, you'll be married and settled down like goofalolly love birds. Like I said, Jake, I'd bet my life on you—you're just the man for my Sally."

Jake snorted in exasperation. Here he was trying to do the honorable thing, and Tom kept tying his spurs together. It was plain he had an ulterior motive. Tom wanted Jake to court Sally, come hell or high water. There was no understanding him. He was purring like a cat in a creamery.

But no matter what Tom suggested, Jake couldn't stand to be near Sally as long as she kept saying, "Make love to me" and "No, I won't marry you" in the same breath. There was no understanding her either. She was not willing, or not able, to give him what he needed—a commitment to spend the rest of their lives together.

Jake rose and gulped the last of his whiskey. "Sorry, Tom. My conscience won't let me take the land without marrying Sally, and I can't do that."

Feeling more alone than he ever had in his life, he strode out of the saloon.

Chapter Twelve

Sally thrust her shoulders between the flailing arms and separated the two boys. "Jim! Brance! That's enough, now. Stop it!"

Jim Eckloff glared at his older brother, his swollen lower lip trembling. "He called me a coward, Miss Maguire. And I ain't no coward." He spat the words into the face of the other boy.

Sally gripped both their shirtfronts with a firm hand and pulled them about to face her. Good heavens, what next? It wasn't enough that the school board was up in arms over her teaching methods. She'd heard that their last stormy meeting in Jake's front parlor had dragged on until two in the morning. Martha had confided that Olla and Dutch Hendricks and old Mr. Baker had been the only ones who'd spoken up for her. Some of the other parents, Martha allowed, apparently thought tar and feathers none too good for a schoolmarm who made up rhymes out of their family names to teach spelling and encouraged the boys to recite poetry. Poetry! "Not the Bible, but *poems,*" the blunt-spoken housekeeper had spluttered. "Poems about 'splendor in the hayfield and gathering roses'!" And now, to top off her troubles, Sally had a fight on her hands.

"So," she demanded of the two glowering boys, "what's this all about?"

Jim Eckloff's mottled face came just to her chin. "It's the race, Miss Maguire. Saturday morning, over at the Bar Y."

"Race? What race?" Sally looked from Jim to his older brother.

"Jake, uh, Mr. Bannister is holdin' a horse race over at his ranch. He says it's sort of a way to let his buckaroos blow off some steam, they been so riled up lately."

"Oh?" Had the drought last summer driven everyone crazy? Sally tapped her foot impatiently and waited for the rest of the explanation.

"There's to be a gents' race," Brance continued, his eyes lighting up. "And a ladies' race, too. Fifty dollars to the winner!"

"And?" Sally prompted. She knew about the impromptu horse races the Bar Y hosted periodically. What she didn't understand was how Jim and Brance Eckloff were involved.

Red-haired Billy Peterman interrupted from the sidelines. "There's gonna be a junior race, too!" His piping voice was breathless with excitement. "Mr. Bannister says the winner can have one of the Bar Y horses. I got one all picked out—he's a real ripper!"

Jim Eckloff's voice wavered at the edge of tears. "And Brance said I weren't a good enough rider to even get close to a Bar Y horse."

"*Wasn't* good enough," Sally said automatically. Oh, my, she thought. There's a lot more to teaching school out here in Oregon than they ever dreamed of in St. Louis.

"Now you boys listen to me," she ordered, hoping her tone was commanding enough to put a stop to all argument. "No one knows who's a good enough rider to win a race until the race is run. It's not fair to decide *before* the race. And it's certainly not gentlemanly to fight over it."

Both boys hung their heads. "Sorry, Miss Maguire," Brance intoned. Jim nodded, scuffing the toe of his boot in the dirt.

Billy danced at Sally's elbow. "You gonna enter the ladies' race, Miss Maguire? I seen you ride. Boy, you sure ride good!"

"Certainly not!" Sally snapped. "And it's 'I *saw* you ride' and 'you ride *well*.'" Oh, what's the use, she thought with a sigh. All those endless hours spent in grammar drill and literature appreciation when all boys wanted to do was grow up enough to cowboy for some trail boss on a roundup. It was the rare ranch hand who was educated past the bare minimum of reading and writing. Most couldn't even do that.

Jake Bannister was a notable exception. Sally sniffed in disdain. Around his hands on the ranch, even Jake talked—and swore—fit to burn dry grass.

She sighed again and released the Eckloff brothers. Without a backward glance she swept into the schoolhouse. The male of this species, she decided, was simply not civilized.

At supper that night, her father, too, joined the ranks of the uncivilized. "You gonna ride in the ladies' race on Saturday, honey-girl?"

Sally opened her mouth to speak but stopped short when Louisa raised her head "I'm riding, Pa," she answered in a calm voice.

"You!" Sally was thunderstruck. Louisa could ride, it was true. Both girls had been taught to handle a horse before they could read, but Sally never thought of

Louisa—demure and fragile looking in yellow-sprigged lawn—as tough enough to compete in a race. Whereas *she*...

Sally looked down at her worn jeans and the faded blue flannel shirt. She was still half-wild, she acknowledged. Jake was right, she hadn't grown up yet. Maybe she never would.

Louisa's quiet voice penetrated. "There's a fifty-dollar prize. If I win it, I can buy a new saddle for Will, for a wedding present." She flashed a quick glance at her father. "There's one he's been mooning over at Mr. Baker's store."

Tom looked from one daughter to the other, and Sally detected a twinkle in the blue eyes.

"Hell, honey, we've got enough money for you to buy that saddle. You don't need to ride for it."

"I know, Pa. But I want to ride. And I want to win. I want the money for Will's wedding present to be mine."

Tom scanned his younger daughter's face, then shifted his gaze to Sally. "What about you, daughter? I hear there's more to the prize than fifty dollars. There's another twist to it."

Sally stared at her father, a question in her eyes. "Twist? What sort of twist?"

"Well—" Tom laughed "—you know Jake's got sort of an overgrown sense of fair play. Just to make it more of a horse race, so to speak, the mounts you'll be ridin' will be drawn by lot. Sort of a way to make the odds more equal."

Sally sucked in a gulp of air. "You mean Louisa won't be riding her own horse, one she's used to?"

"That's it, all right. The horses will be a jib-job lot, loaned out to the ladies by the owners. Some may be gentle as you please, others could be real shadow dancers who'll throw you on the first turn. And the twist comes in at the end, honey-girl. Whoever wins the race gets the horse owner for a supper partner."

"Supper partner!" Sally sniffed. "I can just imagine who thought that up."

"As a matter of fact," Tom answered blandly, "it was George Peterman. He's entering that little sorrel mare he's so fond of. Think about it, Sally. It's practically the only way in the world a respectable married rancher like George can enjoy an hour in the company of a pretty young woman without Mary Ellen gettin' her dander up."

"That's just like George," Sally said with a laugh. "Like a bull in a hornet's nest. Who else is entering horses?"

"Will's entering his gray stallion," Louisa ventured.

"And Nate Randall's entering that mare he bought last spring. Ned Barker's in, too." Tom chuckled and threw a quick look in Sally's direction. "Jake's entering that black gelding you took such a fancy to."

The black gelding! There weren't many horses that could outrun that one, Sally conceded. To win, Louisa would have to win the draw and ride the black. No other horse could touch him.

"What about it, honey-girl?" Tom pursued. "You gonna ride?"

Oh, wouldn't she love to ride that black! She'd do just about anything to show Jake she could. But she wouldn't do anything to compromise Louisa's chances; it was plain her sister had her heart set on buying that saddle for Will.

Sally looked into her father's blue eyes and shook her head. She'd step aside for Louisa.

* * *

On Saturday morning Sally and Louisa and Tom arrived at the Bar Y in plenty of time to arrange themselves along the corral fence. Nebraska and Cole Sieversen joined them, simultaneously hooking their boot heels over the rail.

Sally nodded to the men, then drew in a deep lungful of the warm spring air. It smelled of sage and dust and wood smoke, and inexplicably she found herself thinking of Jake.

Her breath gave a little catch as she exhaled. Jake hadn't been around much since he'd sent her home after the picnic. She hated to admit it, but she missed seeing him.

Dozens of onlookers from neighboring ranches lounged against the fence or climbed up on the plank rails for better views. Some had even driven buggies out from town. Jake's horses were known throughout the valley, and his horse races, held when chores at the ranch were "between seasons" and the hands got a little restless, were the talk of the state. This spring, with the continuing drought on the mind of every rancher in the valley, people seemed more keyed up than usual. "More clabberbrained" were her father's words.

Jake strolled out in front of the assembled crowd, his hands stuffed into his jean pockets. "Well, folks, the Bar Y boys settled down to a little buckaroo geography this morning. The course runs from the corral fence just past where Ned's sitting, across the meadow—" he gestured with his head "—down through that little flat valley and around Blackberry Hill, and then back by the stock pond at the far end of the pasture."

Sally strained her eyes as Jake talked and pointed. She noted that Slim had been stationed at the halfway point, his bulky frame appearing almost sylphlike in the distance. A bale of hay marked the turn toward Blackberry Hill.

Perched on the other side of her father, Nebraska pointed a half-rolled cigarette at the pudgy cowboy far down in the meadow. "Think ol' Slim'll be quick enough to get out of the way when they round that turn?"

Sally gazed across the field in the direction Nebraska indicated and stifled a giggle at the thought of the rotund cowboy moving that fast.

"Hell, there's no animal big enough to run over that tub of lard," Cole joked. "The horse'd spook hisself just lookin' at him!"

Sally bit her lip.

In the distance, Slim waved his battered hat to signal that the course was ready.

"God-a-mighty," Cole groaned as he resettled himself on the fence rail between Tom and Nebraska. "Where's Slim keep that hat, anyway, under his mattress? It's mashed flatter'n one of his biscuits!"

Nebraska exhaled a puff of blue smoke. "A fancy hat don't make a cowboy," he rasped. His voice, usually a bit hoarse, was extra rough because of the dust. He eyed the conchos on Cole's impeccable new hat.

Cole glared at him. "Don't hurt none to look decent."

Nebraska snorted. "You gone loco? No hat's gonna make that big bucket of grease look any different. Hell, Cole, your brain's plum gone to mush! If I knew anybody smarter than you, I'd get him out of the rain 'fore he drowned from his mouth flappin' open."

Sally saw Cole flash a quick look in Louisa's direction, then reach with elaborate care into his vest pocket and withdraw his canister of tobacco.

"Last time I measured it," he drawled, "my mind was as sharp as a razor." He shook some tobacco into a cigarette paper.

"Mebbe just as wide, too," Nebraska joked, his voice throaty. He jabbed an elbow into the cowhand's ribs. Tobacco flakes spilled onto Cole's jeans, but his attention had shifted to the corral where the horses and riders were lining up, and he lost interest in his smoke.

The junior race was first.

The jingle-bobs on Jake's spurs chinged rhythmically as he and Dutch Hendricks moved among the seated riders, giving last-minute instructions. Jim and Brance Eckloff, mounted on almost identical roan mares, glared at each other across the backs of the four other riders.

Billy Peterman, mounted on his father's prize sorrel, nervously adjusted his reins, then his hat, then licked his lips, then adjusted his hat again. Rob Blane was riding Sally's bay mare. His twin brother, Richie, fidgeted on Tom's spirited sorrel.

Between them, eleven-year-old Francie Varner from town perched on a satiny chestnut mare with black mane and tail. Sally watched the girl grip her reins as Jake outlined the rules to the onlookers.

"How come a girl's ridin' that chestnut?" a male voice challenged.

Jake directed his gaze at the speaker. "If she can ride well enough, there's no reason a girl can't race. I've seen young Miss Varner ride. She'll do."

Sally nodded in agreement. Some of the things Jake said made a good deal of sense.

Dutch Hendricks rechecked each rider, then raised his pistol. When the gun fired, Sally jumped.

Jim Eckloff led across the meadow, but was overtaken first by his brother, Brance, and then by Rob Blane on Sally's bay mare. The riders bunched so close together the cloud of dust hindered identification of the leader.

Squinting into the sun, Sally watched young Francie Varner and Billy Peterman push their mounts into a dead heat. Little by little they gained on Brance and Rob ahead of them. When they started down the long valley, Francie pulled ahead. Billy dogged her heels. As they disappeared around the hill, Sally clenched her hands tight in her lap.

"It's Francie!" someone shouted when they reappeared.

"No! It's the sorrel!" Nebraska rasped. "It's that kid Richie Blane on the sorrel!"

"Come on, Francie! Ride that devil!" An unlit cigarette bobbed in Cole's mouth.

Sally had to laugh. To a man, all the Bar Y hands were cheering themselves hoarse for the Varner girl.

On the return stretch, the riders were so close the crowd lapsed into a tense silence. Sally half stood on the fence rail to see better through the cloud of powdery dust kicked up by the horses' hooves.

Brance Eckloff and the Blane twins fell behind as Billy, Francie and Jim Eckloff battled for the lead position. Jim rode with determination and skill, but as the horses thundered past Slim and neared the tree stump serving as the three-quarter mark, Jim's roan was overtaken first by Billy Peterman's mare, and then by Francie on the beautiful chestnut.

It was Francie who gave Billy the most trouble. Sally watched the boy lower his fiery red head down along the mare's neck and move in rhythm with the big horse, working to stay ahead of the chestnut's flying front hooves.

Francie hunched her slim body low in the saddle and rode for all she was worth. Fifty yards from the finish line, she overtook him.

The crowd cheered. Sally's nails cut into her flesh.

Billy leaned forward, lifted his buttocks out of the saddle and surged ahead. He pulled his mare up even with the chestnut, but at the last possible instant Francie edged past the boy to win. Flushed and panting, she stood in the stirrups and waved her hat to acknowledge the shouts of the crowd.

Sally shook with excitement. Both palms bore the imprint of her fingernails. She threw her arms around Louisa. "She won! Francie won! Isn't it grand?"

"Her horse must've got a whiff of Slim's socks!" Ned Barker shouted to Cole.

"Nah," the rangy cowhand scoffed. "She just didn't want to be so slow on a cow pony that the only outfit that'd give her a job'd be the Lazy J!"

The foreman of the Lazy J scowled. He straightened his compact frame from the fence and jumped down into the corral. "You ridin'?" Ned intoned to Cole, his dark eyes glinting, "or is this a gentleman's race?"

Cole unkinked his long legs and spat off to one side. "I'm ridin'. I guess I'm as much of a gentleman as the next fellow—seein' as how I never insult anybody *un*-intentionally."

Ned sneaked a surreptitious look at Louisa on the fence rail. "Come on, then. Let's lay them out and let the ladies decide."

Absorbed in tightening his saddle girth, Cole made no response. Sally noticed that his gaze, too, never strayed far from her sister. This race was over a good deal more than horsemanship or friendly gibes. She wondered if Will Boessen saw what was going on.

The men's event got off to a shaky start. Both Ned and Cole jumped the gun three times and had to be brought back to the starting line. At last Dutch fired his pistol, and they were off cleanly.

The race narrowed at once to a contest between Ned on his magnificent roan stallion and Cole on a tough little piebald mare he prized. The other eight riders spread out behind them.

Jake was not racing, Sally observed. When Ned and Cole rounded the turn and disappeared behind the hill, Sally momentarily let her attention wander to where the Bar Y owner lounged against the fence with Nate Randall. Paula fluttered close to him, dressed in a beautifully cut dark brown riding costume that reminded Sally of a painting of an English hunt scene she had admired in the museum in St. Louis. She watched the young woman smile up at Jake, then circle her fingers possessively around the top button of his dark leather vest.

Sally's spine stiffened.

"Sally, what's wrong?" Louisa whispered.

"Paula," Sally answered. "Look at her. She acts like a cat in heat."

"Sally!" Louisa gasped.

Sally turned toward her sister. "Well, doesn't she?"

Louisa watched for a moment and then giggled. "She's sure got her claws in him."

Sally sniffed and looked away. Watching Paula and Jake together was unusually bothersome. She shifted her attention back to the race.

Cole and Ned pounded across the meadow neck and neck. Suddenly Cole's mare broke stride. The hands from the Lazy J, bunched into a cheering section at one end of the corral fence, yelled and hurrahed for their foreman.

The Bar Y hands sat silent on the sidelines, intent on the outcome.

The two horses thundered side by side for five or six lengths while the crowd roared. Just at the finish line, Ned's roan pulled past Cole, and the Lazy J boys went wild.

Cole slowed his mare to a walk and headed for the corral yard. "Mistakes come easy when you mess with things you don't know nuthin' about," someone yelled.

A triumphant Ned trotted his mount over to Jake, swept off his hat and held it out for the prize money.

Cole dismounted and ran his hands down his mare's foreleg. Frowning, he tossed the reins to Dutch and stumped back to the fence. He kept his gaze averted from Louisa.

"It could have been a lot worse," Nebraska remarked to the defeated rider in his characteristic wheezy undertone.

"How's that?" Cole snapped.

Nebraska tossed a cigarette butt onto the dirt. "The fodder-waster horse with the game leg could have been mine! Now, when you get old enough to have brains, you won't do things like that!"

The other men guffawed.

Sally suppressed her laughter. Ranch loyalty certainly ran hot and cold. At bottom, it was every man for himself. She watched Cole grimace good-naturedly and reach into his vest pocket for his tobacco.

Out in the corral yard Jake took the hat out of Ned Barker's hand and planted a sheaf of green bills in the crown. Then, lifting off his own Stetson, he sought out George Peterman, and the two men conferred for a few moments. At last George climbed the fence rail and the crowd quieted.

"The next event is the ladies' race," George boomed. A murmur ran along the fence.

Ned trotted the roan stallion into the corral yard, dismounted, then swaggered over to Cole.

"Do me a favor," the Lazy J foreman said as he passed. "If you're gonna feel sorry for yourself, make it short. Miss Louisa don't like a sulky man."

Cole glared at him. "Ya know, Ned, it's hard sometimes tellin' the difference between a drunk and a damn fool." He took his time tearing a cigarette paper out of the packet he withdrew from his vest pocket. "Sometimes a drunk is sober," he continued, his voice light. He stared into Ned's eyes. "A fool never is."

Nebraska chortled, slapping Cole's broad shoulder as a glowering Ned eased himself onto the fence rail.

"Conversation's cheap," Ned snapped. He sneaked another look at Louisa.

George Peterman raised his hand for silence. When the crowd quieted, he spoke. "We've got five horses entered, and four ladies to ride so far," he shouted. "The horses' names are on slips of paper in this... you call this a hat, Ned?" He held up Ned's battered black hat. "The ladies' names are in this one." George gestured with Jake's gray Stetson.

The crowd buzzed. George sauntered over to the fence where Cole and Nebraska perched and held a hat out to each of them. "Draw, gentlemen."

Each man dipped a hand into the cavity and pulled out a slip of paper. George snagged the selections, glanced at the names and cleared his throat.

"Riding the white mare entered by Judge Randall will be..." He consulted the paper. "Mrs. Lydia Varner."

Sally felt Louisa's body tense. "Lou," she whispered, "don't be nervous." She looked at her sister's rigid figure, trim in a borrowed pair of Sally's jeans and a long-sleeved shirt.

"Lydia's a good rider," Louisa whispered back. Her slim hands kneaded the black leather riding gloves in her lap. "And that mare of Judge Randall's is a strong horse. To beat her, I need to draw Jake's black gelding."

George waved another slip of paper. "Next horse is Ned Barker's chestnut mare," he announced. "The rider will be..."

The crowd hushed.

"Mrs. Olla Hendricks."

Olla! Sally was astounded. Not only was Olla middle-aged, she walked with a decided limp from a riding accident years before.

"Olla," Dutch demanded of his wife. "Vat you do?"

"I'm riding a horse," Olla retorted. "Maybe I can't walk so good, but the horse, he don't know that!" She rose from the fence rail and limped toward Jake, who stood holding the chestnut's reins. He looped the stirrup safely out of the way over the saddle horn and cupped his hands for Olla to mount. When she was seated, he laid the reins in her hands.

Dutch shook his head helplessly, and his eyes sought George's. "Can't you do somet'ing?" the wrangler pleaded. "Get my vife down off dat horse?"

George Peterman rolled his eyes. "Can't handle my own wife, let alone yours. Leave her be, Dutch." Again he proffered the two hats to Cole and Ned seated on the fence.

"The next horse is . . ." George paused and squinted. "The black gelding owned by Jackson Bannister." The crowd murmured, then fell silent as George bent to read the rider's name. "Miss Paula Randall."

"Oh, no!" Louisa moaned.

Paula moved forward with elegant ease. Sally watched her lift the reins from Jake's hand with an almost caressing gesture and smile up at him as she waited for him to help her mount.

Damn! Even if she couldn't sit a jackass, Paula would win riding that gelding.

George's booming voice rose again. "And my prize sorrel will be ridden by . . ." He paused and scanned the crowd for dramatic effect. "Miss Louisa Maguire."

Sally shot a look at her sister. Louisa's face was calm, but her eyes were shut tight. Sally's heart lurched. She knew how much buying that saddle for Will meant to her. Louisa would have a difficult time catching Paula on the black.

Louisa clutched Sally's arm. "The only horse left is Will's gray stallion, Sally. They're short one rider. . . ."

Sally shook her head.

"Please, Sally. You're a good rider. One of us should win that fifty dollars."

"No."

"Oh, Sally, please!" Louisa begged, her voice low and urgent. "Don't let Paula just walk away with it—and Jake, too. Ride, Sally! Oh, please?"

And Jake, too? What did she mean? Sally glanced at Paula, mounted on Jake's beautiful black horse. She sat up very straight in the saddle. She looked just like her father's pampered barn cat, smugly licking its chin after lapping up some spilled cream. Unbidden, a word flashed into Sally's mind. Arrogant. Paula was so proud of what she was, of what she had. Well, what *did* she have? Just the horse, not Jake. Something niggled at Sally's mind. Or did she?

Anger surged through her. Then she smiled as another thought flickered into her brain. Maybe the gelding would throw her.

George Peterman strode up and down, scanning the excited onlookers crowding along the fence. "And the lady who will ride Will Boessen's gray stallion is...?" He lifted his head and melodramatically cocked his ear. The silence stretched.

"Please, Sally!" Louisa whispered.

"I can't, Lou. I just can't."

"Sally..." Louisa's voice sounded desperate.

"Lou, I haven't even got my riding gloves."

Louisa fished in her pocket. "Here. I brought an extra pair, just in case." Her clear blue eyes held Sally's in a long look.

Sally stared into her sister's face. At last she nodded, took a deep breath and slid off the fence, her heart beginning to pound. She was more than a little wary of Will's gray stallion.

"Miss Sally Maguire will ride Will Boessen's stallion," George announced.

Louisa squeezed her hand, hard, and Sally followed her into the corral yard. Before she mounted the big gray horse Will held steady for her, Sally flicked a glance at Jake.

His tanned face was impassive, but a light shone deep in the midnight blue eyes. She thought she saw his mouth twitch, but when she looked back, he was un-smiling. He tipped his Stetson in a silent salute.

Her pulse leapt. Was he sorry *she* wasn't riding the black? An odd, exultant feeling of power swept over her, savage and almost frightening. She wanted to win. She wanted to beat Paula! She was shocked at the primitive intensity of her feelings. Now she prayed the black would not throw the cool, elegantly clad woman who had clung so possessively to Jake. Sally wanted to beat Paula fair and square.

She leaned down and lifted the reins out of Will's hand. As she reached for his quirt, he caught her arm. "Don't whip him, Sally," he said quietly. "Let him have his head and just go with him. He's got a mind of his own."

She nodded, her heart beginning to thrum.

"And Sally," the foreman added after a moment's hesitation, "whether you win or not, I'm glad you're riding Dancer. He'll know what you want of him."

Dear Will. What a treasure Louisa was getting. If she won this race, she'd buy that saddle for Will herself!

The women riders moved their mounts to the start-ing line in front of the corral fence, gentling their horses with soft words and pats. Sally purposely positioned herself between Louisa and Paula. Holding her breath, she waited for Dutch to signal the start of the race.

Paula's gaze traveled from Sally's jeans to her plaid flannel shirt. A cool smile spread over the perfect lips. "Think you can beat me?"

Sally gasped at the blatant challenge.

"You really needn't bother, you know," Paula con-tinued. "In one sense, I've already won."

"If you mean supper with Jake, you're welcome to it," Sally replied evenly.

"No, not just supper," Paula replied, her tone silky. "Jake."

Jake! Appalled, Sally shut her lips firmly over the words rising from her throat and turned away. So she'd won Jake, had she? The spider had caught the fly.

Suddenly she was furious. Who did Paula think she was, bragging like that about a man as if he was nothing but a sack of wheat? And why tell it to her? Paula might be rich and citified and cultured, but it was plain as day she had no breeding.

Sally pressed her lips together in fury. Well, Miss La-di-da, we'll just see who's the better rider! She jammed her black hat down tight over her pinned-up hair and gripped the reins in her palm.

Next to Sally, Louisa nervously stroked the neck of George Peterman's sorrel. Graceful Lydia Varner sat astride the Randalls' white mare, and next to her, buxom Olla Hendricks, an old hat of Dutch's covering her bun of graying hair, spoke in an undertone to the shiny chestnut she rode. As a young woman, Olla had been a superb rider. Sally wondered if such skill waned with age.

The older woman sat her horse calmly, looking serene and confident. Sally shot a glance at Dutch. Poor man. Olla's husband looked positively sick.

The aging wrangler raised the starting gun in a hand that shook like quaking leaves. Twice he lowered it, still unfired.

Finally Jake lifted the revolver out of Dutch's twitching fingers and fired into the air to start the race.

Sally clamped her lips tight in determination, and the gray stallion leapt forward.

Chapter Thirteen

Olla Hendricks astounded not only the onlookers but her husband, as well. Sally smiled to herself as the gray-haired woman took an early lead and held it all the way across the meadow. Sally and Louisa trailed behind, along with Lydia Varner on her white mare. Paula, clumsy in her handling of Jake's black gelding, lagged at the rear. Sally almost laughed out loud at the difficulty the town-bred girl was having. Then she forgot about Paula and concentrated on keeping out of Louisa's way. She wanted her sister to have the advantage.

Halfway to Blackberry Hill they both caught up to Olla's chestnut. My heavens, how that woman could ride!

When they started down the long, flat valley toward the hill, Sally dropped back, giving way to Louisa. Lydia Varner was just ahead of her.

Louisa overtook Lydia's mare, and then Sally watched, dumbfounded, as both her sister and Lydia widened their trail to make room for her.

Sally took a deep breath and moved into the offered space. Bless them both, Sally prayed. She'd need all the help she could get to stay ahead of Paula and that black gelding.

She rounded the curve and heard the steady thrum of hoofbeats behind her. She shot a quick look over her shoulder. Paula and the gelding were gaining.

As they neared Blackberry Hill, Paula overtook Lydia Varner and moved closer to Louisa. Louisa struggled to stay ahead of the black, but little by little she lost ground. Any minute, Paula would make her move.

What a magnificent horse! Sally put her head down alongside the stallion's neck and concentrated. Without a backward glance she knew the hoofbeats thundering behind her were those of the black. Paula had caught Louisa and passed her. In just a few seconds the black would overtake her gray stallion.

All at once the black surged forward, and Sally pounded toward the hill neck and neck with Paula.

Then the black cut abruptly into Sally's path.

What in the world was she doing? Sally caught a fleeting glimpse of Slim's white, startled face at the halfway mark, and she veered off course as he scampered out of the way. She laughed out loud. Never in her entire life had she seen Slim move that fast.

She struggled to control the gray as Louisa and Lydia Varner pounded past her. She let the stallion reestablish his rhythm, then nestled her cheek alongside his neck and gave him some head. Far beyond her she could see the flying hooves of the black gelding and Paula's arm rhythmically raising and lowering the whip.

Dust stung her eyes. Her breath came in jerky gasps, and the labored breathing of Lydia's white mare and Louisa's sorrel filled her ears as she caught up to them.

For the second time, Louisa moved over to let her through. When Sally emerged from behind the hill and headed back down the long valley stretch, she glanced ahead.

Paula and the gelding had caught up with Olla's chestnut. Sally gritted her teeth in frustration. Olla's riding ability far surpassed Paula's, but the chestnut mare was no match for the black. Paula flew past Olla and took the lead.

Sally clamped her jaws shut and lowered her head. "C'mon, boy," she breathed. "Let's catch her."

Little by little she began to gain on the riders ahead of her.

She was amazed at the noise—the erratic staccato rhythm of hoofbeats on the hard packed earth, the distant roar of the crowd. Her own breathing rasped in her ears, and the gray's steady breath whooshed in and out of his nostrils in hoarse gusts. Every one of her senses seemed heightened. The faint chink-chink of the bridle carried over the snap of Paula's quirt biting into the gelding's hide. The dust smelled bitter, sagebrush and wood smoke blended into an acrid, earthy scent. The blood pounded in her ears.

Sally drew abreast of Olla and edged past the chestnut while Olla held the beautiful mare steady. Her heart swelled in admiration for the older woman. She wanted to be like that some day. Skilled and sure.

She flicked her gaze up for an instant. Paula still held the lead, and they were almost to the finish line. She would have to catch the black gelding in the next few moments or it would be too late.

She turned her cheek into the gray's neck, tightened her thighs and raised her buttocks out of the saddle.

Paula glanced behind her. The startled expression on the perfect oval face made Sally grin. She drove toward the black gelding's rump.

Paula laid the quirt furiously into her horse, but Sally kept gaining ground. All at once they were racing side by side, and then Sally swung out to pass.

The breath tore through her lungs. Victory was close, so close! Just as she began to pull ahead, Paula lashed her whip into the gray stallion's neck.

The horse veered and broke stride, and Paula pulled ahead on the black. Sally could scarcely believe what had happened. Paula had purposely interfered with another rider's horse!

A hot flush of anger surged through her. Paula Randall, with all her fancy duds and fine manners, was a cheat!

Sally clamped her lips together. She wasn't beaten yet, no matter what Paula did.

She bent forward and spoke into the gray's ear. "Don't let her do it, boy! Come on, we'll show her!"

The rushing air burned her eyeballs, and she closed her lids over them, trusting the stallion to drive toward the finish. "Now!" she sang into his ear. "Go like the wind!"

The horse surged under her. Her hat flew off, and the wind tugged at her pinned-up hair. Stray tendrils whipped across her face. Inside her, something wild, almost primeval, leapt to life. In a flash she thought of that night with Jake, when he had touched her, made her moan in ecstasy.

A hand squeezed her heart. She knew she could win.

"Now," she shouted to the horse. *"Now!"*

Less than ten yards from the finish, she caught up to Paula. At the last possible moment the gray stallion edged past the gelding's nose.

The crowd went wild. Sally closed her eyes and flung both her arms up in triumph. She'd done it! She'd won!

With trembling knees she guided the gray in a wide circle, letting him cool down before she brought him back to Will in the corral. She didn't care to see Paula's face. She wanted to see Jake's.

Across the corral, Sally watched him hold the gelding's bridle steady while Paula dismounted. But he wasn't looking at Paula. He was looking at her.

Still mounted, Sally saw Jake's blue-black eyes seek hers over Paula's head. For a moment all the noise and commotion in the corral fell away, and there was just the two of them, staring at one another in a world all their own.

Then Jake pushed the gray Stetson up off his forehead, and his face broke into a broad smile. He tipped his hat in her direction.

"Miss Salty," he mouthed to her. "Well done." He turned away to help Paula dismount.

The young woman glanced at Sally over Jake's shoulder as she descended. Keeping one hand on Jake's arm, Paula tossed her head, sending Sally a silent, unmistakable message. *You may have won the race, but I still have Jake.*

Sally's heart slammed into her rib cage. She tore her attention away and turned to find Louisa. Her sister cantered up at that instant and jumped down off the sorrel.

"Sally! Sally, you were magnificent!"

Sally had never heard such excitement in Louisa's voice. She smiled down at her. "I'm going to buy Will that saddle myself, honey. This horse deserves it!"

Her entire body shook with exhaustion. "Help me down, Lou," she said in an unsteady voice. "My knees feel like they've turned to applesauce."

* * *

"June the eighteenth," Louisa announced at breakfast the following morning. Sally stared at her, and her father's bushy eyebrows rose.

Louisa laid down her fork and smiled at them. "Will and I are getting married next month."

"Oh, Lou, that's wonderful!" Sally hugged her sister. Her breath caught, and an odd, sweet hunger surged through her. She blinked hard as an inexplicable sob rose in her throat.

"Sure took his time about it. It's almost June now!" Tom chuckled. His eyes shone with telltale moisture.

"He's been busy, Pa," Louisa said quietly.

"Busy? Too busy to get married? Busy doin' what?"

"Building a house," Sally blurted.

Louisa looked up with widened eyes. "How did you know that?"

"Jake told me. I'm sorry, Lou. I didn't know it was a secret."

Louisa gave her older sister a penetrating look. "It wasn't, really. I'm just surprised you talked about it with Jake."

"He—"

"Sally," Louisa interrupted, "come upstairs with me after breakfast and try on your bridesmaid's dress. You can help me decide on my veil."

Tom laughed. "That's what all this dressmaking's been about all these months, is it? I should have known, daughter. You're always way ahead of most folks, your own kin included."

"Lou," Sally began, then hesitated. "I have to grade papers. The term ends soon, and I don't want to get behind."

As happy as she was for Louisa, she didn't want to think about the wedding. When Louisa married Will, she'd move out of the house. Sally hated the thought of losing her sister.

"Let's fit your dress first, honey." Louisa rose and laced her arms around Sally's shoulders. "If I don't keep at you, you'll stand up as my bridesmaid in your petticoat!"

On the last day of the term Sally dismissed her pupils for the last time that year and sat at her desk, marking papers. When she heard the horse outside, she raised her head, waiting for the door to open.

Jake stepped inside, pushing his Stetson up with one lean finger. "Sally." His voice rose at the end of her name.

Sally's pulse pounded. Ever since the horse race, Jake had avoided her. She had wanted to see him, and yet in a way, she was afraid to. Whenever she was near him, smelling his leathery pine-soap scent, her heart hammered away under the prim tucks of her white lawn blouse. Now, looking at his tall frame looming in her doorway, she felt the old mixture of fear and excitement rise in her belly.

"I—I was just finishing up some schoolwork."

His glance unnerved her, and she rattled on. "You've missed the children. Elsa Baker and Rachel Varner gave a reading today. *Evangeline.* I was so proud of them. They—"

"I came late on purpose, Sally. To bring your salary for the term. And talk some."

A flutter of panic skittered into her chest. "We can talk on the way home, if you're riding that way."

"I'd rather it would be here. There's more privacy. And," he added, "better memories."

Sally's fear skyrocketed.

Jake reached into the pocket of his blue chambray shirt and pulled out a crisp one-hundred-dollar bill. He tucked it under the dictionary on her desk. "Your salary for the year."

Sally stared at it. "Thank you." Satisfaction surged through her. The payment validated her worth as the Honey Creek schoolmistress. She knew she was a good teacher, knew she had spent these hard months since September when school opened doing what she did best—bringing knowledge to her students. She knew this was her life's calling.

She kept her head down, her eyes focused on her desk, wondering what was coming next. Did he guess how much she loved teaching, watching her pupils' minds come to life and grow under her tutelage? She tried to concentrate on the papers before her, but Jake's silence pressed in on her, unraveling her facade.

"Sally, we've got to talk."

Sally stole a quick look at the leather boots planted near the corner of her desk. She knew what was on his mind—the school board. Her teaching methods were now the talk of the county. Had he come to fire her? Resolutely she stared down at the floor. "Say it. Get it over with."

Jake stared at her bent neck. Damnation, he wanted to touch her. "Sally, I can't talk to you when you don't look at me." He grasped both her arms and pulled her up, kicking the desk chair out of his way as he moved in close to her. Her hair, piled up on top of her head, smelled of lilacs.

"Jake, please—"

"Sally, I have to know something, and I have to know it now."

"Know *what* now? Whether I'll quit? Well, I won't, even if that's what the school board wants. I can't. You can tell them they'll have to fire me before I'll give up teaching."

"Fire you!" Jake's eyes blazed. "You think I rode out here to talk about—"

"Well, didn't you? I've heard the talk about me, and about my school. Isn't that why you wanted—"

Jake groaned. "God in heaven, Sally, be still a minute." He drew in a ragged breath and turned her to face him. "Your job's secure, if you want it. It's true, some of the ranchers are riled up over your, uh, rather unusual methods, but more families are for you than against you. Olla and Dutch Hendricks, the Bakers, they all spoke up for you. As far as I know, your job's secure. That's not why I'm here."

Sally's heart tripped. "It's not? Then why? What's so important that you rode all the way out here today?"

Jake closed his eyes for a moment. "There's something I've got to know, Sally. It involves giving up being the Honey Creek schoolmistress, but not in the way you think."

Comprehension hit her like a bolt of lightning. Jake wanted to know about the two of them, whether... Good heavens! Married women couldn't teach school— it wasn't allowed. Jake wanted to know if she'd give it up and marry him.

Jake's hands tightened on her shoulders. "Sally..."

"Oh, don't, Jake. Don't," she pleaded. Her fingers curled into tight fists.

He hesitated. *Careful, old son,* he cautioned himself. *You're about to roll the universe up into a ball and toss it to her. Better take it slow and easy.* He took a deep breath to steady his voice before he dared continue. "Sally, I need to know whether you…do you care for me at all?"

"Why, of course I do, Jake. You know I do. Once I got over hating you for treating me like a child, lecturing me behind the Petermans' barn that time, I—oh, Jake, you know I like you," she finished lamely.

He groaned. God forgive him, no, he did not know. For an intelligent woman she could be unbelievably obtuse at times. "It's more than that, Sally. I need to know if you…love me."

"No," Sally said quickly.

Jake felt his world slip sideways. "Are you sure?" he pursued, his voice thickening.

"No. Yes! No."

"No, yes, *what?* Dammit, Sally, don't you ever give a man a straight answer?"

Sally twisted away from him. "Yes, I'm sure. No, I don't lo—care for you in that way. What made you think I did?"

Jake closed his fingers on her arm and pulled her toward him. "I'll tell you what made me think so—that night in the storm. What was that all about, Sally? If you don't love me, what was it that happened that night?"

"I—" Her throat closed.

Jake watched her face as she struggled for control. He'd never seen her so at a loss for words.

"It wasn't just wanting, was it, Sally? Some folks think love is just lust misspelled, but I'm not one of them. And I don't think you are, either. I think you care for me."

"Oh, Jake, you know I do. But not in that—"

"And I want to know something," he continued, his voice husky. "And I want to know it now. Today." He drew in a deep breath. "Are you ever going to marry me?"

She looked up into his face, her eyes wide. Frightened. Lordy, she was scared. Not in all the years he'd known her had he seen such fear in those darkening green eyes.

His stomach tightened, and he swore under his breath. In the silence he waited, balanced between heaven and hell like a tightrope walker. Then her lips parted.

Jake held his breath.

"A month ago," she began, "after the picnic social, you said you didn't want me."

He studied her face, trying to master his ragged breathing. "I wanted you, Sally. Hell, I'm in love with you. I told you then I wanted you in my bed, in my life. But you weren't ready. I was hoping, if I waited a while, you'd be ready by now."

Sally avoided his gaze for as long as she could. Finally he gave her a little shake and forced her eyes to meet his.

"I don't know if I'll ever be ready, Jake." Then more words spilled out all at once. "I—I'm afraid of something. I don't know what, exactly, just . . . something. I know it sounds funny, but sometimes, outside of this schoolroom, I don't know who I am. Or what I really want."

Her eyes softened suddenly into fathomless emerald pools. Jake tightened his fingers on her arm. "Whether you know it or not, Sally, that night you let yourself go with me you were closer to being your real self than you'd ever been. I know it scared you. To tell you the truth, it scared me, too. But, hell, Sally, it showed us something. Something important."

She tried to twist out of his grasp, but he pulled her toward him.

"Marry me, Sally! Let yourself love me. Marry me! You know I need you. And whether you'll admit it to yourself or not, you need me."

She was good and scared now—he could see it in her eyes. And when she opened her mouth, he knew he'd gone too far.

"No, Jake," she said, her voice quiet. "I'm not ready to get married. I think I will never be ready."

"For heaven's sake, what is it you're waiting for?"

"I'm waiting to... to find out something. Something I—oh, Jake, I don't even know what it is. I just know I've got to wait."

His voice hardened. "You think you're going to die when you're thirty-five, like your mother did, is that it?"

"No." Sally sighed. "I'm not afraid I'm going to die, Jake. I guess I'm afraid someone I... someone I care about will—" Her voice broke. "Will go away and... and leave me alone."

Jake groaned. "Sally, honey. I'm ready to settle down, raise a family. I want you to do it with me. I want us to do it together."

Sally shut her eyes against the tears that stung under the lids. An ache settled in her chest as she felt the hands holding her tremble. "I can't, Jake," she whispered. "I don't think I'll be anybody's wife. Ever. I'll teach your children, but, God forgive me, I guess I don't want to raise them."

Jake said nothing. An image of Paula Randall rose in his mind. Lately she'd been making it very clear she was available. But he didn't want Paula; it was Sally he wanted.

"You do understand, don't you, Jake?" Sally pleaded. The pain in her darkened eyes tore his insides out.

"No," he said shortly. "I don't understand. And I'm damned sure you don't, either." He kissed her, hard, and when she moved her body into his, he felt her tremble in his arms. He closed his eyes and held her. How could he live without her?

"Jake," she whispered. "I'm so sorry."

"Don't talk, Sally. Just let me hold you."

"This is—this is worse than fighting, isn't it?"

"Much worse," he said, his voice almost inaudible. "Like dust and ashes. Sometimes it's like . . . flowers, I guess. You always smell like flowers."

"I wish—I wish I could always make it like flowers for you, Jake. I really do."

Jake wrapped his arms around her and rocked her with him for a few quiet moments, back and forth, her head pressed hard against his chest, her warm breath warming his skin through the cotton shirt. For a moment he thought his heart would explode. After a while he held her at arm's length.

"Sally, years from now, when you look back, I want you to remember something."

"Yes? What is it?"

He studied her face for a long moment before he spoke. "I want you to remember this."

He pulled her into him again and bent to her, felt her mouth tremble, then open under his like soft silk. He kissed her until he thought he'd burst with need, and then released her.

"Remember that I never wanted anyone but you."
He turned toward the doorway.

When the door banged shut, Sally stood unmoving, the taste of him lingering on her lips, her throat tight with unshed tears.

Chapter Fourteen

Sally tipped the mound of sticky pie dough out onto the floured board and patted it into a rough oval. In the past three days she'd made eight pies—four apple, two peach and two wild blackberry. This would be the ninth. She was a bit restless, she acknowledged as she divided the dough into two portions and flattened one with her fist. Well, maybe more than a bit.

The truth was, now that school was out for the summer, she felt at a complete loss. She missed planning her lessons, missed her pupils, even missed correcting essays after supper each night.

She reached for the rolling pin and skimmed it over the blob of pastry, pressing it into a ragged circle. Heavens, whatever would she do with herself until the fall term? She couldn't just bake pies all summer, and she'd already split enough kindling to last Martha a month.

She lifted the circle of pie dough into a blue-speckled enamelware pie tin and pressed her thumb around the rim. Maybe she'd whitewash the inside of her schoolroom. The rose she'd planted near the schoolhouse door had begun to bloom the last week of school; maybe she'd plant a climbing Cecile Brunner to twine over the outhouse, too. Wouldn't the boys hate that!

Sally smiled. So what if they did? She knew her students adored her. Even the most undisciplined of the boys accepted anything she did, even her wildest, most creative schemes for teaching them to spell and do sums. Her whole life revolved around teaching.

She pushed away the twinge of pain at the memory of Jake's face when she had told him so a week ago. She loved teaching, plain and simple. Not Jake. And to think they paid her one hundred dollars a year! She'd never let on, but she'd teach for nothing if they asked her. It gave her a sense of purpose in life. A sense of who she was.

She hummed a snatch of "Green Grow the Lilacs" as she dumped a colander full of sugared blackberries into the pie shell. She sealed the top crust with her thumb, then cut two slashes in the top for the steam to escape. Just as she opened the oven door, Martha poked her head into the kitchen.

"Land o' Goshen, another pie? Your father'll bust outta his vest if you keep bakin' all summer."

Sally grinned at the housekeeper and slid the pie tin onto the rack. "Not with Hank and the twins around. By the time Pa comes in from the barn at night, only the crumbs are left!"

Martha snorted and tied a clean apron around her generous form. "You go on, now. I'll clean up. Mr. B's in the parlor, waitin' to see you."

Sally blanched. "Jake? To see me? What about?"

"Dunno. Your school, maybe—I hear tell there's been some kinda rumpus at every board meetin' all year long." Martha shook her graying head and waved Sally away from the stove. "Go on along, honey. I'll watch your pie."

Sally untied her blue-checked apron, rinsed her hands under the sink pump and smoothed back her hair. Her chest tight, she entered the parlor.

Jake rose to his feet, his gray Stetson in one hand. "Hello, Sally. I—"

"What are you doing here? There must be a thousand things to do at the Bar Y at this hour of the morning—is anything wrong?"

Jake drew in a deep breath. "There's a school board meeting at the ranch tonight, Sally. I think you should be there."

Sally studied the strained expression on his face. Something was wrong. She could see it in his eyes. "What's happened?"

"Nothing, really. Just that some of the ranchers are up in arms about your, uh, modern educational ideas. They've been jawing about it all year long, and now things are finally coming to a head. I thought you might like to be there to defend yourself."

"Defend myself!"

Jake flinched. "Things might get a little heated."

"Heated?" Sally's throat closed. She'd known that some of the parents of her pupils had questioned her methods. Ladislaw Wolnowsky would never understand why his son suddenly preferred reading poetry to mucking out the stable. But there were others—Olla and Dutch Hendricks, George Peterman, and the Bakers, who brought their daughter Elsa all the way out from town in a wagon each day so she could learn to "read proper." Surely there were more parents for her than against her?

She turned toward the tall rancher. "Oh, Jake, I didn't want this to happen. What should I do?"

"Just be there. Eight o'clock. Olla'll serve cake and coffee." He patted her shoulder. "I'd lay my money on you any day. Once you put your mind to something, your opponents won't stand a chance."

He gave her a lopsided grin. "Try not to worry."

Sally groaned as he headed for the door. Don't worry, indeed. Teaching was her whole life. How could she *not* worry? It meant everything to her.

Jake stopped in the open doorway and faced her, surveying her jeans and worn shirt. His grin widened. "Be sure to wear a petticoat, Sally. You may not teach like a run-of-the-mill schoolmarm, but I think maybe you should try to look like one."

In spite of herself, Sally laughed. "I promise. I'll dress the part. And . . . and I'll try to keep my mouth shut."

"I'll believe that when I see it." Chuckling, Jake pulled the door shut behind him.

Sally listened as his boots thudded down the porch steps and onto the gravel walk. She *would,* she swore to herself. She'd wear her white lace blouse and a dark blue bombazine skirt and act the perfect lady. She'd be polite and friendly, and she'd try like anything not to open her mouth. It would be a struggle, but she'd do anything, absolutely anything, to make sure she was allowed to teach her pupils next September.

Tensing her stomach muscles against the panic she felt rising in her belly, she went to fetch the iron and heat it on the hot stove.

Sally tugged the blue wool shawl tighter across her shoulders and stepped through the open front door of the Bar Y ranch house. She was glad the meeting was here. Jake's house always seemed quiet and serene to her, a sharp contrast with the rambunctious Maguire household with Louisa buzzing continuously on her sewing machine or playing Schubert sonatas on the piano, and the Blane twins tearing about in their rough-and-tumble games.

A sharp pain lanced through her. Jake's house would be like that, if he had a family—noisy and full of life. He wanted a wife, children. He needed a family. He seemed so alone at times. Different.

Sally could never figure out why Jake seemed to stand out from the other ranchers in the valley. Maybe it was his back East education. She would enjoy teaching his children, if he ever had any. With a father like Jake, she knew they would understand the value of the finer things in life—music and art.

But, she thought with a sigh, that would all be in some future year. Right now she had problems of another sort.

Her shoulder muscles tightened. To control the tension that knotted her belly, she raised her head and took in a deep breath. Nobody was going to frighten her away from her schoolhouse. Nobody.

Jake met her in the front hallway. He didn't say a word, just looked at her and smiled. His eyes, so deep a blue they looked like soft black moss, flared briefly as he lifted the shawl from her shoulders and let his gaze roam over her lace blouse. The look was gone in an instant, replaced by a studied calm. Sally winced at the pain in his eyes.

"Glad you're here," he murmured. "The vultures are assembled in the parlor. Watch out—they're out for blood."

"I'm sorry I'm late," she whispered. "Flapjack threw a shoe just as I left the barn."

"Just as well," Jake breathed. "Gave them a chance to sort out their feelings before you got here." He ushered her into the already crowded parlor.

All conversation ceased.

"You sit here, Miss Sally," Dutch Hendricks whispered. In silence Sally took the chair vacated by the bobbing Dutchman. "Haf some of my Olla's lemon cake mit us. Vill be good cake!"

Sally smiled at the wrangler, then froze as a voice boomed, "What's she doin' here, Jake? This here's a school board meeting, not a social gathering."

Sally recognized George Peterman's deep, forthright bass and sucked in her breath. She always thought of the Petermans as friends. Neighbors, at least. But she suddenly realized neighborliness had nothing to do with this. Evidently, George had come to disapprove of her teaching.

"Fair's fair, George," Jake said, his tone mild. "The way I see it, if someone's accused of not doing his— her—job right, they ought to be allowed to confront their accusers."

An uneasy hum circled the room. Jake waited for things to quiet down, and Sally took the opportunity to glance about her. Dutch and Hank Blane, to her left, exchanged looks as Emma Wardwell hunched her chair closer to George's and leaned over to whisper in his ear.

A prickle traveled up Sally's spine. Widow Wardwell had three daughters at her school. None of them ever arrived on time or attended more than two consecutive days. Their spotty attendance explained their lackluster performance and, except for the youngest girl, Letitia, none of them showed any aptitude for learning whatsoever.

George nodded and motioned to Tommy Pearson. "You want to make the motion, Tom?"

Tommy shrank into his chair. "I, uh . . ." He flashed an embarrassed look in Sally's direction, and his face flamed. "I kinda thought you'd want to do it, George, seein' as how it was your idea in the first place."

George opened his mouth, but before he could utter a word, another voice interrupted. "I do it." Ladislaw Wolnowsky jerked to his feet. "I—me and my wife—we want no more Miss Sally to teach our Bobby."

Emma Wardwell nodded her gun gray head in agreement.

Hank Blane slammed his fist into the chair arm. "Now wait just a darn—"

"Nothing against you personal, Sally," Emma began, her tired voice dropping even lower. "It's just that my girls need practical learning, things that ranch wives need to know. Cookin' and canning and—"

"How to raise chickens and birth a calf," George finished for her. He directed his gaze at Sally. "We hear your teachin's kind of dreamy-like. Not practical. Hell, my son's got his head so far in the clouds he can't saddle a horse without gettin' it on ass-backwards!"

Sally blinked in amazement. "You want me to teach Billy how to saddle a horse?" The words were out before she could stop them. She glanced at Emma. "And how to clean chickens and iron dresses? Don't you care if your children can read and write?"

Tommy Pearson squirmed on the sofa next to George. "Now, Miss Sally, Emma didn't mean that exactly—"

"Did, too!" Emma snapped.

"Emma, vait a minute." Diminutive, bearded Reuben Crees shook a bony forefinger at the angular woman opposite him. His daughter, Katrin, could barely speak English, but there were no mathematics problems she could not do in her head. Sally waited to see what he'd say.

"The chiltren need to learn dose t'ings, too, but dey should learn dem at home, Emma. School, it iss for..." He searched for a word. "Upper t'ings. You know... higher, dat's it—I mean higher t'ings."

"Like what?" George boomed. "Silly poems and drawin' up maps of places we never heard of and aren't never gonna visit?"

Sally had to bite her tongue to keep from responding. So George was upset because of Billy's failure in geography.

She glanced at Jake. At the imperceptible shake of his head, she clenched her fists in her lap. *Let them argue it out,* his look said. *You can't reason with people when they're angry.*

She knew he was right, but it took all her willpower not to speak up.

Sol Baker shot to his feet. "My Elsa, she learned to read from Miss Sally in one month—one month! I think she's goin' to be a teacher one day, too. Her mama is so proud. It is a good thing, education. It is good to know about the rest of the world!"

"Is better to know about a ranch," Ladislaw Wolnowsky shouted. "The world, it never go away. A ranch, now." He thumped one heavy boot on the floor. "When it does not rain for years and years, a ranch will go away. Better you should know about t'ings right here."

"Den you are a fool!" Dutch retorted. "Dis iss a new country, Lad, not like the old ones you and I know. Ve get along better here, I t'ink, because ve can send sons to school. For free! Oh, excuse, please, Emma—daughters, too. For free! And maybe dey learn iss better way of life dan in old country? I t'ink Miss Sally, she know what she iss doing. Our son Donald, he writes, all the time writes. I bet he maybe be writer when he iss big."

George leapt to his feet. "Ranchin' ain't good enough for him?"

"Ve do not own a ranch, Mr. Peterman," Dutch said quietly. He turned watery blue eyes on George. "Olla and I, ve vork for Mr. B. Maybe if my son has more education, he von't haf to vork for anyone else. He vork for himself, maybe."

Sally's heart swelled in sympathy for the man. Uneducated as he was, Dutch still understood. But the others?

She cast a wary gaze around the room. Emma Wardwell regarded her in stony silence, while Ladislaw Wolnowsky fiddled with his bushy mustache, his eyes on the floor.

George Peterman raised his hand, as if to call the gathering to order. An awkward quiet descended.

Sally concentrated on the ticking of the clock on the fireplace mantel until she thought she'd scream. Finally Jake cleared his throat.

"Anyone have anything else they want to get off their chest?"

Silence.

"Then I suggest we come to grips with the basic issue that's brought us all here tonight. Some of you seem to feel Miss Maguire's teaching methods are too...advanced for the Honey Creek school. As parents and school board members, you have the right to hire the teacher. But as I see it, you don't have the right to tell her how, or what, to teach. So the question you've raised is this—do you want to hire Miss Sally Maguire to teach the Honey Creek school for another year?"

"Yes!" Dutch Hendricks shouted.

"No!" A chorus of voices rose in opposition.

Jake glanced at Sally and lifted one eyebrow. He was asking her if she had anything to say. Did she! She'd like to tell them all a thing or two.

Oh, heavens, what should she do? She had to speak out, had to defend not only her ideas, her methods, but education in general. But she couldn't afford to lose her temper. She raised her gaze to Jake's face and saw him nod his head. Without further thought, she rose from her chair.

"Mrs. Wardwell, gentlemen," she began. "I know you think it forward of me to come here tonight, but the truth is that I'm just as concerned about your children's future as you are. And whether you believe it or not, we're all on the same side."

She paused and looked about her, trying to make eye contact with every single parent in the room. Emma Wardwell's eyes hardened into two black stones, and Sally saw her give George a nudge in the ribs with her elbow. Emma ran her ranch alone. The overworked mother of three lonely, undisciplined adolescent girls would be hard to win over.

George, too, seemed unreachable. Next to him, Lad Wolnowsky scuffed a boot heel back and forth across the polished wood floor. The scraping sound ceased when Sally opened her mouth to continue.

"It's hard to explain what education really is, what it's 'good for' in life out here in Oregon. And it's harder still to point out the benefits of knowledge to people who haven't had much..."

Lad's head jerked up. "Go ahead, you can say it, Miss Sally. Haven't had much—any—education themselfs." A dull red color suffused his neck.

Out of the corner of her eye Sally saw Jake roll his eyes skyward. She'd gone too far.

"Mr. Wolnowsky, I mean no harm or insult to you, or to anyone else who has had little formal schooling. But surely you want better for your children?"

"Sure, we want better," George blurted. "Just not so crazy-like."

The knot in Sally's stomach tightened. She was going to have to fight hard to keep her position as schoolteacher. "Let me be honest," she began, her throat tightening. When George groaned, she pinned him with a look and willed herself to stay calm. "There is a difference between what is taught and how it is taught. What some of you don't like is how I teach. Others disagree with my choice of what your children need to know."

"Damn right!" someone muttered.

Sally ignored the laughter that followed. "I believe—" she raised her voice as she did in the classroom to command wandering attention "—I believe that everyone should be able to do three things. One—say clearly what they mean and understand what others say. Two—understand where each of us came from and how hard we worked to get where we are. And three—be a part of our community and our state. And our world."

George opened his mouth to interrupt, but Sally stared him into silence. Looking straight at him, she continued. "If your son plans to work your ranch some day, won't it help him to know how hard his father worked? How he treated people? Mr. Peterman, that's why I teach history—so we can all know where people came from, how they lived and why they lived that way. And when your sons and daughters have grown up—"

"Hell, they grow up anyway, schoolin' or no schoolin'," George retorted.

Sally drew in a long breath and pressed on before anyone else could interrupt. "You're right, Mr. Peterman. At least in part. We all live here in Hope Valley. Some of us came from far away—" she slanted a glance at Lad Wolnowsky "—and some of us, like myself, were born right here in Honey Creek. We all have different backgrounds, maybe even religions. It doesn't take a school—or a schoolteacher—to be educated."

She glanced quickly at George. "What it takes is to know what it was like before we came, to have some clear idea of what we may do next, and skill in reading, spelling, arithmetic and geography that will help us do what we want to do in life. It's these things that I try to teach your children."

Sally stopped and gazed at Emma Wardwell. An odd, closed expression descended over the tanned, weathered features of the older woman, but not before Sally caught a glimpse of something startling in her eyes. Fear. Emma was afraid of the future, afraid her daughters would leave her to run a ranch she couldn't manage on her own.

She moved her gaze to George, then to Lad and Tommy Pearson. Lad stared down at the toe of his boot. Tommy stared at her, his pudgy cheeks a bright pink, his pale blue eyes puzzled. Oh, it was no use. They didn't know—or even care—what she was talking about!

But across the room, Jake caught her gaze and held it. A half smile crinkled his lips and he gave her a surreptitious thumbs-up sign. Well, at least *he* understood. Not that it would do her any good when it came to a vote—the board president voted only in case of a tie.

"Now," Sally continued, "as for my methods." Her voice trembled, and she stopped to draw in a steadying breath. At the back of the room Jake gave her a smile. *Give it all you've got,* he seemed to say.

"My methods might seem unusual—"

"Harrumph!" Emma interjected. "Just plain back East addlepated, in my opinion!"

Sally blanched. It wasn't working. Nothing she said seemed to make a dent in their way of thinking. Well, she wouldn't give up without a fight. If that's what it took to teach another year in Honey Creek, she'd do it. This wasn't much different than trying to ride a green horse, she told herself. Just more difficult. She'd just have to climb back in that saddle and try again.

"Maybe my methods are unorthodox. But it's my father, Thomas Maguire, who's responsible, not the teachers' seminary in St. Louis. Pa always says you catch more flies with honey than with vinegar. And that's what I try to do with my pupils' lessons. I try to make learning interesting. Fun. It's true, we do make up rhymes and play games to test the students' ability to do sums, and we act out scenes from a poem or a story and hold spelling bees and—"

"Rhymes about what?" Tommy Pearson interrupted.

"People's names, that's what!" Lad glowered at his boots. "*Last* names."

"Yeah?" Tommy shot Lad an interested look.

"Yeah," Lad growled. "Know what rhymes with Wolnowsky? *Old sow tree!*"

Sally's heart sank. It had been an exercise in counting and sounding out syllables, to help in spelling. She should never, never have chosen the name of the most sensitive foreign-born rancher in the valley to illustrate. Her pupils had had a field day.

"Old sow tree!" George chortled. "That's rich. By God, Miss Sally sure was in the lead when tongues were handed out."

Sally felt her control slip. She would *not* lose her temper! "It probably was a silly thing to do," she admitted. "But it worked. Did you know that your son Bobby came up with the longest word of the day? Supercilious. It has five syllables."

Lad seemed unimpressed. "Super silly? That's a real word?"

George guffawed, and when the others joined in, Sally felt tears sting under her eyelids.

Jake stepped forward. "Okay, folks, we've heard how you feel, and we've heard what Miss Maguire offers by way of explanation. What do you say we resolve the matter and have some of Olla's cake and some coffee?"

"Let's vote on it," George bawled. "Yes, Miss Sally stays. A No vote means she doesn't. I vote No!"

Sally gasped. Surely they wouldn't—couldn't—vote to fire her? Jake's troubled eyes met hers. They could. Now it would depend on how much support she had garnered by her speech. Dear God, she prayed it would be a majority.

"I vote Yes for Miss Sally," Dutch called out.

"Me, too. Not just anybody could handle my twins the way she does," Hank Blane offered. "And they're learnin', too!"

Emma waved one arm. "I vote No!"

"No from me, too," echoed Tommy Pearson. He ducked his head to avoid Sally's eyes.

Both Reuben Crees and Sol Baker voted for her, and Sally felt a glimmer of hope. The vote was now four to three in her favor. Only Lad Wolnowsky had not yet voted.

An uneasy quiet descended over the room as everyone waited for the stocky Russian to speak. Sally thought she would pop if it stretched out another second.

"Lad?" Jake prompted at last.

Lad raised his gaze from the floor and gave Sally a long look. "I vote No."

An ache built in Sally's chest. Could this really be happening? Could the board remove her from her job as teacher? Never let her set foot in her schoolroom again, just when Elsa Baker had started to read? Oh, there were so many wonderful books she'd planned to introduce this next term. And Billy Peterman—she'd find some way to spark his interest in geography, she swore she would. Oh, she simply couldn't bear not to teach!

The vote was four to four. Jake would have to break the tie. Sally closed her eyes. What irony! Just a week ago Jake had begged her to give up the school and marry him. Now he held her future in his hands. Would he vote No, hoping she'd change her mind about becoming his wife?

She glanced across the room to where he stood, looking oddly at ease amidst the tension in the room. No, she thought. Jake wasn't that way at all. Jake was known to be the most fair-minded man in the county. He didn't let outside things influence him. He'd vote his conscience.

His conscience? Good heavens! He'd never given her the least hint about what *he* thought of her methods. As president of the school board, Jake had spent more time in her classroom than any of the assembled parents. She knew how he felt about her, personally. But what did he think about her *teaching?* Did he approve of her as the Honey Creek schoolmistress?

Oh, she felt so alone! Nobody understood, nobody knew how much it meant to her to continue teaching in the fall. She cared about her pupils as if they were somehow part of her own family. And the feeling she got in the pit of her stomach when an idea took hold, when Elsa or Robbie or even Billy Peterman got excited about what they were learning that day, that heady rush of emotion and pride in having done something valuable, something that mattered far beyond the day-to-day struggle of ranch life in eastern Oregon—she couldn't live without it. It was what she loved most in life. It was where she belonged.

She sucked in a deep breath and met Jake's eyes. He was smiling.

Suddenly she didn't want to know what he thought. She just wanted him to put his arms around her.

George Peterman shattered the silence. "We've got a tie vote, Jake. You gonna step in and break it?"

Jake moved to the center of the room. "I am," he said quietly.

"Well?" George exhaled noisily. "Come on, man. Let's get this over with."

Jake paused and sent Sally a long, penetrating look. Keeping his gaze on her, he cleared his throat and spoke to the expectant board members.

"Despite her rather... interesting methods, Miss Maguire is a fine teacher. I've spent time watching her, and I've seen the results." He gave Sally a lopsided smile. "Also, she's extremely dedicated. In my opinion, such a teacher is worth her weight in gold. No one in his right mind would try to keep her out of a schoolroom. I vote that she stays."

Sally closed her eyes tight. Relief washed through her like cool rainwater. Jake understood. Absurdly, she wanted to cry.

She opened her eyes to see Jake watching her, an odd, pained expression on his face.

He held her gaze for a long moment, then turned to his guests. "Okay, folks, that's it. Olla, let's have some of that cake!"

Chapter Fifteen

Louisa stepped out of the ivory silk wedding dress and arranged it with care across the foot of the bed. "It's just perfect," she said with satisfaction. She turned to Sally and adjusted the hem of the peach silk dress she had made for Sally. "And, if you ever want it, it'll fit you, too, Sally. We're the same size."

"I won't ever need it, Lou. I'm the schoolmistress. I'm never going to marry."

Was it just a month ago Jake had asked her to marry him? School was out for the summer, and she and Louisa had been so busy with plans for the wedding, Sally had hardly had time to think. Well, that wasn't quite true. She found herself thinking about Jake quite a bit. Then, before she knew it, it was the day before the wedding. Tomorrow Louisa would become Mrs. Will Boessen.

Louisa knelt before her, her mouth full of pins. At her tug, Sally rotated a quarter turn to the left. "Don't move," Louisa muttered. She pressed the pincushion into her hand.

Sally stared at the top of her sister's golden head. Everyone in the valley had been invited to the wedding. Martha had been baking for a week, and in between long afternoons of sewing with Louisa, Sally had pitted buckets of cherries and sliced apples for pies. Just this morning she had risen early to ice three chocolate layer cakes.

Shorty had pruned up the branches of the apple trees in the backyard so the wedding guests could walk under them, and had helped her father widen the road in front of the house to accommodate the additional horses and buggies he expected from town.

Louisa moved through the turmoil in her usual calm manner, unruffled by last-minute changes in plans, unperturbed even when Reverend Mathews came down with the grippe. Louisa sent him some peppermint tea and was sure he would recover in time.

Louisa, Sally thought with a tinge of envy, was sure of everything.

The ceremony would be held outside. Sally craned her neck to peer out the open window in her sister's yellow-wallpapered bedroom. The rose garden blazed with scarlet Tuscany and pale pink Celsiana roses. Golden honeysuckle and pale peach blooms of the climbing Belle of Portugal intertwined on the fence enclosing the backyard.

"Hold still," Louisa mumbled over the pins. Sally sighed and patiently made another quarter turn to the left. She tried to stand as motionless as possible while Louisa pinned the hem of her bridesmaid's dress.

The odor of vanilla-scented roses hung on the balmy air. Sally drew in a shaky breath and closed her eyes. For some reason she felt like crying.

Louisa repositioned Sally and made a quick mark with her dressmaker's chalk. "Jake's going to stand up with Will, as best man," she said carefully to Sally's back. The rustle of silk petticoats ceased. Sally retied the peach taffeta petticoat at her waist with hands that shook. She knew Jake would be at the wedding tomorrow. She longed to see him, yet dreaded it, all at the same time. "Why are you telling me this?"

Louisa shook her pale hair back from her face and took up the dress hem again. "I thought it might matter some." Her voice was quiet and cool, as always.

"Matter? Why should it matter?" Sally snapped.

Louisa sighed and rested the hem in her lap as she gazed up at her sister. "Because, you goose, as I've been trying to tell you for months now, you're in love with him."

"That's ridiculous!" Sally blurted. "I most certainly am not in love with him!"

"Oh, yes, you are, Sally. You've been in love with Jake Bannister since you were fourteen years old. I never saw anyone work so hard to hate someone in my whole life."

In love with him? In love with Jake? Impossible. Sally stared at her sister's head bent over the peach silk material spread across her lap.

She had not seen Jake since the school board meeting in his parlor. And, she acknowledged with a start, she had missed him. Missed him!

But that didn't mean she… No! Of course she didn't. She would never let herself love anyone.

But even though she had not wanted to admit it to herself before, had not wanted to remember the pain in Jake's eyes, the ache in his voice when he told her he loved her, had never wanted anyone but her, when she saw his anguish at her refusal, it hurt, deep inside. She cared how he felt. At times she cared more about how he felt than about her own distress.

Sally gasped. Was that what love, real love, was? It wasn't just wanting a man, though that was certainly part of it. Was it that warmth she felt whenever she saw him, that strange, humming happiness that flowed through her when she was near him?

She didn't want to love him, didn't want to love any man. It had just sort of crept up on her, taken her unawares. But it was true. She had never, ever, wanted anyone but Jake.

The realization hit her as if a horse had just kicked her in the chest. Dizzy, she shut her eyes. She didn't *want* to love him.

But she did. The wedding was tomorrow, and Jake would be there.

A hard bud of joy swelled in her throat, and for a moment her breath stopped. Yes! She *was* in love with him. The truth resonated deep within her, as clear and strong as her physical yearning for him these past weeks. She loved him! Why had she not acknowledged it before? Was it because she'd been frightened of life, real life? Because it was unknown? Unpredictable?

What a fool she had been. What a damned fool. She wanted to be with him, share his life, even if she *was* frightened.

"Lou, I've got to tell him!"

Louisa was silent. Then she rose and reached a smooth hand to Sally's bare arm. "Sally, I had to tell you about Jake because . . . He'll be coming tomorrow, for the wedding, and you had to know—" She broke off.

"Had to know what?" A cloud settled over Sally's heart.

Louisa tightened her hand and sought her sister's eyes. "Honey, Jake's going to marry Paula Randall."

"Paula!"

"Yes." Louisa sighed. "Paula."

"But he can't! He—"

Louisa smoothed her hair. "He wanted you, Sally. I know he did. Will told me he doesn't think Jake's slept for a month. He gets up in the middle of the night and rides that black gelding of his all over the county. Someone saw him at Sweetwater the other night at three o'clock in the morning. He loved you, Sally, and you threw it away."

A lancet of pain pricked her heart. "Why tell me all this now," she asked, weeping, "now that he's going...going to marry Paula?" She smoothed the tears off her cheek with one trembling hand.

Louisa fixed her sister with a look. "Don't let him," she said simply.

Aghast, Sally stared at her sister. "Whatever do you mean, Lou?"

"Just what I said, honey," Louisa repeated. "Don't let him."

Sally turned away, struggling to hide her anguish. Don't let him? How in the world could she stop him?

Sally avoided her sister's eyes all during supper that evening. "But I don't *want* to go to the social," she explained to Louisa and Will for the twentieth time in the parlor after the meal. "Everybody will be there, and there'll be music, and dancing, and—"

"And Jake," Louisa supplied. "Jake will be there." She handed Sally her blue wool shawl. "It's just a pie social, Sally, not a big whing-ding. And since you didn't bake anything to bring, you won't have to eat with anybody, or talk to anybody if you don't want to."

"Lou, sometimes you are the most..."

Sally's voice trailed off as Louisa smiled at her. "Sally, Will and I want you to come. The social's in our honor. Naturally, you don't have to go if you don't want to. We just thought you might."

"Yes, I guess I might." Sally looked into her sister's face. "Remember the day we threw all the dishes out the window? It seems so long ago. Tonight I feel like doing it all over again!"

Louisa's arms reached out to Sally, and suddenly they were hugging each other, alternately laughing and crying.

Will looked uncomfortably puzzled until Tom appeared in the doorway. "Don't trouble yourself, son. We'll never understand them." He drew the Bar Y foreman into the study.

Sally gave her sister a final hug. "Oh, all right, Lou. You and Will go on ahead in the wagon with Pa. I'll ask Shorty to saddle up the bay and I'll ride over later."

Jake stood in the far corner of Peterman's barn, talking with Nate Randall, while George tuned up his fiddle. He felt restless and empty. Lonely. The pies had all been auctioned, and couples had drifted off together to share huckleberry or gooseberry tarts and thick wedges of the rhubarb or cherry or apple pies the women had baked that afternoon. Will Boessen had had to shell out ten silver dollars for Louisa's cherry pie. Even though they were to be married the following afternoon, Will still had to fight for the privilege of eating dessert with his bride-to-be.

He wondered where Sally was. He hadn't seen her during the auction, and that bothered him. He felt tense and out of sorts. Hungry, he acknowledged. But not for pie.

He needed to see Sally. With a jolt he realized he would always need to see her. He knew now that she was never going to marry him. He'd waited the longest weeks in his life for her to change her mind. He'd even imagined how it would be.

She would saddle her bay and ride over to his ranch, fling herself into his arms. Night after night he lay awake thinking about her, wanting her, until he couldn't stand it any longer. Will joked that if Jake didn't get more sleep, he'd have to get another best man. Louisa wouldn't want anyone snoring during the ceremony.

He didn't know exactly when he'd given up on Sally. One evening he'd ridden into town to see Nate Randall about some mares he wanted. Paula had insisted he stay to supper, and the next thing he knew, he found himself engaged to her. In a moment of weakness he'd mentioned settling down some day, and Paula had accepted on the spot.

But even when he was married to Paula, Jake knew he would still need to see Sally—just see her—occasionally. Now he listened to Nate with only half an ear and tried not to think about the Honey Creek schoolmistress.

Suddenly the older man stopped talking in midsentence. "Son of a gun, that Maguire girl has turned into a real beauty!"

"Don't get your hopes up, Nate." Jake laughed. "She's marrying my foreman on Sunday."

"No," the judge breathed. "Not Louisa. The older girl, Sally."

"Sally!"

"Now that you and Paula have an agreement, surely you don't have any objections to my paying court to Sally Maguire, do you, son?"

Jake glanced at the rapt expression on the judge's face, then turned to look in the direction Nate stared.

Sally moved slowly across the barn toward her father and sister seated on a pine bench near the refreshment table.

Jake's first glimpse of her knocked the breath out of him. She wore a simple, soft-looking blue dress, with a ruffle of white lace outlining the low neckline and elbow-length puffed sleeves. The gored skirt clung to her hips, then fell away from her slim body in graceful folds when she walked. Her hair was piled up on her head, as usual, but tiny tendrils had escaped the pins and curled invitingly on her bare neck.

Jake started involuntarily. God, he wanted to smooth his fingers down her exposed skin.

He certainly did have objections to Nate's interest in Sally, but he had forfeited his right to object.

He stared at Sally and felt his entire body tighten.

Chapter Sixteen

Jake watched Nate Randall's eyes devour Sally, and a stab of irrational jealousy pierced him. He didn't want anyone else to admire her, see how beautiful she was. Or how desirable. He knew he had no claim to her, but God knew he didn't want anyone else to lay a finger on her. "She's too young for you, Nate," he heard himself say.

The judge chuckled. "Maybe not. My Mary was younger than I was by quite a few years. I hear Miss Sally thinks like a lawyer and dances like an angel. I'd say that's a most interesting combination."

Jake clenched his jaw and turned away. He had to get his mind off her. She wouldn't have him, but she'd not be likely to have anyone else, either. The thought didn't help. He still longed for Sally with every fiber of his being. His hands balled into fists, and he jammed them into his jeans pockets and moved away in search of Paula.

Sally danced almost every dance, but her mind wasn't on either the music or her various partners. Once George Peterman got his fiddle warmed up, he whirled through waltzes and polkas and reels at a dizzying rate. Sally never lacked for partners as long as she didn't talk.

Somehow the minute she opened her mouth, men drifted away.

Tonight, though, she didn't feel like talking, and with the pace George's fiddle set, she scarcely had time to breathe between sets. Even Judge Randall asked her for a waltz, and then another. Unlike most of the men in the valley, the judge didn't seem to mind if she talked while she danced. He even encouraged her. But for some reason, she didn't have much to say.

Over the judge's broad shoulder she searched for Jake. And when she found him, she looked quickly away. He had his back to her, talking to Paula Randall.

Sally danced again with Ned Barker, then Nebraska claimed her for a polka. Judge Randall asked for another waltz, and at last her father came for her to head up the grand reel with him.

Late in the evening the fiddler began a slow ballad, and without quite knowing how it happened, Sally found herself in Jake's arms.

He had removed both his jacket and dark leather vest and rolled his shirtsleeves up to his elbows. His arms as he held her grazed her rib cage, and she felt his body heat through the thin material of her bodice. A little ache started deep down in her belly, and she closed her eyes. He smelled of leather and pine soap. For a moment she didn't think she could stand being this close to him and not wind her arms around his neck.

Neither of them spoke, and they danced a long while in silence.

He had to touch her, Jake acknowledged. Had to. No wedding with Paula was ever going to erase that need. He didn't want to say anything to her, just wanted to touch her, hold her.

As if reading his thoughts, Sally looked up at him. "Jake," she whispered, "could you—"

"No," he said quickly. Then after a pause, he groaned. "Yes," he amended. He pulled her close to him, close enough to rest his cheek against her hair, smell that lilac-spicy scent and feel the fluttering of her heartbeat against his chest.

She sighed and missed a step. Jake tightened his arms around her and closed his eyes. She was trembling. What the hell was he doing? He had to stop this! *God in heaven,* he prayed, *help me walk her to the edge of the floor and go find Paula.*

But he couldn't. She moved in his arms, her body in tune with his, and he was powerless to break the spell. He heard her light, shallow breathing quicken, and he moved his mouth near her temple.

"Jake—"

"Don't talk, Sally. Just be with me for a while. I have to go back to Paula soon. Just be here with me, for now."

Jake! She wanted to scream. *I love you, Jake! I don't ever want you to let me go!* Why couldn't she tell him how she felt? *Why?* She parted her lips and drew an unsteady breath into her painfully dry mouth.

"Sally," Jake murmured. "Don't say anything to stop this."

"I wasn't," she said softly. "I was going to tell you—"

"Sally, don't."

"But—"

"We're getting into deep water, honey. Just dance with me, okay?" He ran his palm down her spine.

"Oh, Jake, I want you so much!"

His body stilled instantly. "I know," he said. "That's what makes this such heaven and such hell at the same time." He closed his eyes and spoke quietly into her hair. "Sally, if I ask you to do something for me, will you?"

"What is it?"

"Step away from me. Then turn around and walk away. I've got to get you out of my arms."

She hesitated for a heartbeat. "Yes, Jake. I will. But you know that I still want you. I—"

"Now, Sally," he urged, his voice hoarse. "Do it now."

Sally looked up into his face and saw the pain in his eyes. She'd do anything he asked if only he wouldn't look at her like that.

She let her hands slide down to his forearms, let them rest there for a moment on his warm skin. Then she took one step backward, turned away from him and walked deliberately to the edge of the floor.

He didn't see her go. He kept his eyes closed.

Sally gave the porch swing another nudge with her toe and concentrated on not spilling the contents of the bottle cradled in her hand. The ruby liquid sloshed near the top, and she gulped down a double swallow of the fiery, sweet liquor. Her tongue tingled, then heat spread through her mouth and into her throat.

She leaned her head back against the swing cushion and closed her eyes, listening to the crickets. Tears slipped down her cheeks. She had left Jake in the center of Peterman's barn and walked resolutely away from him, away from his warmth, his arms, his hard body molding itself to hers. The instant she separated herself from him she felt cold, as if an intangible bond between them had been broken. When she left him, she felt desolate. Now she waited for the liquor to take the edge off her pain.

When she had downed her first mouthful, her father ambled up the path from the barn. After one look at her ravaged face and the bottle of sloe gin from his liquor cabinet, he tramped up the steps into the house. A moment later he returned to the porch with a wine goblet.

"Ought to at least drink it out of a glass, honey-girl. It's more ladylike." He chuckled, rolled himself a cigarette and sat down next to her in the dark. "Also, stretches it out a bit."

Abruptly, Sally turned her head into her father's chest. "Oh, Pa, what's wrong with me?" she sobbed.

Tom wrapped one arm around his daughter and patted her shoulder. "Nothing's wrong with you, honey. You just haven't learned yet how to handle what you've got."

He sat with her in the gently rocking swing, saying nothing, until Will brought Louisa home from the social. When Will rode out of the yard and headed toward the Bar Y, Tom rose and stretched. "Think I'll go on in to bed, honey-girl. Don't be drinkin' too much of this brew, now—it'll melt your wits."

"Sally," Louisa began, her voice hesitant. She touched Sally's arm. "Are you all right?"

Tom coughed. "She's fine, daughter. Go on upstairs to bed, now."

Louisa sent her father a quick look, then hugged Sally and followed her father into the house.

Sally poured herself another glass of the syrupy liquid. She sipped it slowly, listening to the crickets and the creak of the swing rope rubbing against the roof beam.

With each swallow, her anguish over Jake softened. Bit by bit she began to enjoy the loose, relaxed feeling the liquor brought. Her body felt warm and slow. A glow moved up from her toes, heated her thighs and settled in her belly. The yearning hunger still gnawed, but its sharpness blurred to a dull ache. Another hour and she wouldn't feel a thing. She raised the glass to her mouth and froze.

Steady hoofbeats sounded on the road in front of the house. Sally peered into the darkness. A lone rider slowed, seemed to hesitate, then reined in at the front gate.

"Jake!" Sally spluttered. "What are you doing here at this time of night?" She tipped her glass to her lips and took a swift swallow.

Jake leaned forward, resting his left forearm on the black gelding's saddle horn. He tipped his gray Stetson back with one forefinger. "I wish to God I knew, Sally. I took Paula back to town after the dance. I've been riding around the county ever since." He hesitated, then dismounted and walked up the path toward her.

When he reached the porch steps, he peered at Sally. Her cheeks glistened and looked flushed. She'd been crying. Her lips were soft looking, stained red from whatever she was drinking. He watched the flutter of the white lace around her neckline where her breast curved and had to stuff his hands into his pockets to keep from touching her.

"Come and sit down, Jake," Sally said, her voice unsteady. "Have some gin."

Deliberately he lowered his frame onto the step at her feet and took the bottle she offered.

"Would you like a glass? Pa brought me a glass. He said it would str—stretch it out."

Jake tipped the bottle up and took a long pull. "I don't want to stretch it out. I want to get good and drunk, good and fast."

"Me, too!" Sally giggled. "It feels wonderful, doesn't it? I feel all soft inside and kind of swirly."

Jake chuckled. "How much of this have you had?"

"I don't know," Sally said honestly. "I couldn't count anymore after the second glass. The more I drank, the nicer I felt."

He laughed and took another swallow, then corked the bottle and set it on the porch.

In the semidarkness Sally studied Jake's lean face. Lines of fatigue marked the areas around his mouth, and in the glow of a lamp left burning inside the house, his deep blue eyes looked almost black. "It was hard to leave you tonight, Jake. You know I didn't want to."

"I know."

"Very hard." She sipped again and leaned her head back and closed her eyes. "When I walked away, I felt cold all over. Like I did when Mama died."

Jake watched the pulse throb in the hollow of her throat. "I know," he repeated, his voice gravelly. Her skirt fluttered each time the swing rocked back and forth, and the white dust ruffle of her petticoat peeked out from underneath the blue muslin. Each puff of lilac-scented air made him dizzy. Finally he reached out one hand and stopped the swing. Oh, God, he wanted to kiss her.

"Nate Randall was quite taken with you," he said, working to keep his voice light.

She kept her eyes closed. "Nate Randall? You mean Judge Randall?"

Jake stared at the fringe of dark lashes on her cheeks. "The same. He's been lonely since Mary died."

Sally gave a little hiccup. "I thought he was just being nice, since I had no dessert partner. Why, he's old enough to be my father. Wouldn't it be funny if..." She giggled. "I'd be Paula's stepmother."

Jake's gut wrenched. "That would definitely not be funny, Sally." Sally was no older than Paula. It was not funny at all. The thought of Sally in someone else's bed was torture.

Without thinking, he rose from the step and slid onto the swing beside her.

Without opening her eyes, Sally languidly brushed her skirt aside to make room. He caught her hand, and her fingers curled warmly around his.

"Jake..." she said lazily.

"Sally, let's not talk. We always get in trouble when we talk."

Her voice softened into silk. "It's when we *don't* talk that we get into trouble, you said so yourself."

He released his breath a little at a time. "Would you like to hear about the roundup next fall?"

"No."

"Would you like me to—"

"Yes," she said dreamily.

"Oh, the hell with it!" He leaned over and kissed her. She didn't move. She tasted sweet, like ripe cherries.

"Exactly," she murmured after a moment.

"Exactly what?"

Her breath fanned his chin. "Exactly the hell with it."

He kissed her again, more slowly, and felt her mouth open under his. The glass in her hand tipped precariously. He drew away and lifted it out of her fingers and set it on the porch. Then he kissed her once more.

"Put your arms around me, Sally."

Her lids fluttered open. "Would you like me to tell you about Elsa Baker's progress in reading?" she said unsteadily.

"Not for at least an hour." His lips found the hollow at the base of her throat, and she drew in a sharp breath. He felt her body move against his, and he laced his hands into her hair, loosening the hairpins.

She pulled her arms from around his neck and reached them up, over her head. Slowly she began removing the tortoiseshell pins.

Jake watched her until he couldn't stand it any longer, then caught both her hands and brought them to his face. Her hair tumbled to her shoulders in disarray, and his breath caught. He bent his forehead against her curled fingers and closed his eyes.

"We've got to stop, Sally."

"I know," she breathed. "But I don't want to, Jake. I don't want—"

His mouth stopped her words. "You're lying," he said gently. "You do want. *I* want to stop."

"*You're* lying," she whispered against his lips.

He made a growly sound in his throat. "Prove it."

She reached her hand to his chest and unbuttoned the top button of his shirt.

His body tensed into an aching hunger. "Sally—"

She looked at him steadily and worked the second button loose.

"Sally, stop." He caught her hand and returned it to her lap. But a battle started inside him. *Don't stop, Sally,* he raged inwardly. *Don't stop!*

"Do you really want me to stop, Jake?"

"Yes." Inside his head, his brain exploded. *No! Touch me.*

"Yes." He bit out the word through gritted teeth. Then, after a long pause, he whispered another, more truthful word. "No. Honey, don't stop...."

"Jake. Oh, Jake! I don't know what you're doing to me, but I'm feeling—"

"You're drunk, Sally." He laughed softly. "Good and drunk."

"I am *not* drunk! I'm ... happy."

Watch it, old son, he cautioned himself. *The next thing you know she'll want to go swimming in the river, and right this minute that sounds like a damned good idea. In fact, that's the best idea you've had since you took Paula home.*

Jake stiffened. Paula! Oh, God. Paula.

Sally opened her eyes. "What's wrong?"

"Paula."

"Paula! Can't you forget about her for one minute?"

"That's the problem, Sally," he acknowledged, weariness making his voice grainy. "I've forgotten about her for a whole evening."

In spite of herself, Sally smiled. "You make me feel wonderful, Jake. All quivery inside, the way sloe gin tastes—sort of sweet and hot." She laughed softly and looked into his face. "Do you know what I mean?"

Her candor startled him. "Oh, God, Sally, you know I do. Would I be sitting out here with you if I didn't? Wanting you, when I should be wanting Paula? Or at the very least trying to get some sleep?"

What the hell *was* he doing out here? he asked himself. With a girl who'd got a bit of liquor inside her and who had him tied up in knots, anyway? Just what the hell was he doing? Unless he was seventeen kinds of a fool, he should get up off this porch and get away from her!

Sally sighed, and a little giggle escaped her. "I never understood before why I feel the way I do with you, Jake."

"You don't understand it now, Sally. You don't know what you're doing, honey. It's just a game with you."

"It isn't a game, Jake. I—"

He laid his finger on her lips. "Don't say it, Sally. Tonight I don't want to hear about swimming in the river with you."

"But Jake, I—"

"Sally, I think I'd better—"

"Don't think, Jake," she breathed. "Just kiss me."

He groaned. Her mouth was sweet, sweet.

"Do you think it's the gin?" she asked when she could breathe.

"I wish to hell it were." He stood suddenly and pulled her to her feet and into his arms. He held her for a moment, listening to the crickets throb in the pregnant darkness, feeling the blood thrum in his body. She was so soft against him, her flesh warm and responsive under his hands. She still wore no corset, he thought. He could feel her heartbeat through the thin bodice.

"Jake, Jake," Sally murmured. "Don't let me go." She felt the heat of his kisses all the way down to her toes.

"Don't worry, Sally. I've been trying like hell all night to do just that, but I can't." With a groan he tipped her face up and pressed his mouth against her swollen lips. Then abruptly he wrenched himself away from her and turned toward the yard.

He couldn't let himself stay, couldn't end up aching again for something he could never have. Sally had

made it painfully clear how she felt about marriage.
She'd tied his heart up in knots, all right, but he
couldn't have her, not the way he wanted, anyway—not
permanently. She was still playing a game, a dangerous
one, considering how he longed to crush her body under his.

But afterward . . . He shook his head. Afterward, she
still wouldn't belong to him. Sally Maguire would never
belong to anyone but herself. It was too late. Besides,
now he had obligations in other quarters.

Before Sally could stop him, he had mounted the
gelding and reined away from her into the road.

Shaking, she felt ice bite deep into the pit of her
stomach. Tomorrow Louisa and Will would be married. Her sister would promise to love . . . And later she
would slip into the white lawn nightgown she had
stitched and be together with the man she loved.

Feeling more bereft than she ever had in her life, Sally
listened until the crickets gradually obliterated the
sound of fading hoofbeats.

Chapter Seventeen

Louisa's wedding day dawned hot and still. Sitting across from her sister at the dining table, Sally sipped her morning coffee and nibbled at a buttermilk biscuit slathered with Martha's strawberry preserves. The ceremony, planned for four o'clock, was hours away, but already Sally was nervous. Unable to sit still, she fidgeted on the upholstered dining chair.

Louisa looked up from her plate. "For heaven's sake, Sally, sit still. I'm the one who's supposed to be nervous."

Sally sighed. "You haven't been scared of anything since you were ten years old, Lou. I guess I'm making up for it."

Louisa gave her one of her patient smiles, and Sally rolled her eyes toward the ceiling and pushed back her chair. She paced to the window and peered out at the riot of flowers blooming in the yard. "Paula Randall will be coming, won't she?"

Louisa sighed. "Nate Randall hasn't missed a wedding, or a funeral, since he was elected judge four years ago. Paula's sure to come with him."

Abruptly Sally turned to her sister. "Lou, there's

something I want to give you. It's upstairs, in Mama's old jewelry box."

"You mean Mama's old wedding band? Will ordered a ring from Chicago, but it hasn't come yet."

Louisa's face was so transparent Sally had to laugh. She grabbed her sister's hand. "Well, come on, then!"

Upstairs in the blue-papered bedroom, Sally pulled the small, velvet-covered box from the bottom drawer of her chiffonier and silently handed it to her sister. Side by side on the narrow bed, the two girls sifted through the collection of brooches and buttons and hatpins, handling each piece with reverence. At the bottom of the box, wrapped in a piece of folded tissue paper, Sally found their mother's wedding ring.

The plain gold band had a beading of tiny rosebuds circling the edge. Sally read aloud the date and an inscription engraved on the inside. "September 12, 1862. Bordered with roses." Her eyes filled. "Oh, Lou, do wear it! I should have given you all of Mama's jewelry before this, but—"

Louisa cut her off. "Sally, don't you want any of her things?"

"I—I never thought I'd need them."

"Need them?" Louisa imprisoned both of Sally's hands in hers. "But why not, honey?"

"I guess I never thought I'd grow up, Lou. For a long time I know I didn't want to."

Louisa's dark blue eyes flicked over her older sister's face. She nodded to herself and smiled imperceptibly. "Mama's ring says something special about love between two people, don't you think?"

Sally dropped her eyes before her sister's penetrating gaze and watched Louisa slip the band onto her finger.

Her heart swelled. Oh, she wanted so much for Louisa to be happy.

By three in the afternoon nearly all the guests milled about the tree-shaded backyard. When Jake and Will rode up to the front gate, the buzzing of the throng ebbed, then mounted again, louder than ever.

Sally watched from an upstairs window. Will looked a bit nervous, she thought with an inward giggle. Jake, though, looked lean and poised in his dark suit and vest. Both men wore their usual Stetsons and boots, which in honor of the day had been polished to a metallic sheen.

Jake turned toward the house, and the sight of his tanned, fine-featured face made Sally's heart jump.

"Kinda late, aren't ya, Will?" Ned Barker called. "We figured if you didn't show up in time, somebody else'd get to marry Miss Louisa." The crowd laughed, and Will saluted them good-naturedly.

Tom circulated among the guests, enjoying himself, whispering occasionally to Martha, who bustled between the kitchen and the tables set up outside, making sure there would be enough cake and lemonade for the reception. Martha had bought all the lemons at Mr. Baker's store, but she worried about running short, and it would be hours before any hard liquor was offered. Sally's hands still smelled faintly of lemon oil from slicing and squeezing the fruit earlier in the day.

Tom positioned himself near the rose arbor with Judge Randall and Reverend Mathews. Jake and Will sought the shade of the apple tree while they waited for Louisa.

Upstairs, Sally carefully arranged the folds of ivory silk over Louisa's starched lace underskirt and taffeta petticoat, then settled the sheer veil on her head, letting it drift down over her sister's pale gold hair. Louisa's face was luminous with joy, her demeanor calm, as always. She was stunningly beautiful, Sally thought with pride. Will was fortunate. For all her apparent delicacy, Louisa would make a good ranch wife.

Sally's peach silk dress rustled with her every motion. She fussed and fidgeted with the short veil until Louisa finally lifted it out of her hands and laid her fingers on Sally's arm. "Stop shaking, Sally! You'd think *you* were getting married today instead of me."

"I can't stop. Oh, Lou, I'm so nervous. Jake is here, and I—I'm going to tell him that I—" She broke off. The words she wanted so desperately to say to Jake kept getting stuck in her throat.

Louisa studied Sally's face. "Tell him what?"

"Tell him...tell him that I..." Oh, why was it so hard to say? What was so frightening about admitting you loved someone? "That I l-love him."

Impulsively Louisa reached out and hugged her. Then she took Sally's face between her cool hands and gazed into her eyes. "Yes, do that, Sally. Fight for him. He's worth it."

Sally gave a little strangled laugh. "Remember when I got bucked off that black gelding? For some reason, telling a man you love him is worse than that. Much worse!"

Louisa gave her arm a squeeze, and Sally drew in a deep breath. She linked arms with her sister, and together they moved toward the stairs.

At the landing Sally paused and turned to Louisa. Her heart caught. Louisa was so young, and life could be so unexpected. She prayed that nothing would ever hurt her. "Be happy, Lou," she whispered.

"We will," Louisa whispered back. She squeezed Sally's hand and started down the stairs.

Sally drew the folds of her full peach silk skirt out of Louisa's path, then descended the staircase a few steps behind her sister. Her thoughts whirled. Fight for him, Lou said. But how? She knew she loved him, but what should she do now?

Tell him, of course. She quailed at the thought. But, she reasoned as she followed Louisa down the stairs, she had lived through the black gelding episode. Maybe it wouldn't be so frightening after all to tell Jake how she felt about him?

But when she stepped off the back porch and saw him, standing tall and silent beside Will, her stomach clenched into a knot. She picked her way through the throng toward the rose arbor where Will waited beside Reverend Mathews.

Jake's dark blue eyes sought hers, and under the tucked peach taffeta her heart lurched. She stepped to the reverend's right, positioning herself opposite Will and Jake.

Will gave her a solemn nod. Jake's gaze never left her face.

Louisa floated through the assembled guests on her father's arm, and Sally's attention shifted. Tom's face flushed with pride as the crowd quieted, then parted to make room for him and the exquisite creature at his side.

Lou looked like an angel. Sally watched Will's eyes widen at the sight of his bride, and in the sudden silence she heard Martha begin to sniffle. The older woman pulled a lace handerchief from under her sleeve and dabbed at her eyes.

Tom stepped to one side, and Louisa moved on toward Will. Taking the hand he extended to her, she turned with him toward the waiting minister.

Jake turned his body toward Louisa, but Sally could still feel his eyes on her. Her cheeks grew warm. Trembling, she tried to concentrate on the reverend's words as the ceremony began.

"Dearly beloved, we are gathered together..."

Jake, she prayed, *please, please look somewhere else.* Her breath slowed, and warmth curled into her belly. *Don't watch me, Jake.* It must be plain as day that she wanted him, but she prayed he wouldn't see it. Not yet. Her knees felt so weak she knew she'd never make it through the ceremony if he looked at her. Desperately she strove to quiet her erratic breathing and concentrate on the minister's words.

"...join this man and this woman in holy matrimony..."

Sally looked at Louisa and Will standing together before the minister, and her pulse hammered. Suddenly she knew she was going to cry. They were so calm, so sure. So...beautiful together. Her throat ached. Tears gathered at the corners of her eyes and spilled over, sliding silently down her cheeks.

She stifled a sob and glanced away to find Jake watching her. The pain in his face tore at her, and her heart turned over. Unable to look away, she stared into his darkening eyes as if hypnotized.

"Wilt thou have this man, to have and to hold, to love and to cherish until..."

At Louisa's quiet "I will," Sally blinked hard. A moment later the minister pronounced them husband and wife, and a radiant Louisa turned to face her guests.

Sally struggled to keep her gaze from straying to Jake. She focused on her sister's face, then closed her eyes for an instant. Her whole body trembled.

The next thing she knew, Jake was beside her. He gave her a fleeting smile and offered his arm. "Miss Salty," he said quietly, inflecting the last syllable upward.

She laid her hand on his sleeve, her fingers shaking violently. Without looking at her, Jake covered her hand with his, and they followed Will and Louisa through the hushed crowd into the backyard where tables laden with food and pitchers of lemonade waited under the apple tree. George Peterman struck up his fiddle, and conversation bloomed.

"Thank God," Jake breathed. He pulled Sally around the corner of the house, away from the other guests. "I've wanted to say something to you all afternoon, but I could never get near enough."

Sally felt she could float up off the ground when he looked at her that way. Just being near him made her light-headed. In the space between their bodies an electric current sizzled. Oh, it couldn't be true about Paula and him. It just couldn't. Perhaps Louisa had been wrong.

"Sally," Jake began, "there's something I want to tell you."

She looked into his eyes and her heart stopped. What she saw was resignation. "I know," she said, her voice grainy. "It's about you and Paula, isn't it?"

Jake's pupils dilated, but his face remained impassive. "I guess you know we're getting married in a week."

His words sliced into her. She felt ice-cold inside. Dead. "In a week! Is that...is that what you wanted to tell me?"

"That's one thing, yes. And there's something else."

"Something else?" she echoed. She didn't know if she could stand anything else.

He hesitated. "I wanted to tell you how beautiful you look today. And I wanted to tell you again, Sally—I never wanted anyone but you."

She turned away from him, moving into the shade beneath the apple tree. Jake followed and stood at her back. He closed his hands on her upper arms and pulled her backward a step until she felt her spine press against his hard chest. His breath warmed the back of her head.

"Do you love her?" Her voice sounded unsteady.

Jake exhaled a long, slow breath. "No. But she knows that. I care about her, though. And she loves me. Or at least, she says she does."

"You don't feel it from her?"

"Sally, to tell you the truth, the only woman I've ever felt that with is you. You know I love you. I'll always love you." He hesitated, struggling for words. "I'll be a good husband to Paula. But I'll always love you, Sally. Always."

Her heart leapt at his words, then shrank as she realized what he was saying. He loved her, but he was going to marry someone else. Jake's fingers tightened on her arms, and she felt the warmth flow from his body into hers. It was now or never. She had to tell him how she felt.

She drew in a long, steadying breath. "Jake, there's something I've been wanting to say to you, too."

He waited, and when she didn't speak, he bent and brought his lips close to her ear. "And that is?" he whispered.

Her throat closed. Jake's warm breath ruffled the tendrils of hair on her neck. Her heart thudded in ragged, shallow beats, and for a moment her senses reeled. Then she inhaled a shaky breath and spoke the words of her heart.

"I'm in love with you."

Jake inhaled sharply, and a tremor shook his body. "Sally—"

"I didn't know it before," she blurted. "Oh, I guess I must have, underneath. Especially after... after that night in the blizzard. But I just couldn't admit it to myself. Or to you. Now I can."

She let out a long breath. She had to speak now, she told herself. Now, or remain silent forever, her secret locked in her heart. She closed her eyes. "I love you, Jake."

"Sally! Oh, God, Sally. Why tell me this now, when..." He stopped, his voice breaking.

She made a motion as if to turn toward him, but he tightened his hands to prevent it.

"You little fool. Why the hell didn't you tell me sooner? Oh, Sally..."

"Jake, kiss me!"

He groaned. "I can't, honey. I'm engaged to Paula. I promised to marry her."

For a moment Sally stood very still. Then she made a small sound and pulled away from him, one hand pressed over her mouth.

The simple gesture brought tears to Jake's eyes. "Sally," he said, his voice hoarse. "Don't go just yet."

She waited, dull pain thudding in her chest. It seemed to her that a cloud slid over the sun, dimming it to gray shadow around them, but when she looked at the grass beneath her feet, the lacework of light and dark shadow under the apple tree was still there. She closed her eyes. "Hold me, Jake. Please, hold me."

"Sally, darling..." He made a move toward her, then caught himself. "I can't let myself touch you, or I'll..."

When he spoke again, a resignation she had never heard colored his voice. "Sally, for what it's worth, you know I'll always be near, if you ever need me. I'll always be there for you, just down the road. But now that's all I can offer."

Sally turned toward the man she loved and looked up into his eyes. "You don't know what that means to me, Jake. Sometimes I feel so awfully alone." She reached out one hand, laid it on his arm. "Thank you for that."

Jake's throat closed at the sight of her ravaged face. Her cheeks glistened with a sheen of tears, but her eyes, though dark with pain, were calm. When she spoke again, her voice was very quiet.

"I will miss you all the rest of my life, Jake." She smiled up at him, a hesitant, trembling smile. "I hope you and Paula will be happy."

Deliberately she moved away, into the throng of wedding guests.

Jake watched her seek out Paula, saw her graciously extend her hand, smile, speak some words and then move away as if walking in a dream. Without looking back, Sally mounted the steps into the house.

He closed his eyes and thought his heart would burst.

Sally spent an hour in her bedroom pacing back and forth between the chiffonier and the bed, her heart leaden. Jake was going to marry Paula. He loved *her*, but he would spend the rest of his nights in another woman's bed.

Through the open bedroom window the sounds of laughter and chattering voices drifted up to her. She sank onto her bed and struggled to quiet her breathing. Never in her entire life had she felt so alone. When her father's rich tenor rose in a song, she thought her heart would break.

> "Oh, the summer time is comin',
> And the trees are sweetly bloomin'
> And the wild mountain thyme
> Grows around the blooming heather,
> Will ye go, lassie, go?"

When his voice faded away, Sally wiped her eyes and gave herself a little shake. She rose, splashed cool water on her face and fixed the hairpins in her thick, upswept hair. Then she resolutely descended the stairs again and walked out into the garden to circulate among the guests.

All the rest of the afternoon and well into the evening, Sally helped Martha serve cake and pour lemonade. Often she felt Jake's eyes on her, and she steeled herself to smile at him, and at Paula, who clung possessively to his arm. Once, Jake nodded at her over Paula's head, his eyes agonized, his smile lopsided.

When George Peterman finally packed up his fiddle and the last wedding guests had departed, Sally sank onto the front porch steps, drew her knees up and lowered her head onto her arms. She felt completely drained.

The wedding was over. Will had driven Louisa away with him in Jake's buggy, and all Sally wanted to do was weep.

She sat on the front porch without moving until it grew dark. When her father strode out the front door, eased himself down beside her and drew his cigarette makings out of his vest pocket, she looked up briefly, then buried her head in her arms.

" 'Twas a fine weddin', honey-girl."

Sally nodded without looking up. "Pa, tell me about you and Mama. Tell me about that inscription inside her wedding band."

Tom sighed and exhaled a puff of blue smoke into the soft night air. "That was a long time ago, honey. The words are from an old Irish blessing. 'May there be a road before you, and it bordered with roses.'" He inhaled on his cigarette and blew the smoke out slowly. "My life with your mother was like that, bordered with roses."

Bordered with roses. Sally's throat tightened. Life would never be like that for her. She would spend all her days loving other women's children, maybe even Paula and Jake's. Abruptly she turned her head into her father's chest.

"Oh, Pa, why is life so complicated? I feel like I got lost somewhere, a long time ago," she sobbed. "And now it's too late."

"I know, honey-girl. I know." He patted her quivering shoulders. "Lord knows, it's hell to be young."

They sat together in the dark until the crickets launched their evening serenade. Sally poured her heart out to the silent man at her side until the sound of approaching horses and a wagon made her stiffen. When it finally rolled into view, she gasped.

A motley assortment of hands from the Bar Y and Ned Barker's Lazy J crew, all more than slightly drunk, spilled over the sides of the bulging wagon. Someone was playing the fiddle—very badly, Sally noted. Raucous laughter and off-key singing split the evening stillness. A sense of foreboding washed through her.

"Evenin', Tom, Miss Sally," Nebraska roared. "Guess you won't mind if we hunt up the honeymooners and serenade 'em a bit, will you now? Up at Will's new house, are they?"

Tom grunted.

"Oh, Pa," Sally whispered, "they're going to give Will and Louisa a shivaree."

Tom nodded, his eyes twinkling.

"Pa, you've got to stop them!" she hissed. "Louisa will—"

The wagon jerked, then rolled on down the road. When it was out of sight, Sally turned on her father. "Pa, how could you? I can't imagine anything worse on Lou's wedding night than—"

"Aw, honey, let 'em go sing their hearts out at Will's place. Will and Louisa aren't there."

Sally stared at her father. "What do you mean, they're not there? Where are they?"

Tom chuckled. "Jake thought somethin' like this might happen, so he let them use the line shack he built last summer. He even laid in a supply of firewood. That cabin's way the hell up in the timber—nobody'll find 'em for a week!"

"Pa, are you sure?"

Her father grinned and patted her shoulder with one work-roughened hand. "About Jake?" He gave her a long look. "You bet I'm sure, daughter."

Sally turned away from her father's too-knowing eyes. "Pa, did you know Jake is going to marry Paula Randall?"

"Is he now," Tom observed, his demeanor unchanged. He gazed at his daughter. "Well, now, I wouldn't stake my life on that. Jake's a man of his word."

"Oh, Pa, that's just the problem! He gave his word to Paula, and now he... Oh, Pa!"

She couldn't stand to think about it for one more minute. Choking back a sob, she gathered the folds of her silk skirt in one hand and rose from the porch step. "Why do you men put such store by things like that? What's a man's word got to do with it?"

"Well, daughter, there's words and there's words. It's how we live out here." Tom chuckled as she bent to kiss him good-night. "Ol' Jake's got a healthy dose of real old-fashioned honor."

Sally shook her head. On her way to the staircase inside the house, she paused at the door to her father's study. After a moment's hesitation she crossed quickly to the liquor cabinet and lifted out the half-empty bottle of sloe gin.

"Sultana Maguire," her father's voice ordered. "Get up, now. It's half past noon. You've got to eat something."

Sally groaned and pulled the heavy quilt up over her head. "Leave me alone, Pa. I'm not hungry."

"Maybe not, honey-girl, but it's not just your breakfast that brought me up here. There's something in the yard you ought to be seein'."

"Go away, Pa. My head aches. I don't care if I never eat again."

"Don't be daft, lass. You've a hangover is all. A bit of Martha's coffee's just the thing for it. Come on, now, get yourself up."

Her eyes shut tight, Sally lowered the quilt from her face and lay still a moment. "What's in the yard that's so important?"

"You'll see" was all her father would say.

Gingerly Sally shifted her body to the edge of the narrow bed and slid one toe to the floor. She reached for her flannel dressing gown just as her father exited her room and clumped down the stairs. After a moment she sat up.

The room tilted, and she averted her eyes from the sunlight pouring in the bedroom window. Lord, her mouth felt like a dry thistle. She'd never again take a drop of spirits. Never.

When she swung open the front screen door and looked outside, she froze. Tethered to the front gatepost was the black gelding. His coat and mane shone like ebony silk, and around his neck hung a floppy red ribbon, looped into a bow. Pinned to the bow was a note.

Sally moved to where the magnificent animal stood, unfolded the paper with shaking hands, and scanned the few words. "Happy Birthday. All my love. Jake."

"But my birthday's not until—"

She stopped in midsentence. Jake had said he wanted to give her something when she had grown up. The black gelding was the gift he'd promised. Stunned, Sally stared at the beautiful creature.

The horse looked at her with soft, intelligent eyes, and Sally's control wavered. She leaned her head against its fine, warm neck.

Jake was telling her something, telling her she'd grown up at last. But it was too late. Too late for sharing a life with the man she now knew held her heart, too late for happiness in life save what she could salvage in her schoolroom.

Too late for Jake. He had given her the only thing he had left to give.

She wound both arms around the black's quivering neck and wept as if her heart would break.

Chapter Eighteen

Tom Maguire ran a callused hand through his red-brown hair and studied his younger daughter. A week had passed since the wedding; tonight, Will and Louisa had ridden by to take supper with them. The newlyweds sat side by side in the porch swing, their fingers interlaced.

Tom tilted back his chair and propped his boots on the porch railing. "Sally's taking it pretty hard," the Irishman said. "Oh, she's all right on the outside, but she's back to splittin' the kindling for Martha. And you know with Sally, that's always a bad sign."

Will turned warm gray eyes on his father-in-law. "Might get worse. Jake and Paula Randall are getting married tomorrow afternoon, in town. You goin' to the wedding, Tom?"

Tom nodded. "I don't think Sally will, though. She's held up pretty well so far, but—"

"Pa," Louisa interrupted from the swing. "This is just plain crazy. Jake's in love with Sally, not Paula. And Sally loves Jake. They should be marrying each other!"

Will sniffed. "They probably would be if Jake didn't have his honor so polished up it's blinded him. Hell, he doesn't love the Randall girl. But he said he'd marry her, and . . . well, you know Jake. Once he's given his word, he won't budge. Seems like he's got caught in his own loop.''

Louisa pushed back and forth in the swing. "I think," she said slowly, eyeing her husband with a preoccupied gaze, "it's time we did something drastic."

Tom snorted. "Drastic, now, is it? You must have something in mind, daughter, or you'd never say such a thing."

Will nodded at his wife, his eyes thoughtful. "Tom, you remember that land you offered to Jake? You said you'd been saving that hundred acres for Sally, when she and Jake got married. But now that—"

"Jake backed out of the deal we made before he got involved with Paula," the older man said. "Said he didn't care about the land, just Sally."

Will smiled. "That may be the key."

Louisa's eyes sparkled oddly. "Sally never knew about it, that . . . arrangement, did she?"

"Huh! Not on your life." Tom let his gaze rest on Louisa. "There's more under this hat than just hair, daughter."

"Pa, what if we . . ."

Tom frowned. "Surely you're not thinkin'—"

"That hundred acres is the only shotgun we've got, Pa." Louisa stopped the motion of the swing with the toe of her shoe, clasped both hands under her chin and smiled. "Let's see how far it will shoot!"

Tom regarded his younger daughter in silence, one bushy eyebrow quirking upward. "I dunno, honey. If Sally ever got wind of—"

"That's just it!" Louisa interjected. "She's *got* to get mad! When she's mad, sometimes she sees things more clearly. This may start her thinking, and then . . . Oh, I just know it's going to work!''

Tom blinked. "What's going to work, honey?" Puzzled, he glanced from his daughter to her husband.

Will nodded, a thoughtful look on his face. "Sally's gonna be mad as a hornet." He chuckled. "Everybody in the valley ought to be warned."

"That's the whole idea," Louisa said. "Otherwise, Jake's going to end up married to Paula Randall!"

Tom drew on his cigarette. "Maybe you're right, daughter. I never figured things would work out this way—Jake marrying someone else and Sally chopping wood to hide her heartbreak. You're right, we have to do something. I'd go to the moon to make Sally happy. I'll do anything."

"Anything, Pa?" Louisa smiled at him.

Tom sent his daughter a keen look. "Honey, you look like a cat that's swallowed a coupl'a dozen canaries. Why don't you spit out your idea and let an old man and his new son-in-law have some supper?"

Louisa bent toward her father. Briefly she outlined her plan.

Supper that evening seemed strained. Sally, pale and preoccupied, struggled to keep her mind on the conversation as Will and Louisa shared their plans for a start on a small herd of their own. Her father and Will discussed water and winter pasture, and the best location for the corral Will would build next spring.

Sally toyed with her fork. How could they sit there and talk about cows and fence posts at a time like this? All she could think about was tomorrow afternoon, when Jake would marry Paula Randall. Oh, it just couldn't be happening. It was *she* who loved him. Wanted him.

But it was too late. Tomorrow afternoon her life would stretch before her like an endless barren road, without Jake.

She jerked to attention at the mention of Jake's name.

"You might as well have that land, Will," Tom remarked, his tone deliberate. "Jake won't need it, now that he's, uh, going to marry Paula."

"What land, Pa?" Louisa's voice was light.

"What land?" Sally echoed.

"Oh, just some acreage with some water on it that Jake thought he might be interested in if—"

"If?" A prickle laced up Sally's spine. "If what?"

Tom's voice was careful. "Jake said he'd marry you if I'd give him a hundred acres he wanted down by the creek."

"*What?* Jake said . . . One hundred acres? To marry me?" Her voice thinned to a hard edge. "Jake said he'd marry me for. . . for land?" Her eyes blazed into emerald fire. *"For one hundred acres?"*

"Now, honey-girl . . ."

"Sally," Louisa said quietly, "the whole county's been laying bets on whether he'd pull it off or not."

"The whole county?" Leaping to her feet, Sally headed for the front door. "Shorty!" she shouted through the screen at the figure lounging on the porch step.

The handyman jerked upright. "Yes'm, Miss Sally?"

"Saddle that black for me. And be quick about it!"

Shorty snapped his jackknife shut, bolted to his feet and ran for the barn.

Sally flew to the hat rack outside the parlor, jammed her black Stetson onto her head and tore out the front door.

The screen door slammed behind her.

Will and Louisa looked at each other, then at Tom.

His eyes sparkling, the Irishman worked to suppress a smile. He took his time reaching one work-hardened hand across the table toward the sauceboat.

"More gravy?" he offered.

Never in her life had Sally ridden a horse so hard. She pounded through the Bar Y gate, her face rigid with fury, her narrowed eyes searching for Jake. And he said he loved her! How dare he bargain for her as if she was a prize heifer! *How dare he!*

She had no clear idea of what she was going to do when she found him, but she'd come up with something—something he'd never forget. She felt a bit unreal, as if she were dreaming. One part of her brain acknowledged that she wasn't thinking clearly, but she shrugged off the message. She knew only one thing for certain. When she got through with Jake Bannister, he would never be the same.

She found him at the corral yard, working a roan mare with Dutch. When she galloped up, Jake turned away from the mare and came toward her.

Sally yanked on the gelding's reins and brought him to a halt near Jake's sorrel, tied up to the fence rail. She swung her leg over the saddle horn and slid down to the ground.

"What the—" Jake bit off the sentence. Sally looked madder than he'd ever seen her. He watched, dumbstruck, as she strode to his horse, yanked the Winchester from its saddle scabbard and swung to face him.

Jake stared at her. Her face was white and set, her eyes crazed. "Dutch," he intoned. "Clear out of here."

The wrangler's eyes widened, and he stepped away, pulling the roan mare with him.

Sally raised the rifle. She cocked it in one jerky motion and with shaking hands pointed the barrel at Jake's heart.

"Sally! What the hell are you doing?"

Sally squinted one eye to take aim. Her vision blurred with tears and she blinked them back.

"Sally?" Jake took a cautious step toward her.

The gun wobbled.

"Dammit, Sally..."

She began to cry. Gasping for breath, she struggled to hold the rifle steady. "It's perfectly obvious what I'm doing, Jake Bannister. I'm going to kill you!"

"Why?" he demanded. He was afraid to move, afraid she'd jerk and pull the trigger.

"You wanted me for a hundred acres!" she sobbed. "You told Pa you'd marry me for one hundred measly acres!" She steadied the gun. "And I'm going to kill you."

"Sally, let me explain."

She sighted down the steel barrel and paused. "Well, did you? Did you say you'd marry me for that land?"

He hesitated so long she thought she'd scream. "Well, did you?"

"Yes, I did."

Her finger squeezed the trigger.

The bullet thudded into a fence post behind him, and a spray of splinters flew up.

In the next instant Jake was on top of her, knocking the gun out of her hand and toppling her to the ground under him.

"You little fool! What the hell do you think you're doing?"

"I told you, I'm going to kill you," Sally shouted. "Let me up and I'll prove it." She twisted under him, and he pinned her arms to the ground above her head. She kicked him, but he propped himself on his knees and pressed one thigh down on her legs. She couldn't move.

"Jake Bannister, you let me up this instant!"

"And get my butt shot off? Not likely."

She tried to squirm out from under him. Breathless, she heaved with all her might, to no avail.

"Don't make me hurt you," she snapped.

Jake threw back his head and laughed, relaxing his hands for a split second.

The instant she felt the pressure ease, Sally punched him in the midriff as hard as she could.

Jake pinioned her arms. "Lie still, Sally," he ordered, his voice taut. "I'm stronger than you. You'll only hurt yourself if you don't quit."

"I won't!" she screamed.

"You will," he countered. "And you're going to listen to what I have to say."

"I won't listen to you! I won't listen to you or speak to you, ever again, you lousy, flea-bitten skunk!"

She thrashed under him, and her voice rose to a shrill wail. Disconnected phrases spilled out in incoherent, jerky bursts. And then she began to scream.

Jake stared down at her, his blood freezing. She was out of control. The girl he loved so desperately was completely irrational. Hell's bells, she was hysterical!

He hesitated a moment, then crashed his fist into the side of her jaw, and she lay still.

Oh, God, forgive me! He picked up the limp form and ran for the ranch house. "Olla! Olla!"

When Sally opened her eyes, Jake was bending over her placing something wet and cool against her face. It smelled of vinegar. There wasn't a sound in the room except for Jake's ragged breathing.

"What happened?" She lay stretched out on the green velvet sofa in the Bar Y front parlor, but she couldn't remember how she got there. Before she could open her mouth again, Jake laid his fingers over her lips.

"Listen to me, Sally. You're all right. You were hysterical, so I...I knocked you out. Do you understand me?"

She nodded weakly. How odd he looked, his face pale, his lips tight. And his eyes... She cringed at the anguish she saw there. All the fight drained out of her.

"If I take my hand away, will you listen to me for a minute? Let me explain?"

She nodded again. Her head pounded. Tears welled in the corners of her eyes and spilled down her dust-streaked cheeks. Her shoulders shook, and her breath came in shuddering gasps.

Jake gathered her to him and let her cry it out. At last she quieted and lay still, her face pressed against his shirt.

"Did you tell Pa you'd..." Her voice choked.

Jake hesitated. For the first time in his life he considered not telling the truth. It would just hurt her. But he knew sooner or later she'd worm the whole story out of Tom. Anyway, he had to be honest—he'd never lied to anybody in his entire life. Out here, a man's reputation was built on his word; he'd worked hard to fit in to the ranching community, to be respected. He wasn't about to throw that away.

"Yes, Sally, I did. Tom offered me the land. It was good pasture land that I needed—it had water on it. And I accepted his condition. But that was before you came home from St. Louis. Before I fell in love with you. When that happened, I told Tom the deal was off. It was you I wanted, not the land. You were worth more to me than both our ranches combined, more than all the ranches in Oregon."

Sally gave a shaky sigh. "But if you told Pa—"

"It was about that time I began to see that I'd never have you, Sally. Really have you. You'd have killed me, one way or the other, if not with a gun, then with your tongue. I couldn't have stood it, loving you and letting you slice me up the way you do. I finally figured I'd be a fool to trade one hell for another."

She sniffled, and he eased one arm from around her shoulders and pulled a bandanna from his shirt pocket.

She blew her nose and wadded up the square of red-and-white cotton, twisting the edge in her hands. "And now?"

He thought for a moment, then smiled at her, his indigo eyes tired. "Some things in life are beyond price."

"Then marry *me*, not Paula."

He gave a half laugh and shook his head "It's too late, Sally."

She pulled in a sharp breath. "Is it?"

A long silence stretched. "Yes."

Sally listened to the irregular thump of his heart and worked to steady her breathing.

She glanced up at him. "Maybe it's not too late."

Jake stared at her, his eyes incredulous. "I'm getting married tomorrow, Sally. You don't have much time. Unless, of course, you're going to shoot me."

A hiccup of laughter escaped her. "Let me up, Jake. I won't hurt you, I promise."

A low chuckle rumbled deep in his throat. He eased her to a sitting position. "Can you ride?"

Sally nodded. Her head throbbed, and her face felt hot and sticky. She knew she wasn't too clearheaded at the moment, but her head ached. Her tongue felt like a herd of cows had trampled it. She couldn't think of one sensible thing to say.

Maybe Jake was right—it *was* too late. In less than twenty-four hours he was going to marry Paula, and there was nothing she could do about it. Nothing, except make it less painful for him.

"Come on, Sally," Jake said, his voice tight. "I'll take you home."

Her legs shook when he helped her to stand, and she swayed against him. He smelled of sweat and leather. Suddenly she longed for him to hold her, kiss her.

Jake set her away from him. "I'll get the horses."

They rode the six miles back to the Circle L in silence. When they came within sight of the two-story white frame house, Jake slowed his horse and reached over to catch the gelding's bridle. He brought their horses to a halt and looped both sets of reins around his saddle horn.

He leaned toward her and cupped her face between his palms, his eyes shadowed with pain. "Maybe it wasn't such a bad idea, after all," he said softly.

"What wasn't?"

"Shooting me. In some ways, I wish you hadn't missed."

Sally's throat ached. "Oh, Jake," she whispered. "Don't marry Paula. You'll be miserable."

"I have to, Sally. I promised, and—"

She jerked away from him. "Jake Bannister, you are the stubbornest man in the county. You're wrong, you know you are. But you just have to keep your word, don't you? You men can be so stupid about those things!"

"It's not stupidity, Sally. A man's word is his code of honor. When the chips are down, it's all he's got."

"All he's got? What about love, and life, and—" Her voice broke. "Oh, to hell with you. I may be in love with you, but you are so pigheaded I wouldn't marry you now if you were the last man in the state!"

He smiled crookedly. "Is that supposed to make it easier? Dammit, Sally, you sure as hell are one free spirit. The next thing you know you'll be wanting to vote."

Sally laughed, but the tears started again despite her attempt to fight them back. Oh, yes, she'd marry him! She'd marry him in a minute, pigheadedness and all. She'd wear petticoats every day, she'd give up being the Honey Creek schoolteacher—she'd do anything he asked her.

Jake tightened his fingers around her chin and bent toward her. Sally raised her face.

He kissed her lightly, and very slowly. At the first touch of his lips, her eyelids fluttered shut. She tasted of honey and salt.

With a little sob, she leaned into him. Instantly he pulled back and dropped his hands to his sides.

She reached out to him, resting her palms on his shirt. After a slight hesitation, he groaned and caught both her hands in his. Gently he lowered them to her saddle horn, pressing her fingers firmly around the hard leather.

"Don't touch me, Sally. I'm okay as long as I don't smell you, or touch you." His voice sounded gravelly. "Tomorrow I'm ... Oh, hell. Tomorrow I'm going to marry Paula. And that's going to be a lot easier if you don't touch me."

He gave her a long look, then reached over and separated her reins from his. He slapped her gelding on the rump, and it jolted away.

Jake watched her move away from him into the deepening dusk, her head up, her back slim and straight He'd never known anyone like her. No matter who he married, slept with, raised a family with, some secret part of him would always belong to Sally Maguire.

He took the longest possible route back to the Bar Y. At the river he pulled his mount up short and spent a long time staring across the swirling green-black water to the sand bar barely visible in the fading summer light.

Chapter Nineteen

Sally tossed on the narrow bed in her small upstairs room. Moonlight slanted across the rumpled blue quilt, and the croaking of thousands of frogs down at the stock pond rasped in the stillness. She closed her eyes against the maddening, relentless sound and pulled the feather pillow over her head to shut out the noise. Her body ached. Her brain whirled with disjointed thoughts.

Jake was getting married tomorrow, and she could do nothing. Nothing! *Fight for him,* Louisa had said. Well, she'd tried to stop him and failed. Now time was running out, and she didn't know what else to do.

Or did she? She stifled the sob that rose in her chest and forced herself to think rationally. Was there really nothing she could do? Was this what grown-up life was like—seeing what *should* be, and having to live with things the way they were? She detested it. But, she sighed to herself, maybe it had to be. After all, what was so wrong with Jake's marrying Paula Randall?

What was wrong with it! *You ninny! You know what's wrong with it. Jake deserves better in life, that's what's wrong with it.* She couldn't stand by and watch Jake waste his sensitivity, his fineness, in a joyless life with a woman he did not love. No matter what, she didn't want that for him. It would kill him. Jake owed himself more than that.

And he owed *her* more than that. She'd offered to give up everything for him—her independence, which she treasured, even her beloved job as schoolmistress. She'd give it all up in a heartbeat if only he'd marry her instead of Paula.

It was so simple, really. Plain as red hair and freckles. She loved Jake, and Paula didn't. Paula loved possession, winning, but she didn't love Jake for himself. To Paula, having Jake was like winning a horse race.

Sally clenched her teeth until her jaw ached. She could not bear to see Jake throw his life away. More than anything else in the world, she wanted him to be happy.

She lay motionless, staring at the paned window silvered in the moonlight. She tried to breathe evenly, tried to control the tears that welled behind her eyelids. By tomorrow afternoon Jake would belong to Paula. What, oh, what could she do to stop it?

Frantically, she racked her brain. Only one thing was clear—she didn't have much time.

Her eyelids snapped open. It was almost three o'clock in the morning; she didn't have *any* time! There was only one thing she could do, and even that seemed futile. Still, she had to try. It was now or never.

She rolled out of bed, grabbed her jeans and the first shirt she found, and pulled on her boots. There was no time to pin up her hair, so she let the thick tresses hang loose down her back. Jake liked it better that way, anyway.

The barn was inky. She propped the door open wide enough to admit some moonlight and found her saddle and bridle. Carefully she felt her way to the gelding's stall, and when she'd saddled the horse, she led him quietly out into the stable yard and mounted. She walked the black out the front gate and onto the road.

Lantern light glowed through the Bar Y ranch house kitchen window as Sally approached. Through the glass she saw Jake sitting at the small oak table in the corner, his head bent, his forehead resting against his balled fist. His other arm lay, palm up, across the table, the fingers knotted.

Quiet as a cat, Sally dismounted and drew closer. Steam puffed from the spout of the blue enamelware coffeepot on the stove. What was he doing making coffee at four o'clock in the morning?

She crept closer, then bent and picked up a small stone and tossed it at the window glass.

Jake did not move.

She threw another pebble, then another. Finally he lifted his head and looked up. She heard his footsteps tramp out of the kitchen to the back door, and she moved around to the back of the house as the door swung open.

"Jake?"

"Sally! What the hell are you doing here?"

"Jake, I—I've come to...to fight for you!"

There was a long pause. "Are you armed?"

Sally groaned. "I haven't got a weapon," she conceded. "Other than my tongue."

"You're armed, all right," he muttered. He descended the steps toward her.

His face was gray with fatigue, his hair unruly, as if he had been combing his fingers through it. Sally's chest constricted at the pain in his eyes.

"What do you want, Sally?" His voice sounded grainy.

"I want to talk, Jake. Just talk."

He raked one hand wearily through his hair. "Sally, I'm tired. I've been out riding most of the night, and I'm dead beat."

Riding? All night? The damn fool, no wonder he looked exhausted. She struggled against tears, then took a deep breath and moved to face him. When he didn't stir, she laid both her hands on his chest and looked directly into his eyes. "Jake, you've got to listen to me."

He stared at her for a moment, then carefully placed his hands over hers and returned them to her side. "I'll listen, Sally. I'll listen to anything you have to say, just don't touch me. Not tonight."

"Jake—" Her voice shook, and she waited, drawing in a breath, then exhaling slowly. "You can't marry Paula, Jake. It's wrong for you."

He sighed, his breath hissing out in a ragged stream. "Sally, a promise is a promise. A man doesn't go back on his word."

Frustration tightened her voice. "Forget your damned honor! You can't marry her, Jake—you deserve more than that."

He stared at her in silence.

Desperate to reach him, to make him understand, she stepped closer. "Think, Jake! This is for the rest of your life, both your lives. You told me once nothing comes for free, that you had to risk things in life. Well, you've got to risk this, Jake. Break your engagement with Paula."

His face twisted. "Sally, I can't do that. I promised I'd marry her. I can't go back on it."

Sally grabbed folds of his shirt material in her fingers and tugged. "You must, Jake. This one time, you must. For yourself."

A muscle jerked in his jaw. His hands moved toward her, then he caught himself and jammed them into his pants pockets.

"Jake, please listen! It isn't just because I want you—"

His breath sucked in sharply, and she stopped short, then plunged on. "It isn't because I want you," she repeated, "it's . . . it's because I love you. I want what's right for you. You owe yourself more than Paula. I'm willing to risk hurting Paula for that. For that, I'm willing to risk the disapproval of the whole county."

She waited a moment, holding on to his shirt, feeling his heart thud beneath her fingers. "Jake, a marriage can last fifty years. Fifty years to spend with someone you don't love will be hell on earth." Her voice wavered, then broke. "I could live the next fifty years without you, if I had to," she said, weeping, "but to think of *you* living it . . . It would kill you, Jake. I know it would. No man's honor is worth that."

Jake gazed at her with pain-dulled eyes. "My father taught me that a man's honor is everything, Sally. I've lived my whole life believing that."

Honor! Sally wanted to scream. What did honor have to do with being fair to oneself? Being honest with oneself? How could he be so blind? "You're an intelligent man, Jake. You're educated, cultured. But even a smart man can be a fool, and you're being a great big damn fool. You don't understand a thing about what your father taught you. Not one thing."

He shut his eyes for a moment. "Sally, don't get started on me. Please. Not tonight."

She ignored his protest. It had to be said, and it had to be said now. "Real honor is doing what's best for people, doing what's *right* for people you care about. That's what your father meant, Jake. *That's* what people should live by. And I'll fight for that—and for you—with everything I've got. That's why I'm here now, you big, dumb lunkhead. I'm fighting for you!"

He stared at her for a long moment. Lord, she had guts. And heart. And it was true—he wanted her, not Paula. *Her.* Oh, God, what was he going to do? He was trapped, square and simple, in a net of his own devising. He hadn't been hoodwinked or seduced by Paula; he'd just found her a willing ear after Sally's rejection. Paula had skillfully let one thing lead to another.

Yet deep down in his gut he knew it *was* wrong. Paula knew he didn't love her. He would never love anyone but Sally. But he'd given his word. *His word!* Out here in the West there was no civilizing force except for the trust of other men and reliance on the code they lived by. That code gave meaning to his world. Adherence to it gave him a respected place in it. And he'd given his word he'd marry Paula Randall.

For a fleeting moment he considered escape. But escape to what? Into a life of dishonor? A life where his word, his very self, meant nothing at all anymore?

Slowly Jake shook his head. "I can't do it."

Sally stifled a sob. The man was beyond her. "Jake, it's your decision," she said, her voice uneven. She crumpled the front of his shirt in her fingers. "But please, think about what I said. You don't have to marry *me*. Just some day marry someone you *do* love, Jake. Please," she sobbed. *"Please!"*

Jake studied the slim girl before him, the dark red hair tumbled about her face, the clear green-blue eyes blazing into his. He'd remember the color of her eyes for the rest of his life.

Sally gazed steadily back at him. "You said once that you have to take risks in life, to gather your courage and start things—important things. You helped me do that, remember? That night we spent in the schoolhouse?"

Jake groaned. "You know I'll never forget that night, Sally. Never."

"Jake, if that meant anything to you, you've got to think about *why*. It was right, between us. And now it's just as important to know when to stop things that *aren't* right."

His mouth twisted. "It's better to know when not to start in the first place. I don't want to think about the rest of it any longer. I'm tired, Sally. Just bone tired." He put his hands on her shoulders and set her away from him.

Sally wanted to cry at the hopelessness in his voice. He wanted *her*, not Paula, but he wouldn't budge. Oh, men and their stupid sense of honor!

She reached out and grabbed the front of his shirt. "Listen to me, Mr. Honorable Bannister. You've only got this one day to settle your life. You've *got* to think about it, Jake. Now! Or else you'll have to think about it for the rest of your days."

She kissed him, letting her lips linger on his, exploring and savoring him one last time. "And so will I."

His arms went around her, and she felt his body tremble. She reached up, pulled his head down to hers and pressed her mouth against each of his closed eyelids.

"Sally, oh, God, Sally, what the hell are you doing?"

"I'm loving you, you damn fool. I'm talking sense to you!" *And it isn't enough,* she sobbed inside. *It isn't enough!*

She held him tight against her for a moment, then stepped out of his arms and turned away. She moved deliberately toward the gelding and pulled herself up into the saddle.

She'd given it her best shot. If Jake was fool enough to marry Paula after what she'd said . . . well, then, he was a fool.

But deep inside, Sally knew Jake was not a fool. He was just a man with a misguided sense of honor. She only hoped he would realize it in time.

Slowly she walked the black out the Bar Y gate and did not look back.

Chapter Twenty

The ax cut cleanly through the pine log, and two chunks of wood toppled off the chopping block onto the ground. A week ago the Bar Y hands had felled the big sugar pine in the meadow and cut it into lengths. Now the stacked logs leaned against the schoolhouse wall, waiting to be split into firewood.

Sally was relieved to find the woodpile still intact; splitting wood would give her something to do, something physical and, she prayed, tiring. Something to keep her body busy while her mind struggled with the ache deep inside her.

She stooped to retrieve one chunk of wood, balanced it on the block and split it in half with one ringing blow. She bent again, and again swung the ax, breathing steadily. *Thank you, Pa, for teaching me how to chop wood.*

The sun climbed higher over the tips of the fir trees and beat down on her back. Her flannel shirt, damp with sweat, stuck to her breasts, and the bare skin of her forearms shone with moisture where she'd rolled the sleeves back.

She was tired. Very tired. Doggedly she lugged another log to the block. Somewhere in town Jake was getting married, standing in front of Reverend Mathews with Paula Randall, repeating his wedding vows. Paula would be dressed in something elegant, something...

She had to stop. She couldn't bear to think about it.

She aimed a vicious blow with the ax. Jake would stand next to Paula, tall and solemn and...

The ax bit into the wood. Everyone in the valley would be there—Martha and Hank, the twins, her father. Even Louisa and Will.

The ax thunked into the wood again. She had filled Martha's wood box long before anyone was up for the chores that morning, then mindlessly split enough kindling to last the month. Her father had raised his eyebrows as she brushed by him on her last trip into the kitchen, but he'd said nothing.

She'd saddled the gelding and ridden out to the schoolhouse before her father and the others had loaded up in the wagon and driven into town for the wedding. Earlier her father had taken her aside and asked quietly if she wanted to go with them.

She had shaken her head. She didn't want to see anyone, talk to anyone. She just wanted to be alone. She'd been chopping wood ever since.

A lead weight settled into her belly, and she battled an anguish so crushing she longed to just close her eyes and never wake up. Jake and Paula, for the rest of his life.

And her life. Oh, God. Jake and Paula.

She filled both wood boxes at the schoolhouse, then began stacking the split pieces against the outside wall. When her arms ached so much she could no longer lift the ax, she leaned the handle against the chopping block and went in search of a bucket.

Trembling with fatigue, she filled the container with water, staggered into the schoolhouse and dropped a bristle scrub brush into the pail. On hands and knees she began to scrub the floor.

She worked methodically from one corner of the schoolroom to the other, dipping and scrubbing, back and forth, struggling to keep unwanted thoughts from crowding in. If it was three o'clock, Jake was getting married. By four o'clock the ceremony would be over and George Peterman would be tuning up his fiddle. By five...

She lost track of time. When she finished scouring every inch of the smooth cedar planking, she refilled the bucket, rinsed out the brush and started all over.

Two hours later her arms and neck ached. Her knees were raw and stiff from hours on the hard floor and she was so tired she could barely stand.

But it was a relief in a way. Exhaustion dulled her agony, and for minutes at a time her mind drifted, hazy and oddly numb. She felt dead inside.

She dumped the last bucket of water onto the rose-bush outside the door, dropped into the chair at her desk and laid her head on her arms. In an instant she was asleep.

When Sally woke it was pitch-black in the tiny room. She raised her head. Outside the open door of the schoolhouse, the black gelding whickered gently.

Weary, she pulled the schoolhouse door shut, stumbled to the horse and dragged herself up into the saddle.

She had no memory of riding home.

The house was dark. Everyone must have come home from town after the wedding and gone straight to bed.

In the kitchen Sally stripped off her jeans and sweat-stained shirt and poured into an enamelware pan the water Martha had left simmering on the stove. She sponged off her aching body, choking back a strangled laugh. It was Jake's wedding night and here she was standing naked in the kitchen taking a spit bath.

She climbed the stairs to her bedroom, dropped her clothes in a heap on the floor and pulled the white cambric nightgown on over her head. When she turned toward the bed, she stood stock-still.

Louisa's ivory silk wedding dress lay spread across the quilt. Dazed, Sally stared at it. Louisa must have brought it to pack up and store in the attic trunk. But why tonight, of all nights?

Too tired to think, Sally tugged the voluminous folds of silk down to the foot of her bed, folded back the quilt and crawled under the covers.

It was Jake's wedding night, and he and Paula... She clamped her hand hard over her mouth and curled her body into a ball. She didn't ever want to wake up.

In her dream Sally heard a dog growl and begin to bark. Then a man's voice spoke. "Quiet, Shep." Then another, different voice. Then the first voice again. "This is between Sally and me."

Something pinged against her window. After a moment, another ping. Then another.

Suddenly wide awake, Sally stared at the square glass pane. Had she dreamed that? She slipped out of bed, raised the window without making a sound and peeked out.

A lean finger pushed back a gray Stetson, and a man's voice said, "Close your mouth, Miss Sally. It's me, Jake Bannister."

"Jake! What are you doing here? You shouldn't be…
Jake! It's your wedding night!"

"Is it?" He looked relaxed and extraordinarily
pleased about something.

She caught her breath. "Isn't it?"

"Sally, to tell you the truth, I've been up all night for
two straight nights, and right now I'm too damned tired
to know what day, or night, it is. If it's my wedding
night, you'll have to content yourself with a good
night's sleep instead of—"

"Jake!"

"Now, Miss Salty, don't get your feathers all fluffed
up."

Dumbfounded, Sally watched Jake jam his hands
into his pockets and rock back on his heels. He took his
time before he spoke, and when he did, his voice
dropped to a rough whisper.

"Well, Sally, first I rode around the valley half the
night, wondering what the hell I was going to do. And
then, when I finally figured it out, I had to ride all over
hell and gone again to spread the word."

Sally's eyes narrowed. "Word? What word?"

"Don't rush me, Sally. I'm a tired man."

"*What word!*"

"Sally, why don't you tie on that ruffly blue apron of
yours and stir up some flapjacks?"

"Flapjacks! Jake Bannister, are you out of your
mind? It's the middle of the— Are you married or
not?" she demanded.

"Right now, I'm not. Paula didn't show up at the
church. She sent the reverend a note saying she'd taken
the train back to Philadelphia."

"Philadelphia! Didn't she want—?"

"Nope. I think she knew all along she didn't really want to be a rancher's wife. She just wanted to..."

He let his voice trail off, then flashed a dazzling smile up at her. "So I'm not married. Tomorrow, though, I might be."

"Tomorrow?" Sally ventured, her voice tremulous.

Jake's face sobered, and he gazed up at her, his dark eyes intense. "You were right, Sally. To tell you the truth, I was relieved she didn't show up. I kept thinking about what I knew I had to tell her. It wasn't right for me, or for her. I couldn't do it to her. Or to you."

"Me!" Incredulous, Sally stared at the man on her front porch, her heart swelling, aching with love. She grabbed a dressing gown and flew out the bedroom door, pulling the robe around her on the way down the staircase. In an instant she was in his arms.

Jake wrapped his arms tight around her and covered her upturned mouth with his. "Oh, Sally," he groaned. "Sally, marry me, dammit. I can't stand any more of this."

She reached her hands about his neck, letting her robe fall open in the front. "Neither can I," she murmured.

He kissed her again, his hunger apparent as his mouth crushed hers. After a long moment he lifted his head and chuckled. "Think Tom'd reconsider about that hundred acres?" he teased.

"No," Sally whispered. "Yesterday Pa offered to sign over half the ranch to me when I got married."

Jake smiled. "Well, then, Sally, girl, we're going to be rich!"

She shook her head. "No, we won't, Jake." She looked straight into his eyes. "I turned him down. I told Pa I was never going to marry. I was going to teach school for the rest of my life."

"Going to teach . . . Sally, are you going to marry me or not?"

Sally kept her eyes on Jake's face. His deep blue eyes searched hers, waiting for her answer. She delayed as long as she could, savoring the moment. Oh, it was tempting to string him along, let him suffer for a few moments as she had suffered all day yesterday. But she couldn't do it—couldn't bear to see his eyes darken, his mouth twist with pain.

"Well, are you?"

Sally smiled up at him. "Mr. Bannister, darling, don't you think you should come courting first?"

Jake groaned. "Courting! Hellfire, what do you think I've been doing ever since you stepped off that train from St. Louis!"

"Oh?" she teased. "I hadn't noticed."

"Sally!" Jake exploded.

She pulled his head down to hers and ran her tongue delicately over his lower lip.

"Sally . . ." his voice warned.

"Hmm?"

His lips met hers, and a warm bubble of joy expanded inside her. Her breath stilled, then her body felt light, buoyant, as if she could float. "How soon do you want to get married, Jake?"

His breath was soft against her lips, his voice throaty. "How about tomorrow morning? I'm so tired tonight all I want to do is sleep."

"I'm tired, too, Jake." Sally sighed. "I spent all day scrubbing floors and chopping wood. Someday I'll tell you about it."

"What about tonight, Sally?"

"What *about* tonight?"

"I brought some jerky and some whiskey. And my bedroll and all the buffalo robes I could tie on the horse."

She laughed in delight and clung to him. "How big is your bedroll?"

"Big enough." He spread open her light silk dressing gown and pulled her tight against him. "We could ride double."

"Yes!" Sally whispered. "I know just the place—it's got plenty of firewood and the cleanest floors in the whole county!"

Jake closed his eyes and inhaled the lilac fragrance of her hair. "We could go swimming in the river on the way."

"Yes, we could," she murmured.

"We could—"

"Yes, Jake," she breathed. "Oh, yes! Yes!"

He paused and looked down into her upturned face. "You think we'll be able to find our way in the dark, Sally?"

"Oh, yes, Jake." She sighed lazily against his mouth. "The road is marked. Well marked."

He frowned, his eyes questioning. "Marked?"

"Yes. All you have to do is know what to look for." She kissed him lingeringly, feeling her lips stir his, his heart hammer to match her blood's beat.

"We'll always be able to find our way, Jake. The wind's at our back, and the road is . . ."

She felt his arms tighten.

"Bordered with roses."

*   *   *   *   *

Author Note

When the school board members met the following fall, they voted unanimously to retain the services of Sally Maguire, despite her marriage to rancher Jackson Bannister. Mrs. Sally Bannister became the first married woman to teach school in Honey Creek.

The Honey Creek schoolhouse also had the first split-rail fence in the county that was bordered with a pink climbing Cecile Brunner.

And Billy Peterman won a county fair prize for his world map of roses.

Coming in April from

Harlequin®
Historical

the
Norman's
Heart

By award-winning author

MARGARET MOORE

"A story brimming with vibrant
color and three-dimensional characters...
emotion and power on every page."
—*Romantic Times*

Available wherever Harlequin books are sold.

UNLOCK THE DOOR TO GREAT ROMANCE AT BRIDE'S BAY RESORT

Join Harlequin's new across-the-lines series, set in an exclusive hotel on an island off the coast of South Carolina.

Seven of your favorite authors will bring you exciting stories about fascinating heroes and heroines discovering love at Bride's Bay Resort.

Look for these fabulous stories coming to a store near you beginning in January 1996.

Harlequin American Romance #613 in January
Matchmaking Baby by Cathy Gillen Thacker

Harlequin Presents #1794 in February
Indiscretions by Robyn Donald

Harlequin Intrigue #362 in March
Love and Lies by Dawn Stewardson

Harlequin Romance #3404 in April
Make Believe Engagement by Day Leclaire

Harlequin Temptation #588 in May
Stranger in the Night by Roseanne Williams

Harlequin Superromance #695 in June
Married to a Stranger by Connie Bennett

Harlequin Historicals #324 in July
Dulcie's Gift by Ruth Langan

Visit Bride's Bay Resort each month wherever Harlequin books are sold.

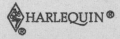

Fall in love all over again with

This Time...
MARRIAGE

In this collection of original short stories, three brides get a unique chance for a return engagement!

- Being kidnapped from your bridal shower by a one-time love can really put a crimp in your wedding plans! *The Borrowed Bride*— by **Susan Wiggs**, *Romantic Times* Career Achievement Award-winning author.

- After fifteen years a couple reunites for the sake of their child—this time will it end in marriage? *The Forgotten Bride*—by **Janice Kaiser**.

- It's tough to make a good divorce stick—especially when you're thrown together with your ex in a magazine wedding shoot! *The Bygone Bride*— by **Muriel Jensen**.

Don't miss THIS TIME...MARRIAGE, available in April wherever Harlequin books are sold.

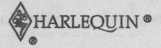
HARLEQUIN ®
®

To an elusive stalker, Dana Kirk is

FAIR GAME

JANICE KAISER

Dana Kirk is a very rich, very successful woman. And she did it all by herself.

But when someone starts threatening the life that she has made for herself and her daughter, Dana might just have to swallow her pride and ask a man for help. Even if it's Mitchell Cross—a man who has made a practice of avoiding rich women. But to Mitch, Dana is different, because she needs him to stay alive.

Available at your favorite retail outlet this March.